A Witch Awakens

A Witch Awakens

by Ellis Elliott

HAWKSHAW PRESS | LOS ANGELES

A Witch Awakens
A Fire Circle Mystery

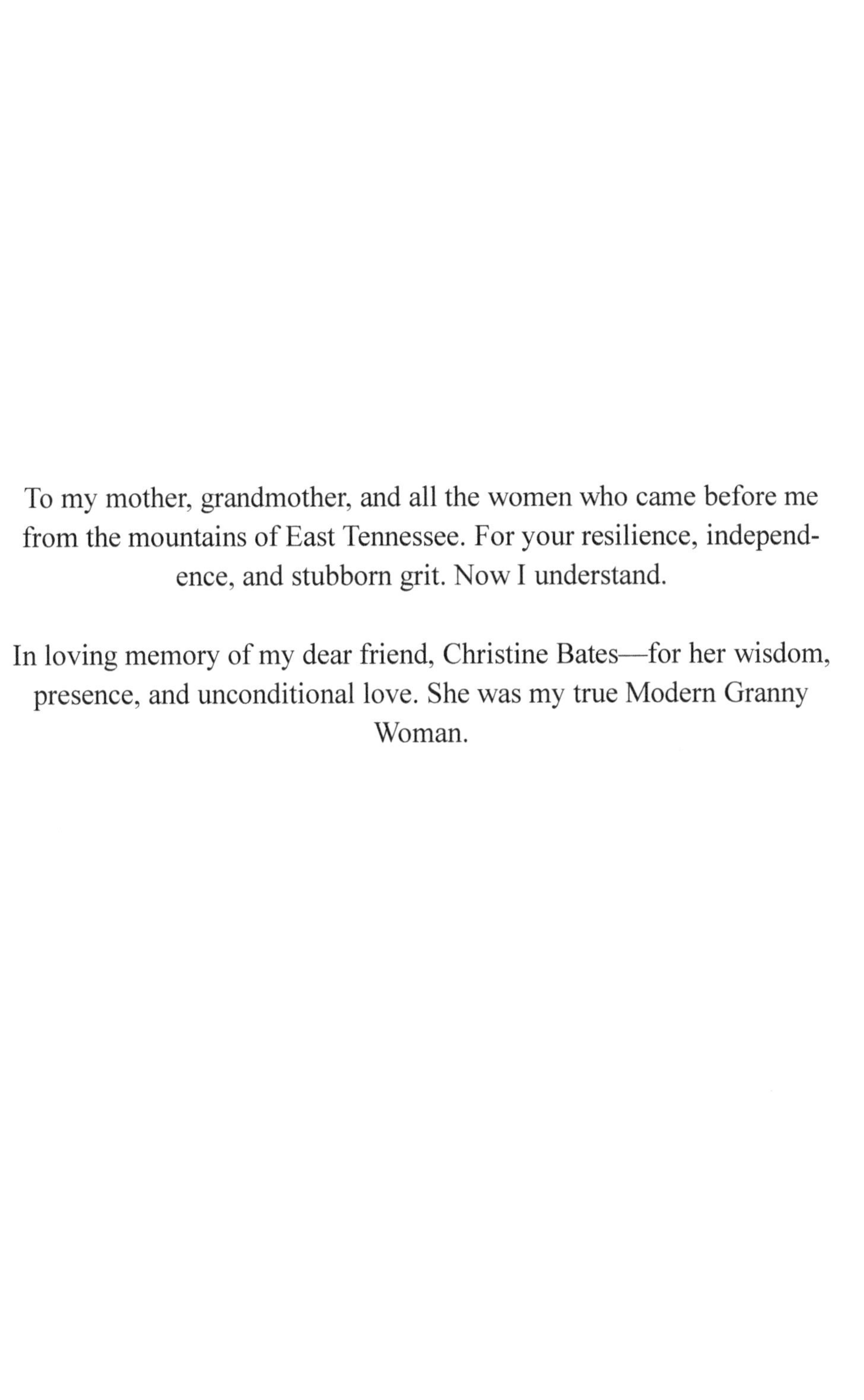

To my mother, grandmother, and all the women who came before me from the mountains of East Tennessee. For your resilience, independence, and stubborn grit. Now I understand.

In loving memory of my dear friend, Christine Bates—for her wisdom, presence, and unconditional love. She was my true Modern Granny Woman.

Also by the author

Break in the Field

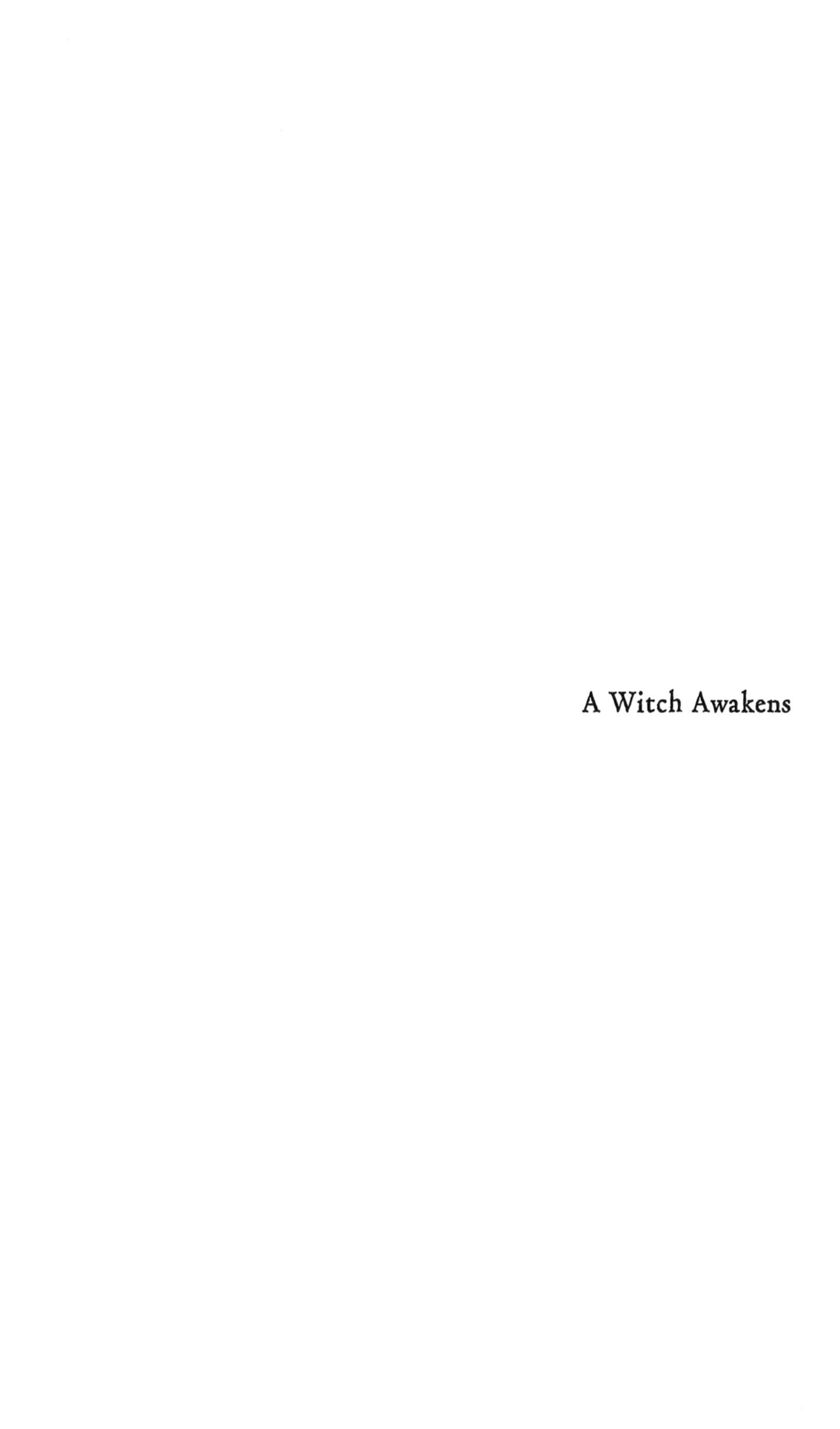

A Witch Awakens

"The witchery of living
is my whole conversation
with you, my darlings."

    —from the poem "To Begin With, The Sweet Grass"
    by Mary Oliver

FIRE CIRCLE

Under a full harvest moon on the gentle slope of hillside behind Aunt Granny Hazel's house, four women gathered around a crackling campfire. The old woman seated next to Hazel leaned over and handed her a small bundle of beeswax candles wrapped in sage leaves and pine needles tied together with string. "This is for the ceremony," she said, her voice casual. "Watch how it burns. That will tell you more than the smoke."

In the valley below, the incandescent city lights of the East Tennessee mountain town, Eureka Grove, were like pinpricks in the veil of darkness. Just beyond the valley were dense forests and rugged hills sprinkled only with an occasional house light, and home to hidden coves and deep hollows spread under an inked night sky. There was not much to see out there except the shadows of cows, weird and otherworldly, on the hillsides, and spirals of smoke rising from chimneys and campfires.

The woman on the other side of Hazel stood facing north into the woods. She held a smoky amber stone in the upturned palm of her hand.

"Why do you have your cairngorm stone tonight?" Hazel asked.

"This is my offering for Beira, the Cailleach, queen of winter. In the fall we are looking forward to the winter season, and I am wishing for the warming air to slow or stop." Her voice was soft and musical. The others nodded in agreement.

Hazel's joints popped as she stretched out her legs and picked up a stained sackcloth sachet from the ground beside her. It was tied with red twine and filled with rosemary, a clove of garlic, and a coyote's tooth. She held the bag over the fire by the twine, gently swinging it back and forth nine times before placing it back on the ground. "This is for my Cece, for her protection. She doesn't understand what's happenin' to her, and I get why she's worried. I felt that same way too, once."

"She's like you in a whole lot of ways, Hazel. She's always been different from the others," came a soothing voice across from her.

Hazel chuckled. "God bless her soul, then." Hazel turned to spit tobacco on the unsuspecting chipmunk behind her. "You know, her peculiars are going to get worse before they get better. We can't do anything about that, but we sure can try to keep her safe."

"Of course we can, and everything happens in the time it should. It always does. You know that as well as anyone. Have you checked in the book?"

"Not yet," Hazel said. She looked at the three women around her, and the silence that held them was comfortable and deep. In the darkness they listened to the fire speak its languages, different for each of them. Hazel lifted her arm and dropped the tied bundle of candles and herbs into the fire.

Their four voices then joined in a song meant only for the night forest: "We sisters gather in Spirit, and the Spirit is power. Protect her; protect her in her needful hours." The women repeated the lines in unison, their voices projecting and then fading like smoke in the night air.

"The book doesn't matter so much now, anyway. Once Cece finds out, she'll have to learn how to accept it first, and only then can she come to understand it. That's when she'll need you, when she learns her power."

"That's when she'll be needin' all of us," Hazel added, giving the others a sideways glance before bending over with a groan to tie her unlaced boot. "I reckon we'll all just have to wait."

I

Little Brennie Conover had managed to cram both her chubby toddler legs into only one of the legs of her pink tights.

"Okay, Bren. We've got this, but I'm going to need your help," Cece told her, managing to get her untangled and wrestling her back in correctly, each leg to its own pink tube. Cece and Bren, confined within the metal walls of the dance studio bathroom stall, were damp with sweat once the feat was accomplished. *Welcome back to the glamorous life,* Cece thought. *New York casting calls were a breeze compared to this.*

"Miss Cece, I wanna be a unicorn!" Brennie declared, yanking a sparkly tutu up one leg.

"Of course you do, sweetie," Cece replied, pulling out another tutu from the bag that was wedged in the stall with them. "Here's one for the other leg while you're at it. In fact, I think it's a two-tutu day. And you know what? Today, you *are* a unicorn. And I am, too."

Having had to move back to her hometown from New York, and turning thirty soon, Cece felt her description wasn't too far off base.

* * *

Classes done, studio organized for Monday, Cece turned off all the lights behind her in the Eureka Grove Dance studio, having finished teaching her Saturday dance classes for the day. She lugged her multiple bags out through the main door into the glow of afternoon light, and turned to insert the silver key and lock it.

As she turned, the sun reflected off the key, magnifying its proportions and making it hot to the touch. At the same time, the scent of sage was so strong it made her eyes water. Cece squeezed her eyes closed and opened them a couple of times in a row to clear her head. It wasn't the first time that Cece had felt a sense of being both off-balance and aware of another layer under her regular life, like the smell of sage. Whenever this happened she felt temporarily jolted out of one reality and into another. Lately, it had been happening more often than it had in all the years before, and differently, somehow: familiar, but also not. She put her hand against the door to give herself a minute to recalibrate and pretend everything was normal, then smoothly locked it, pocketed the key and began the short walk home.

The weather was perfect for walking since the sun had broken through the curtain of dark clouds from the mountaintops, and the fall air held just the right amount of chill. Cece spied something surrounding the trunk of an old oak tree in the front yard of the Colley house ahead. She squatted low to get a closer look at the miniature fairy village encircling it.

"Well, good morning, Littles," Cece said in greeting, delighted by the village scene of multiple small houses. "How is everyone in the Kingdom of the Fae on this fine September day?"

"Is that you, Cece?"

The voice startled Cece, and she turned to see first, knees, then the enormous belly of her former schoolmate, Marla Fines.

"Were you talking to someone? I thought I heard you talking," Marla asked, looking around.

"Oh, no," Cece stuttered, then hurriedly pretended to pull an earbud from her ear and put it in her pocket. It was her old trick for when she was caught talking to herself. "Just finishing a call, and checking out this sweet scene." Cece stood up slowly and pointed at the tree. "Good to see you, Marla."

"I heard you were back in town. How's it going, being back in the Grove?" Marla asked, pulling at the ruffled collar of her tangerine maternity mini dress. Marla had been a cheerleader at their high school, while Cece had been a proud founding member of the Spanish Club.

"Oh, you know, good. I'm back teaching at Nana's studio. At least for now," Cece told her, talking like she already had a plan. "But, hey, congratulations," Cece said, lifting her palm toward Marla's belly. "You must be so excited."

"Oh, yeah, Carlos and I can't believe it's already number three. Jessie Rae and Marlon are so excited for a baby sister."

"Yeah. I bet they are," Cece said, nodding her head while thinking, *Number three? Somehow I missed the other two.* "How's Carlos doing?" The only thing Cece remembered from school about Carlos was that he'd had a full beard by tenth grade.

"Wonderful!" Marla said, twisting the ice-cube-sized diamond on her finger. "Still working at the bank, and on his way up the ladder, you know."

Cece really didn't know, but persisted nonetheless, hoping this interaction would be over soon. "That's really great, Marla. Sounds like all is well, then. I guess I better be heading on home. I promised Nana I'd help with the garden before it rains," Cece said, hoping her voice sounded urgent despite a cloudless sky.

"What's Miss Anna B. up to these days, anyway? Besides gardening? Jessie Rae will be ready for the toddler class at the studio before you know it!" Marla said, calling her grandmother, Anna Beth Chagall, by the name everyone called her, and postponing Cece's departure.

"She's still the energizer bunny she's always been," answered Cece, assuming Marla had been one of her grandmother's former dance students. It seemed half of Eureka Grove had been her student at one time or another.

"And your crazy Aunt Granny, Hazel Brown, how's she doing? Is she even still alive?" Hazel was Cece's great-aunt and her grandmother's sister.

"Yes." Cece winced. "She's alive and well." *Who even asks that?* Cece thought. "She's still taking care of everyone in Charity Hill, like she always has. She was just chopping wood this morning," Cece said matter-of-factly.

"Oh, wow," Marla said, surprised, "Cool. I guess I better go, too. Have to give our nanny a break sometime," she said, her head inclining far to one side. Cece remembered Marla's head dipped into a similar position in seventh grade when she'd handed out invitations to her skating party, to everyone but Cece.

"Okay, well, good to see you, Marla," Cece said, "and good luck with, you know, everything."

* * *

"Yes, Mrs. Callahan, I understand," Cece said, balancing her cell-phone between her shoulder and cheek while kneeling with straight pins in one hand to tack the wide circular hem of Jenny's gorgeous dress for the charity ball. It was three days before the ball, and Jenny's dress needed to be hemmed. Cece was regretting having taken the call from Ashley's mother.

"Yes, Ashley is advanced for her age… Yes, I agree, she does learn the dances quickly. Okay. Well, I really don't think she needs private lessons. She's not that far ahead of the others in her class. Oh, I see. You want her to learn more dances. And why is that exactly? No. No, I didn't know that. Fourteen thousand followers? Yikes. Yes, that is amazing for a four-year-old. Mrs. Callahan, I'm sorry to interrupt, but I've really, really got to go," Cece said, rolling her eyes at Jenny, who was grinning down at her. Cece was in no mood for the overbearing frippery of Mrs. Callahan this morning. "We'll talk later at the studio. See you soon," she said, tapping to hang up before another word could be squeezed in.

"Dance Mom?" Jenny asked.

"Ugh. Yes. Poor Ashley. Her mom takes videos of her dancing and puts them on social media all the time. Even in dance class she acts like she's performing for a camera. Now, take a twirl, and see what you think about this length," Cece said, circling her finger in the air.

Jenny was standing in front of the floor-length mirror hung on the back of Cece's bedroom door, and as she obliged Cece's request with a quick turn, her light jasmine perfume with a hint of spice filled the air, turning into swirling colors of amber and chestnut in Cece's mind. It was truly a spectacular dress, with alternating strips of sapphire blue velvet and matching silk for its skirt.

At almost six feet tall, with chin-length blonde-mixed-with-grey hair, Jenny was perfect for the dress. Jenny's twirling motion had proven too exciting for Cece's beloved black mutt, Maybelline, who was jumping and turning as if the movement was her cue to dance as well. "Come here, May," Cece called, patting the wood floor in front of her and then pulling her in for a snuggle.

"I think that looks perfect, Cece. I can't thank you enough for helping me out at the last minute," Jenny said.

"No problem. Anything for you, Jenny. Now it's off to Mrs. Adams for alterations. She'll have it done by Saturday."

"Dropping that off will be a huge help to me. I've got a really busy day. My sister-in-law, Sandra, is coming into town tomorrow for the weekend, and I've got a council meeting tonight."

Cece already knew Jenny was busy. Despite being retired, she was a town council member and also worked occasionally as a private security consultant. "You are busy!" Cece said, and without missing a beat, she added, "I think we have more bunnies in the yard than I've ever seen before."

"Oh, is that right?" Jenny said, eyebrows lifting, nodding, and grinning to herself at Cece's lifelong habit of throwing the most random sentences into a conversation. It was one of many things that made her unique, and Jenny had known her so long it no longer surprised her. "I'm so glad you moved back home, Cece." Jenny continued, "I know your grandmother has to be over the moon to have you home and teaching at the studio again. And you look great, by the way. I see so much of both your parents in you, and I see your grandmother in your hair," she added with a playful grin.

Cece touched the side of her forehead where silver hair was beginning to grow from front to back like a stripe through her deep copper locks, mirroring the opposite of the one dark streak still left in her grandmother's otherwise all-silver hair. *Back home,* Cece thought, and felt the tension between old wounds and nostalgia. She had been back in the town she grew up in for only six months, and Cece wasn't sure yet if she would be staying. She wasn't even sure she wanted to keep dancing or teaching dance, despite that being her presumed future for as long as she could remember.

One truth that never wavered for Cece was the beauty of the majestic, ancient mountains of East Tennessee. From above, say if you were flying back from a life in New York City that hadn't really gone as one hoped, the Appalachian Mountain range looked like an intricate mandala of lines and swirls, from the dark canopy of forested ridges to the light-filled valleys. The mountains enclosed her small town of Eureka Grove like a warm embrace.

Cece left the bedroom so Jenny could change clothes, remembering what a strong, steady influence Jenny Newport had been for her growing up. *Lord knows I'd needed that,* she thought, nodding to herself. Cece's mom had died just before she started tenth grade. She knew little about her mom's side of the family, and they had never really been a part of her life. At the time, her other grandmother had her hands full with the studio and the inn. Cece's grandparents had bought the old, Victorian house they lived in from Jenny's family years before. Jenny had grown up there, and it was almost as though Jenny had come with the house as a package deal. Jenny had been a good friend to both her grandmother and her mom, and then to Cece too. She had offered a little extra stability to Cece when she needed it most.

It was warm and comforting for Cece to be back, living on the grounds of the old house, talking with Jenny again, but the question remained of whether she would stay put for a while. After college, she couldn't wait to get out of Eureka Grove and managed to live elsewhere for almost ten years. She had danced and taught in Memphis for a few years before meeting a dark-eyed, guitar-playing man who traveled with a flamenco dance company from Spain. She thought she should put all those years of taking Spanish classes to use, and ended up going to dance for a small company in Madrid for a while. Starry-eyed Cece realized fairly quickly that the *idea* of a European life was a lot more romantic than the reality. Then she'd spent the last three years trying to make it as a dancer in New York, following in her grandmother's footsteps. Her brief stint dancing dressed as an M&M at the Times Square store was bad enough. But it took her last audition, when the casting director dismissed several of them almost as soon as they started moving, for Cece to burn out. She'd complained to her agent that, at this rate, she wasn't even going to get to dance enough to keep limber, and her agent had replied that "lots of girls dance as strippers on the side to make ends meet." Cece had hung up on her, and made the hard decision to come home.

Sometimes, Cece found herself thinking, *the universe begins with a whisper to nudge you in another direction, and sometimes it kicks you out and shuts the door behind you.* She decided to count her failures as experience, and she knew she might need to let go of one dream to make space for something else. It was certainly her *intention* to stay put, but intentions only got her so far, and for as long as she could remember, she had demonstrated a perpetual need to delay becoming an adult. She knew it would take time to build up her self-confidence again and make peace with the new direction of her life. She just wished she knew what that new direction was.

"Okay, then," Jenny said, appearing from the bedroom in her sweatpants and bright orange Tennessee Volunteers hoodie. "I think that's the last charity-ball-related chore on my list. How about you? Are you ready? Do you have a dollhouse for the auction this year?"

"I think we're ready," Cece said. "The Children's Hospital takes care of most all the details for the ball. And I *am* actually almost finished with a dollhouse for the silent auction."

Cece and her grandmother, Nana, shared the hobby of miniatures, specifically building dollhouses or remodeling old ones. They would scour thrift and antique shops for old ones and particularly loved when they found one that was custom-made. Both Nana and Cece thought there was something magical about a little house built with love for children who could create any world they wanted within its walls. For Cece, custom dollhouse orders also served as a much-needed extra income.

"But mine is a one-room cabin this year. I'm going with the rustic theme, so I can keep expectations low," Cece quipped. "It's hard to go up against Nana's houses, you know. Speaking of the auction, have you bought your raffle ticket yet?"

"Oh yes, I bought a few. I used to buy dozens, but I've reconciled myself to the fact that I'll never win. It's like thinking we'll ever find my father's gold box. Some people are just luckier than others, I guess," Jenny said, pulling her keys from her pocket.

"Oh, that's right! I'd forgotten about the mysterious gold box. Your dad told y'all he hid it somewhere in Nana's house back when your family lived there, right? Wasn't it supposed to be filled with cash or diamonds or something? I remember I took a turn trying to find it one summer."

"Yep, Dad told my brother, Ed, and me it was our inheritance. He said he'd hidden it in the house for us to find when he was gone, but we didn't find anything when we went through and cleaned out the house after he died. I told your Nana to be on the lookout because if she found it, I told her we'd all go on a lavish trip to Paris, see all the sights, and taste test lots of expensive French wine," Jenny said, with a smile and wink. "It is a shame, though, because Dad was so serious about it back then," Jenny continued with a little chuckle, "that Ed and I thought we were in trouble or something! He made us sit down beside each other on the sofa so he could tell us about the 'gold box that would change our lives.'" Jenny's eyes shifted, remembering the moment. "But it just wasn't meant to be found, I guess." Jenny laughed and shook her head. "Well, anyway, Ed and I had a good time joking about the things we could've bought with all that money we never found! Hey, is Bess doing the decorations again this year?"

"Yep. She's been working on them for months, and she just loves doing it. She gets to make her design boards and mix-and-match colors. It's right up her alley," Cece said as they stood inside her front door.

Bess worked at the historic Eureka Grove Inn, where the charity benefit was held every year. She had handled the details of the ball for years and had been Cece's best friend since they were young teens. The inn had become something of a "preferred getaway" for wealthy city folks, some that came at the same time every year. It was a go-to location for swanky event functions, and had even been used a few times as a movie set.

Cece held the door open to see Jenny out, letting in a cool rush of air and sunlight that had laced down to them through the tree branches overhead. "I'll have Mrs. Adams call when the dress is ready. Should be tomorrow afternoon, she said, and you can pick it up at her house."

Jenny stopped in the doorframe and took Cece's free hand in both of hers. "I'm so glad you're home now. And not just because you're pinning my dress at the last minute, but because I missed you. I really did."

"Thanks, Jenny, I missed you, too," Cece said, drawing in a full breath of fresh mountain air. "And it's good to be home," she said, and she and Jenny exchanged a brief but tight hug.

It's good to be home, Cece repeated in her mind as she closed the door. She believed that, or at least she believed if she said it enough, it just might become true.

2

Cece flicked the tarnished latch and pushed to raise the kitchen window of what she called her "cottage" because it sounded much better than "the guesthouse in her grandmother's backyard." She couldn't complain because it was four times bigger than her previous home, a fifth-floor walk-up in New York with the kitchen sink a few feet from her twin bed.

The cottage was built to match the magnificent Victorian house Cece's grandparents had bought from Jenny's family, one in a row of six Victorians on Eureka Avenue called the "painted ladies of Eureka." Nana's house was a deep hunter-green with elaborate burgundy trim, and was replete with a pitched roof, wraparound porch, and a turret fit for Rapunzel.

Cece's cottage was painted in lighter shades of green and burgundy, and had a living/kitchen area, one bedroom, and full bath with a deep claw-foot tub. She divided her living area in half, one side with a loveseat and overstuffed chair, and on the other, a table made from a re-varnished door held up by two old filing cabinets, placed where the light was best, and used for working on dollhouses.

An assortment of antiques and treasures bought on their travels by Nana and Cece's grandfather, Papa Sam, filled both the house and cottage. Between the guest and main house, Nana had planted raised gardens of what she called her "practical herbs." She had the purple-skirted cone-flower, also known as "echinacea," for stimulating the immune system, and lemon balm, green leaves with serrated edges, for anxiety. She had yarrow, clusters of tiny white flowers like bridal bouquets, with flowers used for their calming effect, as well as the vibrant yellow roots of golden seal, which were for wound care. Nana and Aunt Granny professed that what they grew in their herb gardens could "cure whatever ails you," and

Cece had been taught early on that for most problems in life, she need only look to nature for the answers.

Cece made herself some of the Ceylon black tea that Nana had brought back from a trip to Sri Lanka and sat down at the round oak kitchen table to go over her to-do list. Nana had always loved "high tea" ever since she first experienced it in London, and made a family tradition of having one every Christmas Eve. She would bring out her silver and china and make everyone choose hats from a big trunk she kept in the attic. She made cucumber and cream cheese sandwiches, homemade scones with clotted cream and lemon curd, and enlisted Cece in making and decorating delicious petit fours. Not only did Cece look forward to that tea, but it meant there was always a supply of special tea from exotic places, as Nana didn't believe in saving "special" for only one day a year.

Cece still had to check the lists from fall registration for classes that had just begun at her tea-loving grandmother's dance studio, Eureka Grove Arts, founded almost forty years ago. Nana had gone straight from high school to New York, having never been out of the state of Tennessee before, with a friend she'd met at a dance camp in Knoxville. She had one goal in mind, and that was to become a Radio City Rockette. Aunt Granny would get tickled telling stories about Nana enlisting their friends to try and make a "kick line" when they were kids and how, inevitably, one of them would kick the other or get tripped up, and they would fall down like dominoes. With her impossibly long legs and a lot of hard work, Nana accomplished her dream and became a Rockette.

After a couple of years of dancing with the Rockettes, Nana attended a dinner dance and met the dashing Samuel Chagall, who was attending NYU law school. She quickly recognized his southern accent and made a beeline his way. Not only was he handsome and smart, but it turned out he grew up just forty miles south of Eureka Grove, and his people were a wealthy land-owning family. Sam knew Nana was the one when she immediately took the lead in their first dance together. With a grin, he'd said that he had been following her lead ever since.

After they got married and moved home, Nana opened a small dance studio in the basement of the historic, but crumbling, Eureka Grove Inn. Even though it had been built in 1925, Nana had seen potential in the old inn when all anyone else could see was rotting wood and overgrown gardens. It had once been a thriving tourist attraction, and Nana thought it could be again. Sam was a lot more skeptical, but eventually Nana won him over.

After a few years, they took their savings and sank it into buying the inn. For years, they reinvested their earnings and put a lot of elbow grease into renovation until they had done all they could, and finally resorted to hiring out for help. The inn went on to become a success, so much so that Nana and Sam eventually handed over the reins of the everyday operations to a trusted business friend, while they concentrated on enjoying their lives together. Cece's family had been heartbroken when Sam had a sudden heart attack and died, which was soon after Cece graduated from college. And, despite Cece's repeated attempts, Nana had not been out on a date since. Sam was irreplaceable in her eyes.

Nana no longer taught much at her dance studio, now relying mostly on other teachers she hired. On the other hand, she loved teaching her Senior Swans adult ballet class, helming her "Old Broads Book Brigade" monthly book club, and exercising with her "Not for Sissies" workout group at the gym.

Once the tea had steeped, Cece set her to-do list down so she could pour some for herself. After drizzling a five-second stream of honey into her tea, Cece reached for her cell and tapped in Bess's number. She knew better than to expect a normal greeting and was not disappointed when Bess answered.

"Hello, you've reached Bess Gibson. If you are calling about my stress level, press one. If you have any other requests regarding the quality of your room sheets, the water pressure of your shower, or have a catty comment about my accent, please hang up now and do not call back. *Ever.* Beep."

Cece chuckled at her fake message. "Hi, Bess," she said. "Long day already, huh?"

"Sister, you have no idea. The good news is that it can only go up from here. Like Dolly says, 'If you want the rainbow, you gotta put up with the rain.' What's up?"

"I'm just checking on the Fall Ball. Anything I need to know or do for the performance? We're three days out and counting."

"Oh, are we three days out?" Bess said, practicing what she called her "coping sarcasm." "That's about all I've been thinking about, Cece, and no, I think we've got it about wrapped up. We've got food, decorations, the DJ, and our usual Mercy Hospital Commander-in-Charge, aka Lorna, managing everything else." Lorna reminded them both of the actress Bea Arthur from the *Golden Girls*, and Bess began to sing the chorus to the theme song, "Thank You for Being a Friend." "Lorna's been doing this longer than I have, so it's pretty much a fine-tuned machine, thanks to her. At least I hope so."

Cece had met Bess in the eighth grade, and though they seemed quite different, their differences complemented each other. Bess was tall to Cece's short; Bess was full-figured and curvy to Cece's stick-straight, and Bess complained that her hair was too curly, while Cece lamented hers was too flat. Bess loved to wear lots of makeup and get her hair and nails done, while Cece opted for the more natural look.

Bess had been raised by a single mom who was in and out of rehab, and her dad had been out of the picture ever since the day her mom had picked her up from school with a black eye in second grade. She'd started working at the inn in high school to help her mom pay the rent. She was a no-nonsense, Dolly Parton-loving mountain woman who quickly rose through the ranks to what was one of the most important jobs at the inn: hospitality director. She was the kind of devoted friend who always had your back, and she was also the closest thing Cece had to a sister.

Bess was the kind of woman who wouldn't have thought twice about taking a job as a stripper if it meant paying the bills. She would do whatever it took because she'd had to before for her and her mom. Cece knew that Bess had witnessed her mom being abused by her dad before he left the family, and Bess was fiercely protective of family and friends because of that. Bess had wide-set dark brown eyes, flawless brown skin, and four visible tattoos. She also had thick, wavy blue-black hair, which her relatives said was evidence of the "Melungeon" in her. Melungeon people were a people who came about as a genetic mix of European,

Native American, and African ancestors, and were found in the largest concentration in the eastern parts of Tennessee.

"I'm sure it'll be great, as usual," Cece replied. "By the way, are you bringing Melvin?" she asked, adding, "And did you know about twenty percent of first dates lead to second ones?"

"Umm, okay, no, I didn't know that. But now I do," Bess said. "Very, very funny. You know perfectly well his name is Manny. He's coming in from Nashville Friday night. Maybe we can go out to dinner? I want you to meet him and tell me what you think."

"Are you okay? Since when do you care what anyone thinks? But dinner sounds great. I'm done early on Friday."

"You have a point. I guess I thought it sounded like the right thing to say. I *do* want you to meet him, though. This one might be around for a while. He might even make it to four dates."

"He sounds interesting," Cece said, chuckling and thinking of how many times she had said those words about whoever was Bess's latest love interest. "And I'd love to have dinner. Just send me a when and where."

"Will do. Talk soon. Mmm-wuh." Bess made a kissing sound into the phone.

When Cece put her phone down, her dog May was sitting patiently at the door, her white markings stark against her black fur, and staring longingly toward the yard. "Okay, May, let's go," she said, pulling May's leash off the tall mahogany coat rack by the door.

The trees were still mostly green on this late September day, with a hint of the pending temperature drop. Only a few trees gave a tease of what was to come by sporting an occasional red or yellow leaf. Cece tried to move May along, in spite of the beautiful day, so she could get back to work, but May was busy sniffing. Cece tried placating herself by taking in the view when she spied one of Nana's neighbors, Dr. Morley, with his shaggy black dog, Cleo, ahead and called out to him: "How're your knees doing today, Dr. Morley?"

Dr. Morley had decided, when he'd retired as a physician, to shed any semblance of professional bedside manner and become a curmudgeonly old man, and so far, had exceeded all expectations. And to reinforce to his local community his commitment to this endeavor, he had recently taken to wearing, below his usual shorts, colorful knee-high socks with sayings on them like "I'm too old for this shit."

Dr. Morley shook his head and grumbled, "You'd think that young'un doctor would know enough to help, wouldn't you? Couldn't find his way out of a wet paper bag! And why in God's name doesn't Mrs. Jingles get rid of some of that crap in her yard?" He pointed at the yard next door to Nana's.

"Sorry to hear all that, Dr. Morley," Cece said, with a big smile.

Dr. Morley gave a gravelly "Harrumph" in reply and kept walking.

"Hey, May!" came a voice from behind Mabel and Cece, as a black and white Eureka Grove patrol car pulled up beside her. "Maybe she's born with it, or maybe—"

"It's Maybelline," came Cece's response for the millionth time. Cece had named May after a cosmetic company, and that was one of their old slogans. Cece recognized the voice right away before turning to see Detective Joe Barksdale, with one hand thrown casually over the steering wheel and an elbow out the window. Joe had been her first love, and they had dated all of her senior year before she supposedly "broke his heart" and left for college.

"What're y'all up to on this beautiful day?"

"Hey, Joe," Cece said, coming to a stop on the sidewalk and trying to nonchalantly suck in her stomach. "We're getting a quick walk in before I have to get to work."

"Yep. I've seen a lot of the pink tights and black leotards heading toward the studio lately. I bet y'all are busy getting ready for the big Fall Ball about now, too."

"Yeah, classes just started, and we're ready as we can be for the ball," Cece answered, just as May yanked on the leash, having spotted a squirrel across the street, which forced Cece to step into a wide forward lunge, almost a split. She managed to slowly press herself back up to standing, then awkwardly placed one hand on her hip as if it were nothing.

"Nice catch," Joe said from the car.

Cece asked, with feigned disinterest, "You and Hailey going to the ball?" Cece had heard he was dating Hailey Carmichael from the hair salon.

"Nope," he said, a bit too fast and definitively. "I mean, no," he slowed down. "I think she's working. Besides I'm on duty for the ball that night. You know, all those *city* people coming to town," he said. "Will you be going? I mean, of course you are, I guess…," he trailed off.

"Yeah. I'll be there with my advanced ballet class. We haven't rehearsed the dance piece as much as I'd like, though." Cece hoped the sweat she felt running down her back was not also showing under her arms. She couldn't understand why talking to Joe brought her entire past floating up to the surface, and she felt every bit of sixteen years old at that moment. She also sensed a rush, like a full-body memory, of what first love had felt like.

Cece tried to diminish the feeling by telling herself that she and Joe were just kids back then, but once someone makes you feel that way, it stamps itself into both your body and brain. She subtly shook her head to clear it and did her best to keep her mature, "city girl" façade.

"Oh, I'm sure it'll be fine. I mean, remember when Rona Gail Renner was doing turns and accidentally hit that other girl in the face at your recital that time?" Joe asked, laughing. "It can't be as bad as that, can it?"

Cece laughed. "When had I last thought of that? Seems like a lifetime ago," she said as lights and beeps started coming from the big screen on Joe's dashboard.

"Gotta run. See ya later, Cece." He waved, putting the car in gear and heading off.

Sure hope so, Cece thought to herself. But, no, she didn't want to think that way, because of Hailey, because it was history, because she didn't want to get involved with anyone until she figured out some things about her own life. Cece picked up her pace, and soon she and May broke into a run for home. They both needed to get rid of a little extra adrenalin.

* * *

May and Cece ran right into Nana's backyard and up to the back door of the "big house" because she needed to ask Calvin, Nana's everpresent handyman, if he could come take a look at her dishwasher. As it happened, his stepladder stood near the door, and as she opened it, she walked straight into the ladder. Despite being a dancer, Cece could be surprisingly clumsy.

"Whoa there, Cece," Calvin said in his laid-back, extended drawl as he reached out to steady the ladder. Calvin had a limp brown ponytail, a scraggly beard, and wore a rotating selection from his heavy metal tank-top collection. He had an unusual tattoo on his bicep that looked like a turtle with a pineapple coming out of its shell, which he'd gotten when he worked as a handyman for a resort, and lived on one of the Cayman Islands for five years. Calvin could fix anything, from the light fixture he was currently working on, to computers, to car engines. Given the amount of time he spent at Nana's house, the dance studio, and the inn, he might as well have been on the payroll, but Calvin was in demand all over town.

"The Duchess is in the kitchen," he said, tipping his head in that direction, knowing no one could get away with calling Nana "the Duchess" but him. May ran into the house and straight toward Nana's super-sized calico cat, Blisters. Bliss offered May one slightly lifted eyelid from her place of rest on the jewel-colored pillows of the window seat before returning to her slumber.

"Sorry about that, Calvin. You're the one I really needed to see. Can you come over when you get a chance and look at my dishwasher? It seems to stop after just one cycle."

"Yeah. Happy to take a look later. Might be tomorrow if you're home, ah wah?" he said in his strange linguistic mix of Cayman Creole and Tennessee.

"That's fine, I gotta go to work now anyway. Just text me tomorrow. Thanks, Calvin."

"Tennessee, is that you?" came Nana's lilting voice from the kitchen. Much to her chagrin, Cece's given name was indeed "Tennessee." She was thrilled to later learn her young preschool dance class friends couldn't pronounce it, so she became Cece early on. She would never cease to wonder why her parents thought a name that was already the name of a state, the one they all lived in, and impossible to spell, would make a good name for their daughter.

The only excuse her parents came up with was, "It seemed like a good idea at the time," making Cece seriously question the wisdom of all their choices from then on.

"Hi, Nana," Cece called toward the kitchen. "I can't stay. I'm heading to the studio."

"Okay, darling. Good luck today. I know the first weeks the little ones can be wild as bucks, and it's almost a full moon."

"Thanks, Nana. I'll give you a report later. Let's go, May," Cece yelled out. May came bounding down the hall from where she was busy trying to get Bliss to acknowledge her existence, and they headed out the back door and to the cottage.

Cece threw her hair up into a bun, pulled on a leotard and leggings, then sweatpants, grabbed her bags for class, and was off.

Inside her house, Nana put away her watering can, having just finished attending to her numerous potted plants, and went to give another stir to her latest herbal remedy concoction that smelled of ginger root and cinnamon sticks. She was always extremely careful in her medicine-making, for her remedies called for precise measurements and precise mixing and cooking instructions, or what was intended to be helpful, even curative, could become dangerous.

She pulled an ice-cold bottle of Fanta orange from the fridge and sat down at the kitchen table to write the herbal recipe down for Hazel and Cece. She felt the soreness in her lower back again, which she knew came from overdoing it teaching her Senior Swans class. She was determined to teach Jerome how to do a *changément* jump, even if it killed her.

She crossed her legs to rub some Solomon's seal salve into her foot where it had been cramping, remembering it was also good at calming the nervous system. Even though Sam had been gone almost ten years now, Nana still felt the piercing ache of his loss. Sam had been mowing the yard when she stepped out the front door to bring him a glass of water, and he'd collapsed before her eyes from a massive heart attack. Nana had learned a lot in the school of grief in the years between, and allowed the feelings to wash over her when they needed to, knowing the feelings would recede if she let them have the air they needed from time to time.

Grief was also, in her view, a way of loving Sam's spirit, letting him know he was still very much a part of her life.

Nana worried for her granddaughter, Cece, and she thought maybe that was activating her arthritis and her grief. She wondered if Cece could be happy back in their little mountain town after being in New York and Madrid, knowing the tough adjustment it had been for her long ago. She never expected to meet Sam and end up back where she grew up. Cece had always been wildly independent, just as she had been once, and Nana was convinced she would never move back to Eureka Grove. She had always known dance for Cece was different than it had been for her. For Cece, dance had been what helped her fit in but wasn't her one-and-only passion.

Nana also worried about what the family called Cece's "peculiars," believing that what Cece's doctors and therapists had tried to pin down and diagnose was something entirely different than what those "experts" thought it was. Nana and her sister, Hazel, believed the peculiars to be a gift passed down from the women of the family, a gift that allowed them to experience the world in ways unlike other people. Nana and Hazel both had always possessed these gifts, and they thought Cece was just now discovering hers. Nana pulled her sock back on, still rubbing her foot, and lost in thought. She knew she and Hazel would have to explain it all to Cece. She wasn't sure how, but she also knew it had to be soon.

3

Cece pulled into the back parking lot of the studio, thankful her 2015 Jeep Wrangler didn't have a caution light on for once because it was running on 180,000 miles and had been inherited from her dad well after the first hundred thousand. She parked beside the double-door entrance to the dance studio.

Built in terraced sections into the side of a hill, the massive arts-and-crafts style inn, constructed of stone and wood, held a stately presence in the town. The dance studio was tucked away on the bottom floor, partially underground. On the lawn surrounding the inn, mature oak, maple, and dogwood trees stood among the flower gardens, bordered by pink rhododendrons and mountain laurel, and intersected with pebbled walking paths.

Cece unlocked the doors and promptly flipped on the long row of light switches. Because the studio was built into the ground, it was very dark, prompting Cece and Bess to refer to it as "the catacombs." Luckily, the narrow horizontal windows at the back of the inn, where the ground had sloped down, allowed in some natural light, and wall colors of lacey white with a hint of yellow were evidence of Nana's attempt to lighten things up.

The studio had two dance rooms, a dressing room with benches, a small office, and a storage room cram-packed with old performance costumes, props, set designs, and a sequin-littered floor. On the lobby walls hung two posters from Nana's Rockette days. In one she was in the famous red-sequined "toy soldier" costume, wearing a tall black hat with even longer white feathers coming out of the top. The other was of her in the Rockette's famous kick-line. There were also photos of Cece and the other instructors, and Cece was grateful she was not wearing the infamous M&M costume in hers.

For Cece, the studio, and the inn as well, could be a little off-putting, especially at night. The inn stood like a fortress on the hill, solid and imposing. A railroad tycoon had originally built the inn as a place for folks to enjoy the "rarefied and healing mountain air," and he viewed it as a place for those suffering from respiratory problems and to promote overall health and well-being.

There were all sorts of stories about the inn, some of buried or hidden treasures, and some of scandals from long ago. The inn had a basement with hidden passageways and rooms put to use during both wartime and prohibition. Of course, rumors had circulated that it was haunted, linked to various tragedies from years past. Cece always kept her eyes and ears open when she had to close the studio at night, and Nana was less than reassuring when she told Cece not to be worried about ghosts because all the ones she'd ever met were quite friendly.

Cece's phone vibrated, and, pulling it from her jacket pocket, she answered, "Hey, Dad. What's up?"

"Hi, baby. Just checking on you. I wanted to know how the Fall Ball's coming, and how the first week of classes are going."

Cece's dad, Leo Chagall, was an American History teacher at Johns Town Community College and wrote a monthly local history column called "Backroads" for the *Eureka Gazette*. He lived about twenty-five miles south of Eureka Grove. Cece could hear the tap-tapping of stone hitting stone in the background, which meant her dad was probably out on his front porch "flintknapping," making arrowheads or other ancient tools from rock.

"Doing okay. It's busy, but I like it that way. Don't we have a lunch date next week?"

"Yeah, we sure do. Do you want to drive over here, or you want me to come there?" he asked.

"I'll come there. I need the change of scenery," Cece said, continuing to walk around the studio and turn on more lights. "Dad, I really hate to cut it short, but I have to get ready to teach."

"Of course. I understand. Love on your Nana for me. Bye now."

"Bye," Cece said, tapping to hang up, just as she heard the rumble of a truck pull up half an hour early for class. She knew the truck's owner and took a deep breath to collect herself. Beryl Bridges had a shiny, black, tricked-out Ford F150 with tires so big she thought it might take a rope ladder to get up to the imported leather seats.

Cece was particularly sensitive to southern stereotypes, having lived in New York, where it felt like her accent was a constant source of amusement, abysmal imitations, and unfounded assumptions. She would make it clear to anyone who would listen that not everyone in the South said "ain't," married their cousin, or drove a huge pick-up with big tires. Unfortunately, Beryl could've easily been the poster child for the stereotype of the "Southern Good Ole' Boy."

Beryl was good-looking, in an ex-football player, broad shoulders, thick neck kind of way. As usual he ushered Bridget in, walking straight over to Cece. He was wearing his signature lizard-skin cowboy boots with pressed khakis and a starched white shirt. He always wore a gold serpentine necklace, and that alone made Cece cringe, but on top of that, he would lean his head down too low and close when talking to her, and she smelled his breath, hair gel, and cologne, all at the same time.

"How's Miss Cece doin' today?" he asked, filling the entire lobby with his presence and scent as if marking his territory.

"I'm doing great, Mr. Bridges," Cece said, kneeling to talk to Bridget. "How are you doing today, Bridget?"

"Fine, Miss Cece," Bridget's high, nervous voice answered.

"Cece's looking good these days. She needs to remember to call me Beryl. We ain't that far apart in age," Beryl boomed, winking, his jaw moving sideways as he chewed on a wad of gum.

He always spoke to Cece in the third person, as if she were somewhere other than right in front of him, and he wore a slow grin that sent a surge of uneasiness racing down her spine. Cece had maintained composure for the sake of his daughter, but she wasn't sure how long she could keep it up. Her southern upbringing dictated she not be rude, but this time in history was a different time for all women and called for different responses.

Beryl Bridges was a developer who owned sprawling tracts of land in Eureka Grove and the surrounding area. He was on the town council, divorced, and, even when he had a girlfriend, was perpetually on the hunt for the next one. Cece knew that he was at odds with Jenny, also on the council, over the new waterpark he wanted to build. She and another council member had opposed it, and Beryl had called them "anti-family" because of it. Thankfully, a few more students wandered in, and Cece busied herself putting dance bags in cubbies.

Before leaving, Beryl put his hand on her elbow and leaned in to say, "Just so you know, I fixed it with my ex, so I'm the only one bringin' her to class," his voice low, as if sharing some secret conspiracy. It made Cece feel like she'd just been blasted with noxious smoke, and she couldn't wait until her workday was over so she could wash it off.

Cece ushered out the last ballet class at 7:00 p.m., having finished teaching three classes in a row. There was always one student left waiting after all the others were gone, and for this class, it was Lexi Shafer.

Lexi, age nine, had already called her mom from her cellphone. Cece was pretty sure she hadn't even mastered how to tell time at Lexi's age, watching incredulously as Lexi's thumbs danced across her cellphone's keyboard. Lexi helped Cece pick up trash and put props away while they waited.

Finally, her mom, Amanda, blew in about twenty minutes later, followed by what Cece picked up as a dousing of rose perfume layered over body odor.

"Here I am, sugar. You know Mama just couldn't help it," Amanda gushed in a fake singsong voice, addressing Lexi only. Cece knew better than to expect an acknowledgment, let alone an apology, because every time this happened, there was an excuse. "All the treadmills were busy at the gym, and things just ran late; you know how busy Mama gets."

Amanda was married to the new high school principal, Steve Schafer, and she was his third wife. Rumors had flown that she might have once been his student in the town they had moved from. She certainly was working hard at her marriage, given the apparent surgical help she seemed to have already had. Cece didn't understand it since Amanda was naturally all blue-eyed, blonde gorgeousness. She couldn't imagine why Amanda thought she needed to fix anything, but then again, *Isn't that the way it always is? Others see us differently than we see ourselves.* Cece knew pretty much all women heard multiple voices in their heads whenever they looked in the mirror. *It's just a matter of which one is loudest, which one we choose to listen to.*

"Well, she's all ready to go," Cece said, opening the door wide to encourage them out, and fanning it to let some fresh air in. She hoped it would help get the mix of cologne, perfume, and sweat out of the lobby. Cece turned on all the outside floodlights and gathered trash bags to take to the dumpster. She was hoisting the bags over the rim when she heard something from behind the dumpster. Armed with only two kitchen-size garbage bags, she boldly yelled out, "Who's there?"

She heard a racket coming from behind the dumpster and then a small voice, "Sorry, Miss Cece," as a figure stepped out from the shadows.

"Angel! You scared the bejesus out of me! What are you doing out here? Class was over almost thirty minutes ago." Cece pulled the sleeves of her hoodie down, realizing for the first time how the temperature had dropped. "It's starting to get a little nippy out here. You know you can always wait inside with me. And why didn't you walk home like you usually do?"

"Cassie was s'posed to pick me up. I called her, but she's not answering."

"Okay, well, now it's dark, and you don't need to be out here. Let me get my stuff, lock up, and I'll give you a ride," Cece told Angel, noticing an empty Cheetos bag and donut box Angel had nudged behind the dumpster with her foot.

Angel was thirteen years old and already in the advanced ballet class. Her technique and musicality were off the charts. Cece was thrilled to have her as a student, and even more elated that she worked as an assistant for Cece's classes with her youngest students, which was always like herding cats. Angel lived in a small townhouse on the edge of town with her older sister, Cassie.

"Okay. Yeah. Thanks," Angel said, picking up her dance bag and backpack. Cece locked up the studio, loaded her bags into the trunk, threw Angel's bags in the back seat, and soon they were pulling up in front of

Cassie and Angel's townhouse, but the front porch of Angel's house was dark.

"Are you sure you'll be okay?" she asked Angel, now worried because she knew that Cassie was hypervigilant when it came to Angel. She always left the door light on.

"She probably had to work late or forgot or something," Angel said as she opened her car door and slid out, pulling her bags over the seat and out with her. "I'm good, Miss Cece. Promise. Thanks for the ride." Angel hurried to her front door, went inside, and flipped on the outside light to let Cece know she was in and okay.

Cece sat in her car for a little longer. She wasn't sure if she was hoping Angel's sister Cassie would show up, or remembering what it felt like to be thirteen and come home to an empty house. Either way, Cece made a mental note to check in on Angel again. She had an idea the empty Cheetos bag and donut box signaled a different problem entirely.

* * *

Once home, after multiple kisses from May, Cece couldn't wait to sink into the steaming hot water in her claw-foot tub. It was her favorite way to relax, besides cracking jokes about the *Housewives of Dallas* TV show with Bess while eating popcorn and drinking boxed white wine. Every day after teaching a different part of her body was sore, and a hot bath with Epsom salts was always the remedy. That, and Aunt Granny's wild yam tea for muscle soreness, which required incredible amounts of sugar to stomach. Just as Cece turned the porcelain handles to "off," her phone buzzed.

"Hey, Bess. This better be good because my tub is almost full, and I am totally worn out."

"Oops, sorry about that! I do so hate to intrude on the all-holy bath time. Real quick, I just wanted to tell you Manny called and won't be getting here 'til late. We'll have to do dinner another time, but how 'bout we meet at The Iris for coffee in the morning?"

"Sounds great. Sorry about dinner, but we'll try again," Cece said, adding a couple of drops of lavender essential oil to the bathwater. "Does 8 work?"

"Yep. Great. I'll have all the charity ball info with me, so we can take a last look at when your students will perform. See you in the a.m. Mmm-wuh."

Cece eased into the water and felt the knotted worries in her muscles and on her mind release. Everything, that is, except the image of Joe in his patrol car, the toned cut of muscle in his upper arms, and their easy rapport that was still there all these years after high school. She knew that image might take more than a fast run and a salt bath to work through.

4

"This is the guest and RSVP list, and this is the schedule for setup, including caterer, decorators, and DJ. And this is where your dancers come on the schedule," Bess said, pointing a long, fuchsia, silver-tipped fingernail at the spread of papers on their table.

The local coffee shop, The Iris, named after the Tennessee state flower, was proudly owned and operated by Ricky and Olivia Ferrell. The décor was a mix of dark wood, brick, and exposed beams, with local art and vintage photos of Eureka Grove on the walls. They'd done a great job running it, despite Ricky's complete lack of a personality. The only thing that could produce the slightest spark from Ricky was if you brought up his antique Corvette. Olivia, on the other hand, practically vibrated with personality. She wore colored high-top Converse shoes every day with equally colorful overalls, and she liked to share upbeat quotes with her customers, which annoyed Bess to no end.

Bess came dressed for work, wearing a raspberry-colored tunic top with big multicolored tassels for earrings. She had her hair in a long braid to one side so thick and shiny it looked like the tail of a show horse.

"Seems like you're ready to roll, as usual," Cece said. Cece had always admired Bess's easy way of being in the world, always unabashedly herself, whether it was in how she looked, what she said, or what she believed.

"Well, it's really all Lorna from Mercy; I just get the place ready, decorate, and unlock the doors at the right time. And according to this schedule, I better get moving soon. We've got a final walk-through in a little over an hour," she said, gathering papers into her wide canvas tote that had the words "What Would Dolly Do?" printed in red block letters on the front.

"Wait, I have to hear about Manny," Cece said, putting her hand on Bess's forearm. "At least give me the elevator speech, so I can try to make a stab at small talk tomorrow."

Bess stopped, sitting back down and smiling. "Well, how's this? He's tall, dark, and handsome. He moved up from Florida for college and has lived in Nashville ever since."

"And did you meet him at the hotel?" Cece asked, already knowing the answer.

"Bullseye. How'd you guess?" She grinned. "He was at the inn to visit clients in the area."

"What's he do?"

"He works in the country music industry as an agent. I asked him to give me some inside scoop, but he says he can't 'disclose names due to confidentiality agreements,'" Bess said, making air quotes. "But he laughed when he said it, adding that they were mostly performers who had been popular at one time and still needed to make a living."

"Like 'one-hit-wonders,' I guess," Cece said. "Nevertheless, I'm excited to meet him. I know you're in a hurry, but give me just a few more minutes? I don't even know what's going on at school," Cece said before taking the last bite of a salted-chocolate caramel cookie the size of her hand. Bess had been taking one class at a time at the community college to get her associate's degree and now only had one semester to go.

"Oh, God," she said, putting one palm over her forehead and rolling her eyes. "I don't have time now, but remind me to tell you about Dr. Simkins." Bess emphasized the *doctor* part.

"Hope I'm not interrupting y'all," Olivia said, flitting up to the table.

"No, not at all," said Cece, glancing up. "What's up?"

"I just wanted to tell y'all to be sure and remember to have a blessed day, that's all," Olivia said, with two firm taps on the table for emphasis, before moving on.

"Well, thanks, Olivia. You, too," Cece said, glancing over at Bess, who was pretending to be writing something. "As you were saying?" she said to Bess.

"I forgot since I was busy remembering to have a blessed day." Bess smirked. "I know; don't say it. I know she means well." Bess shook her head. "Anyway, let me know if you want to come over tonight. I'm hoping Shane can come, too, and give his usual unsolicited advice for what we're wearing to the ball. But now," she said, glancing at her watch, "I really need to go. Mmm-wuh," she said, including an exaggerated kiss-blowing gesture as she hopped out of her chair to leave.

Cece headed home to meet Calvin at her cottage, and found him waiting, leaning against her door with a cigarette hanging from the side of his mouth, when she rolled up.

"I thought you'd quit those things, finally," Cece said, knowing he'd quit and started again too many times to count. She picked up her watering can, offering it to Calvin as an ashtray.

"I'm working on it, Cece. It's a work in progress."

"Come on in," Cece said, unlocking her front door, which was painted a deep red and had a half-circle window at the top. "Thanks a lot for doing this. Let me know the charge."

"No prob. I'll just put it on the Duchess's tab," he said out of the side of his mouth since the other side was now busy shredding a toothpick.

"Oh, please don't," Cece told him. "It's bad enough that I live in her backyard and work at her studio. I really would like to pay you myself."

"I hear you. Before I left for the Caymans I lived at home with my parents and worked at Best Buy, so I know the feeling. I'll let you know the cost once I figure out what's going on."

"Thanks, Calvin. I've got to head over to Nana's for a minute. C'mon, May," she called, and May came zooming out from the bedroom to Cece's side. May could always hear, "Going to Nana's," from a mile away because it meant getting to annoy Bliss the cat and maybe receiving a few tasty treats from Nana. The word "bath," on the other hand, had the opposite effect.

Bliss paused from licking her paw barely long enough to glance at May as they made their way in through the back door. Since Nana didn't want Cece to have to ring the back doorbell every time she came in, she rigged up a bell contraption that jingled when the door opened, like in a retail store. Inside Nana's house all the floors were polished heart pine, and every room was filled with potted plants and comfortable antiques. Most of the plants served some sort of medicinal purpose, like the spiky, octopus arms of the aloe plant used for burns, or the starburst leaves in the white sage, used for congestion. Cece walked into the back hallway, peering into an empty kitchen, where the distinct aroma of mud and lemon was coming from, so she knew Nana had some kind of healing plant mixture on the stove. "Nana?" Cece called up the wide staircase with the curving oak banister.

"Darlin', I'm coming down right now. Take a peek at the stove pot for me, will you?"

Nana met Cece in the kitchen wearing one of her graphic T-shirts—this one was her favorite color red with the words "Bless Your Heart" in white on the front—and black corduroy pants. She had on her signature diamond post earrings that Sam had given her, and she wore her shoulder-length silver-grey hair in a low bun, highlighted by one stubborn streak of darker hair running from front to back. With her high cheekbones, still-dark eyebrows, and rivulets of wrinkles on smooth pale skin, she was beautiful in the striking way that only age and experience reveal.

For a rural mountain girl, Nana pulled off sophisticated with ease. She told Cece that when she married Papa Sam she had to learn how to mingle with the wealthy and educated, and Nana was nothing if not smart as a whip. Nana was the first in her family to graduate high school and then college. Dance had truly been her ticket out, having grown up in an isolated hollow east of Eureka Grove. Learning which fork to use or how to write a proper thank-you note wasn't even on Nana's radar, but those things were important in the family she'd married into, so she made it her goal to learn. She said she would carefully observe and study, keeping quiet while memorizing details at their elegant parties. She went into the kitchen, learned the recipes, and watched as the table was set. She watched what the other women wore and how they wore it, along with learning how to play tennis and golf. She read books by Tolstoy and Austen, and poems by Coleridge and Dickinson. She studied the art of Picasso and Monet. She read the newspaper and followed the stock market. Nana learned by trial and error how to play the game, becoming a master of conquering her new world while keeping one foot solidly in her old one.

"Smells like eye of newt and frog toes," Cece joked, remembering how when she was little she wished Nana would just bake rice crispy treats and chocolate cupcakes like other grandmothers.

"Take a load off those biscuits and tell me what's new," Nana said, gesturing to the kitchen table. "I was upstairs trying to get that dang doll-house finished for the auction. Want something to drink?"

"Just some water, thanks. Just came from coffee with Bess at The Iris."

"You got it." Nana opened the fridge and handed Cece a bottle of water. "I still can't believe I actually pay money for water in a bottle. I ought to bottle what comes from Hazel's spring house; I could probably get rich. That, or find that hidden gold box of old Mr. Newport's. Anyway, tell me what's up with the little ones at the studio, and then we can get to Bess."

Cece caught her up on the goings-on in class the night before, and about Beryl and Angel.

"I've known Beryl since he was a baby, and even though he's slick as a snake, he's harmless like a garter. He might pinch, but he won't bite," Nana said.

"That's the point, Nana. Pinching—or, in his case, leering—is no longer an option in today's world, and I shouldn't have to take that along with his gag-inducing cologne overload."

"You're right," Nana agreed, nodding with a sigh. "Things certainly have changed since the old days. And thank the good Lord above. The stories I could tell you about back when I first started…," she gave an involuntary shudder. "It was a different time back then."

Cece absorbed Nana's energy like a magnet. She couldn't imagine what it must've been like for her on her own in New York, let alone when she was just starting out as a woman in business for herself. "Just because it was a long time ago doesn't mean it was okay, Nana. It was never okay," Cece said. "So, guess who I've got in beginning ballet class."

"Who?"

"Marydale Bevins."

Nana's brown eyes shifted skyward, thinking. "That's Millie's granddaughter, isn't it?"

"Yep. I still can't believe you actually taught her grandmother."

"Good God. How can that be possible? That must mean I got old," Nana said with mock surprise. "Or, they must've been very young mothers, like your mama and I were," she said, grinning.

Nana couldn't help but see and hear Cece's mom in Cece. She saw it in the way Cece's head bobbed slightly when she was listening and in the tone of her laugh. Nana also noticed how Cece put her hand on her heart, as if when someone talked she could feel the vibration, which was exactly like her sister, Hazel. *Funny how it's not just what we say that gets passed down, but how we say it, even down to the smallest gestures we use when talking,* Nana thought to herself as she looked at her granddaughter. Nana believed every soul wore a body with its own story to tell, and each person carried generations in their bones.

"We were way too young for young'uns," Nana continued. "I'm glad you're taking your time. Although . . . time has a way of getting away from us. Believe me, darling."

"Yes, Nana, I know. Someday it'll happen. I guess. My track record's been less than stellar, you know. How about this? I'll go out with someone if you will," Cece half-teased, genuinely wishing her grandmother could find a nice companion. "Remember, I'm here for you when you want me to set you up on that dating app."

"You know I'm savin' myself for Snoop Dog," came Nana's usual reply.

"I've told you before, he's too young for you, Nana."

"Tell that to Martha Stewart," said Nana, with a wink.

Cece's track record with men was indeed terrible. Although she'd had a couple of long-term boyfriends, she was too restless to stay too long, let alone settle down.

"Speaking of men, what's new with Bess?" Nana asked.

"She's bringing her new beau from Nashville to the dance. Apparently he's a tall, dark Italian guy named Manny and works in the country music business."

"That's perfect for our Bess, then," Nana said, absentmindedly drawing figures on the table with her finger.

Nana's cellphone ringtone, "Beethoven's Fifth," blared from the kitchen counter, surprising them both. "I better get that, darling. It's Carlene from the beauty shop, and she's been trying to fit me in today. I better not miss it," Nana said, pointing at her hair and making a panicked face.

"I gotta get going anyway. Love you, Nana."

"Love you, too, darlin.' See you soon."

Cece headed back to her cottage to begin her "formal event" prep. In this regard, she was much more like Aunt Granny Hazel than Nana, preferring her hiking boots and jeans to evening gowns and heels. The process of choosing what to wear and shoes to match, how to do her hair, and which accessories to add, was completely overwhelming for her. She learned she had to get organized the day before the event. She was not one to get into hair and makeup, unlike Bess, who reveled in pencils and powders. But Cece had learned from professionals how to get makeup on in a hurry for the stage in New York, which came in handy in times like this.

She already had her gown laid out on her bed, gathering the courage to try it on and see if it would still fit since she hadn't had it on in two years. The gown was one she'd kept from a short-lived off-Broadway show she'd done called *Zombie Prom*. Despite the title of the show, the dress was a lovely plum-colored frock with a wide tulle skirt. The neckline was round and embellished with tiny silver seed-beads and had a fitted bodice to accentuate the wide skirt for elegant turns. Luckily, her old strappy silver sandals went with everything.

Cece's phone buzzed. She checked it to find a text from Bess.

Shane just got here to assess the fashion situation for the ball. You up for bringing your stuff over?

Cece tapped back:

I wish I could, but I have to finish this dollhouse since it has to go to the silent auction tomorrow 😵 Can I just send pictures of me in my dress?

Shane says send 'em on and he'll give his 👍 or 👎 😗

Shane had grown up with Bess and Cece and moved back to town several years ago to run the local bookstore, Stone Soup. Besides loving anything book-related, he had quite the eye for fashion as well.

Later, after trying on the outfit for the ball and getting a thumbs-up text from Shane, Cece heated up some leftovers. She gave May her evening walk and was soon snuggled into her well-worn pink flannel robe. Cece settled down in front of her dollhouse worktable and put on her favorite podcast, *Crime Stories*. She wore a "headband headlight," which made her look like a coal miner, and she had an extra-large magnifier clamped to the side of the table so she could see to work with the tiny pieces and parts.

The miniature house was a log cabin with two large rooms and a loft. Having finished staining the "logs" and interior a deep chestnut, Cece didn't have much left to do. Cece had already meticulously constructed the stone fireplace with miniature pebbles glued to a wooden frame, using tweezers and a syringe filled with glue.

Cece often lost track of time while at work on the miniature houses, becoming so laser-focused that everything else fell away. At her feet, May twitched in a deep sleep, undoubtedly dreaming of finally getting a reaction out of Bliss. Using her tweezers, Cece carefully lowered her hand inside the house to place the last in a set of blue one-inch books on the shelf of an almost-full bookcase. Before she could get the first one on the shelf, she was surprised by a scent so strong it made her flinch. Cece thought it smelled as if someone had put the strongest perfume possible, made of peaches and honey, right under her nose. It caused her to drop the tweezers, knocking over the bookcase and spilling all the other books out in the process.

Cece shook out both hands, interlaced her fingers, and pressed her palms out, taking a deep breath. She rolled her shoulders forward and back. She did everything her therapist had suggested she do after these "episodes."

"Peculiars" was the word her Aunt Granny Hazel used to explain and help Cece understand when this happened to her. For Cece, the sensation poured over her, lasting only a moment, but packing a powerful punch. Aunt Granny would tell her it meant she was "special, meaning secret-superpower-special." The official name for this was synesthesia, which means to feel an arbitrary sensation coupled with an image. And though they come on together, the two don't necessarily go together, such as the color blue is associated with a specific smell, or maybe hearing the number four and tasting lemon.

The downside for Cece was that because of her "peculiars," she would sometimes say or do things that others regarded as strange. She had particular trouble in school math class, once refusing to write the number eight because, as she'd tried to explain at the time, "It burned," and another time in algebra, claiming the equal sign made a high ringing sound in her ears. Since, as a child, Cece didn't know any other way to be, she was baffled by the reactions of others. Her parents worked hard to help Cece become aware of her differences and to learn some coping tools without ever demeaning her. They viewed her neurodivergence, like Aunt Granny did, as her superpower. Her classmates, though, were another story entirely.

But now, as she was on the downslope to thirty, her peculiars were changing in other ways that Cece couldn't quite define. Her therapist suggested she make a diary of what was happening, and her dad was worried enough to suggest an MRI

For now, at least, she knew the best medicine would be sleep. She pulled off the headlamp and turned off the light, giving May a "time-to-move" nudge with her toe, and they headed down the hall to bed.

5

Cece unpacked her Jeep and made her way straight for the inn's Allegro Grand Ballroom. She held her dress over her shoulder in a dry cleaner's bag, her shoes in a box, and another big bag filled with things her student dancers inevitably forgot, like bobby pins, hairspray, and makeup. She pushed open the double doors with her foot, expecting to find Bess and her new man inside, but they were nowhere to be found.

Instead, tall, lanky Nick Adams, the DJ, was busy setting up the sound system, and Lorna, the hospital rep, was shuffling papers at the registration table. The room looked spectacular, filled with autumnal colors of barn red, gold, and saffron. There were clusters of balloons threaded with glittering gold ribbons, which created a backdrop for the dance floor at the end of the large, rectangular room. The round tables that curved around the dance floor each held a fresh arrangement of tangerine lilies, red roses, and amethyst mums clustered around pillar candles with faux flames. Hanging from the ceiling were multiple craftsman-style chandeliers with stained glass borders casting a thousand multicolored glimmers across the room. Burgundy silk curtains hung from fabric-covered cornices in tall windows, framing the quickly disappearing glow of sunlight.

"Well, hello, Cece. So good to see you again," Lorna said, volume on high, from across the room. "What do you think of our decorations this year? I think your friend could make a business of this."

"It's tremendous once again, Lorna," Cece said, making her way over so they didn't have to yell. "I think Bess might've outdone herself this time." Lorna was tall and big-boned, as Nana would say, and she seemed to always be wearing a tunic vest with a satin, tie-neck shirt, and matching knit pants. It seemed, to Cece, quite like an outfit Bea Arthur would have approved of. As a nod to the festivities, her vest had shimmery threads throughout, but she'd kept to her usual sensible low-heeled shoes. Lorna ran this ball like a seasoned ship captain, fantastic at what she did and precise in her planning down to the smallest detail.

"Speaking of Bess, have you seen her?" Cece asked.

"She and her friend were just in here. They're probably close by," Lorna said, turning her head.

Cece guessed they might be out in the inn somewhere and made her way to the door, opened it, and almost ran right into Bess.

"There you are," she said. "So, where is he?" Cece took in Bess's floral and musk perfume, knowing it had to be from the Dolly line of fragrances.

"He's on a phone call; should be back in in a minute. I'll introduce you, then we better change clothes. Good job on the glam hair, by the way."

Cece proudly touched her coppery locks, having begrudgingly used a curling iron for the night, and was just glad the curls had lasted this long. "The place looks great, Bess. I love the balloons. I don't remember you using those before."

"I saw them on Instagram and loved the look. If you squinch your eyes tight and look, you might think you're seeing Fall trees," she said, squinting her eyes to demonstrate.

"Too bad you can't give everyone special glasses for that effect."

"We do. They're called champagne flutes and shot glasses, my dear." Bess mimicked a "mic drop" and laughed.

Just then, the double doors opened, and a group of Nana's Senior Swans came in with a flutter, carrying various folders and name tags, ready for their duties at the registration table. They took the job seriously, even wearing all-white so they would match. Bess headed toward them to give registration instructions while Cece laid eyes on the outstanding male specimen that had come in after them. His eyes were only on Bess, though, until she detoured to the registration table, so Cece took the opportunity to head his way.

"You must be Manny," she said, holding out a hand.

"Yes. Yes, I am. I'm Manny Marinoni. And you must be Cece!"

"Yep. I'm so glad to meet you." Manny looked to be mid-thirties, with wavy black hair, full lips, and chiseled cheekbones. He wore a fashion-forward dark green suit, with pants that skimmed his ankles, no socks, and loafers. "Is there anything you guys need help with? I feel a little useless," Manny commented, his head circling to take in all of the ballroom.

"No, I don't think so. Between Bess and Lorna from the hospital, everything is ready."

Two arms overflowing with audio equipment pushed through the ballroom's double doors, with Nick's head barely peering out from the top.

"There's my answer," Manny said, heading to help. Nick worked as head bellhop at the inn during the day and DJ'd as a side gig. He was a quiet guy with sandy-blonde hair that tended to fall over one eye, causing him to continually flick his head back. He was someone who genuinely listened when anyone talked to him, which made him an outstanding bellhop. He also had an almost photographic memory, which served him well in dealing with the never-ending, and often unusual, needs of guests.

While Manny helped Nick, Cece headed to the room off the lobby where her dancers had gone to change into their costumes. She had to field the usual last-minute emergencies, such as forgetting their pointe shoes or tights, prompting frantic calls home and rushed drop-offs at the front desk. It was for this very reason Cece had the dancers report an hour early for the event. All were present and accounted for, with a couple of parents doing duty as helpers. Cece and Bess had already unrolled the heavy Marley flooring used for the dancers so they wouldn't slip in their pointe shoes.

Manny was talking to Nick when Cece came back into the ballroom and joined them. "Looks like folks are starting to trickle in," he said, as the wait staff, dressed in crisp black and white, began to prepare the tables.

"Yeah, it's going to be like a beehive around here soon. Bess said you worked in Nashville in the entertainment industry?" Cece was eager to get in a few questions and dig a bit before things started humming.

"That's right. I mainly work with older performers who were once popular, or had a hit or two at one time, but now just need a job to pay the bills. It's not very glamorous, but I've met a lot of nice people."

"I bet you meet a lot of talented folks from the Nashville music scene. Are you from there?" Cece already knew the answer but was hoping for more details.

"No, I grew up in South Florida. I ran open-water fishing tours with our family business in the summer until I came up to Nashville for school. I've been here ever since." Manny's dark eyes scanned the room, landing back on Cece. "Feels almost like home now," he continued, "but I miss the water and head to the Outer Banks or down to Florida when I can. But you know I've come to really love these mountains, too. I do a lot of hiking, and I love the trails at Buffalo Mountain Park."

"Oh, I hike, too," Cece jumped in eagerly, glad to latch on to something in common to talk about, "and I love that park. White Rock Loop is my favorite, and the views are incredible. That's one thing that brought me back from—"

Bess took Cece's elbow and pulled her toward the door before she could finish her sentence. "Manny, we'll be right back. Sister, we have to go right now for our quick-change," Bess said over her shoulder, dragging Cece behind her and carrying both of their dresses and a giant makeup bag. Bess came in close beside Cece as they made their way to the bathrooms, whispering in her ear, "Isn't he just delicious?" Before Cece could answer, Bess continued, "Our wealthiest big-bucks donors could arrive any minute. We better not be wearing these sweatpants."

What followed in the dressing room with Cece and Bess involved a frenzy of pulling, sucking-in, zipping, and one possible corneal abrasion with an eye pencil, and is best left to the imagination. In a miraculous turn, they reappeared in a record-breaking fifteen minutes in full Fall Ball regalia. Bess wore her black hair loose, and it cascaded down her back, catching and reflecting light like a prism. She wore a metallic cobalt-blue evening gown with a boat neckline and deep cowl back that hugged her ample curves in all the right ways.

"Whoa," was all Manny could manage to say before pulling Bess to his side with a big grin. The first guests had just come wandering in to find their tables, and Bess headed to greet them.

* * *

It wasn't long before the room was like a multicolored kaleidoscope filled with flickering lights and beautiful jewel-toned dresses. A steady stream of guests were now entering the ballroom and checking for their table numbers and place cards. Outside, the sun had just slipped below the mountains, and thick clouds had begun to gather ominously on the horizon.

Despite some objecting to Cece attending the ball alone, namely Nana and Bess, she liked getting the view solo from the sidelines. From there she got a firsthand view of various interactions that might go unnoticed if she'd had to tend to a date, and like her Nana, human behavior was by far her favorite kind of entertainment.

Cece had just finished her 360-degree scan as Nana made her entrance. She looked stunning, sporting her usual red lip and wearing a turquoise, high-necked gown with silver sequins. Nana had the posture and regal bearing of royalty, which belied her little-known skills of seed-spitting and cussing. Since Nana had lived here forever, she had to stop and chat with almost everyone as she made her way over to Cece.

"Look at you! You're just a picture, and you better hug my neck," Nana said, leaning in. "And doesn't it look gorgeous in here? Bess has outdone herself once again."

"I know. I love the balloons. When she told me about this I was afraid it'd give off a kid's birthday party feel, but this is so not that. Our table's over here, Nana. I think we're sitting with Bess and Lorna," Cece said, pointing close to the dance floor area.

"Great. I hate to say it, but I'm already tired of these heels." She bent her knee and looked down at her shoe. "And these have to be the lowest heel ever made."

"That's because you're old, Nana." Cece threaded her arm through her grandmother's, chuckling. "You might need to rest."

Nana waved her manicured hand to the side. "Old is a state of mind, my dear. By the way, did Bess tell you what was going on earlier with Dr. Simkins in the lobby? He seemed to be kicking up an awfully big fuss over his table assignment."

"Ugh. No. Which one is he anyway?" Cece asked.

"He's the one in plaid pants. Hard to miss."

"Oh, I know exactly who you're talking about. Looks like an Irish garden gnome. Bess had said she had something to tell me about him. I'll have to remember to ask her. Every year at this ball it seems they have at least one person who has to cause some kind of trouble."

Nana kept making her way to their table as Cece sized up the room, checking out who was where and doing what. The wait staff fanned out amongst the round tables in a choreographed dance of their own. They were filling tea and water glasses, balancing hors d'oeuvres trays, and patiently bending to hear requests from guests. Cece watched Beryl belly up to the bar, his faithful lizard skin boots on and his arm around a noticeably younger blonde she'd never seen before. She saw the Schafers, Amanda and Steve, heads close and engaged in what looked like a serious conversation. Amanda wore what looked like a beaded body suit with a scooped front, giving a full display of her ample cleavage as she leaned forward at their table. Cece spied Nick staring at Amanda from behind his sound mixer before Cece caught his eye. He broke into a broad grin and shook his head.

"Okay, let's get this party started, Sister," came Bess's voice from behind Cece. "Time to get your dancers ready. The stage is ready and all yours. You double-checked the Marley floor was taped down good, right?" she asked.

Cece nodded. "Triple-checked," she said, and hurried off.

Moments later Cece reappeared leading a line of twelve high school-age dance students wearing wine-colored leotards, long white tutus, and a head wreath of delicate gold and silver flowers. Cece had tried to teach them how to walk out quietly, but their pointe shoes still sounded like clattering hooves. The dancers took their places as music from Vivaldi's *Four Seasons* began.

Afterward, Cece escorted the dancers out of the ballroom to change clothes in a meeting room, now a dressing room, where she gave advice on a boy in third-period English and sewed a pointe-shoe ribbon back on. She returned to the ballroom with her biggest job behind her. It had gone smoothly, and no one face-planted or forgot the steps, which Cece considered a huge success.

"So, how's it going so far?" Cece asked as Bess sat down for the first time since she'd gotten there three hours ago.

"Well, I think we have about three-fourths of our guest list here, which is about the usual number to be expected."

"Nana said Dr. Simkins was hot about something earlier. What was that about?" Cece asked.

"Good Lord, he is such a colossal pain in the butt," Bess said, shaking her head.

"Didn't you say you were going to tell me some story about him?"

"I was just going to tell you that I have him for a British Studies class this semester. He's a real piece of work. He demands everyone call him '*Doctor* Simkins' after this poor girl made the mistake of saying 'Mister' instead. And he talks in this overdone British accent, like he comes from there or something, and he's never lived anywhere but Tennessee. Tonight he complained he wasn't sitting with the people he'd paid to sit with. He pitched a baby fit because he had to sit with Jenny Newport and her boyfriend, Buck. I double-checked the requests and showed him on my clipboard where his wife, Jackie, had signed off on it. He just stomped off in a huff."

"He sounds like a pompous ass. I'll have to ask Dad if he knows him at the college."

Just then, the swinging doors from the kitchen opened and a line of wait staff entered the ballroom and fanned out, dinner trays balanced on their palms. The menus, printed on framed cards at each table, included filet mignon, shrimp and grits, and mushroom risotto. The inn usually went all out for this event. The tables sparkled with cut glass, crystal wine glasses, and tall silver candlesticks.

Next came dessert and coffee, including a superb chocolate mousse. It was so good that Cece managed to eat both hers and Nana's.

Afterward, the hospital representatives gave their required speeches and acknowledged the big donors for the evening. As the names were called out for recognition, people raised their hands and gave a brief wave, until they got to Beryl Bridges. He stood up, staggering slightly with half of his shirt untucked, and took it upon himself to say a few words from behind the podium,

"I just wanted to say thank you to all the wunnerful people who came to help the children, and I know y'all will support the new waterpark I'm fixin' to bring." By this time, Lorna stood beside him and managed to wrestle back the mic from Beryl.

"Thank you, Mr. Bridges. Thanks so much for your generosity," Lorna said, gently propelling him toward his table before seamlessly finishing the ceremony. Cece and Bess locked eyes and stifled grins.

Somehow Sandra Newport, Jenny's sister-in-law, had ended up in the chair next to Nana. As Sandra rattled on about how great the shopping was on Worth Avenue in Palm Beach, Nana nodded her head, feigning interest. Nana changed the subject to living in Florida since she had toyed with the idea of retiring there one day. She was interested in things like the cost of living, but all Sandra seemed to want to tell her about was where to shop and dine and how "restaurant service just wasn't like it used to be." As she pretended to be listening to Sandra, Nana's eyes followed Cece's every move, as she was now up and out amongst the guests. She just didn't seem herself tonight. Nana knew she'd felt out-of-sorts herself all day. Maybe it was just missing Sam, what with the dancing and happy couples around her, but it felt like more than that. For Cece, at least, she hoped it had something to do with that handsome Joe Barksdale being here and not something else.

"I'm so sorry, Sandra, you'll have to excuse me. I just got the signal to begin the dancing," Nana said, heading straight over to old Mr. Carlisle's table, where he had taken Sam's place with Nana as the first couple on the dance floor. It had become a tradition, Nana and Sam, and then Nana and Mr. Carlisle, leading the dancing, and always worked to get others up and dancing, too.

Mr. Carlisle was quite a bit older than Nana and seemed to have had a crush on her for as long as she'd known him, given the way he never took his eyes off her. She could always count on him to be her partner, and he was quite a good dancer. He wore the same seersucker suit every year with its highwater pants and powerful smell of mothballs. And every year, Nana would have to repeatedly put his wandering hand back up on her waist. Before long, the dance floor was full, and Nana and Mr. Carlisle considered their mission a success.

6

It didn't take long for the temperature in the room to get decidedly warmer as moving bodies heated up. Tempers seemed to rise as well, and Cece couldn't help but notice Beryl and Jenny in a heated conversation by the bar, as well as two of the wait staff arguing as they stood in front of the kitchen doors. Cece couldn't hear Beryl and Jenny, but Beryl looked as if he were making his point by sweeping his glass back and forth in front of Jenny's face, while Jenny responded by shaking her head, lips pressed tight.

There was never a shortage of drama at the ball, Cece thought to herself. *A person just needed to watch closely enough.* She knew, from experience, that you could never tell what might happen as the night went on, especially when the price included a full bar.

"This crowd needs shaking up a bit. Shall we?" Bess said, appearing out of nowhere and offering Cece her hand.

"Why, of course, madame," Cece said, "but where's Prince Charming?"

"It's another work call," she sighed. "He's out in the lobby or somewhere. They never leave him alone. So, sister, this is our chance to show them how it's done."

Just then the percussive beat of tango music began playing over the speakers as Bess shot a look and a wink over at Nick. "They're playing our song," she said, leading Cece onto the dance floor.

Bess had taken ballroom dance classes on a bet in high school. The dance studio had a visiting ballroom dance teacher one year, and Cece bet her that she couldn't do it, which, in hindsight, had been a big mistake. Bess practiced daily for six months with anyone she could find, male or female, learning how to both lead and follow. Cece and Shane were her most frequent partners, but Cece was the one who had to pay up with three months of unlimited chocolate Frosties at the Dairy Barn.

"Let's see what tongues we can get wagging this year," Bess said as she brought her arm out like an arrow, turning her head to the side, chin over shoulder. By the time the song finished, the whole dance floor had stopped and was clapping and stomping around them.

Bess and Cece were just giving their bows when a cannon of thunder boomed from outside, the lights flickered, and the whole inn seemed to shiver. At the same time, the speakers started making a high-pitched squeal. Right away, Nick lowered the volume and was frantically turning knobs and pushing buttons. The room fell momentarily silent, then filled with the din of guests talking over one another.

Cece made her way to Nick first. "What can I do?" she asked him.

"I don't know. I don't know what happened *or* why it did this. It's never done it before." Nick was breathless, his words rapid-fire. "I think it may be inside the speaker that is connected to my computer screen here."

"Do you have a backup? Anything we can use temporarily?"

"Yeah," he said unconvincingly, fumbling around in a large bag beside him, "I've got this smaller speaker. It's better than nothing until I figure this out. I don't know if I can, Cece." Nick's eyes were wide. "I hope…. I just don't know anything about computers, and I think that's where the problem is."

"Why don't you let me call Calvin? He knows computers, and I think he's home tonight. Would that help?" Cece asked.

"Yeah. That'd be good. Any help at all would be great."

By this time Bess, Manny, and Lorna had joined them, and poor Nick pushed his hair back, now wet with sweat. Cece quickly punched in Calvin's number, and he answered on the second ring.

"He says he'll be right here," she said to Nick, and then to Calvin, "Thank you so much. I'll be waiting for you at the front door."

Nick set up the smaller speaker, and Lorna grabbed the microphone on the podium to say, "We're going to take a short break and will be back," to the guests.

Cece made her way through the ballroom and out the door, pausing long enough to pull both shoes off to carry in one hand. She headed to the front door of the inn and hoped Calvin would appear soon. Cece was almost there when Denise Callahan stepped directly in front of her.

"I have got to get some answers about Ashley, Miss Cece, and I really need them now," she said, sliding the long front fringe of her choppy bob haircut behind her ears. "Her Insta numbers have not gone up in a week, and you need to do something!"

As if on cue, Calvin burst through the heavy double front doors of the inn in his rain-soaked corduroy jacket and Star Wars flannel pajama pants. He was carrying his red metal toolbox and an inside-out umbrella.

Cece deftly sidestepped Mrs. Callahan, saying, "Sorry, have to help with the sound system," and marched forward without looking back.

"Hey, Cece. Got here as quick as I could. Rain's coming down hard, and the wind's come up out there," said Calvin as he pulled the drenched hood of his jacket off.

"I can't thank you enough for coming out in this. I'm sure you can get something figured out. Let me take you to Nick."

Cece ushered Calvin over to help Nick and turned almost headfirst into Bess.

"Is there anything else we can do? I'm so glad Nick has backup just in case."

"I don't think so. We've got the best in town on it right now."

"I sure hope you're right," Bess said, taking a deep breath. "I guess I better go pay some attention to my date."

Cece glanced over at their table, where his chair sat empty. "I think he's figured out how to live without you."

"In that case, I better hurry," Bess said, picking up her stride.

Cece spied Joe wandering around the perimeter of the ballroom in his police uniform. She began working her way between the tables and toward him when Jenny Newport lightly touched her on the arm to get her attention.

"You look lovely tonight, Cece. Especially for someone just back from the Zombie Prom." She smiled, remembering Cece's story about her dress. "I just want to thank you again for doing that last-minute hem job on my dress."

Cece laughed, "Oh, no problem. We can thank Nick's mom, Mrs. Adams, for that. And I must say we did well because it sure looks great on you."

Jenny's long-time partner Buck Taylor leaned forward as he put his arm around Jenny. "Have to agree with you there. You both look great. But I think you must've put some kind of batteries in Jenny's skirt because I cannot get her off the dance floor. She's 'bout worn me out," he said, sweat glistening on his forehead.

"I consider that a great problem, Buck. Jenny, didn't I see your sister-in-law around here?" Cece said, glancing around the table. "I don't think I've ever met her before." Cece had noticed Sandra sitting by Nana earlier. She had a dramatic coal-black bob haircut with bangs and enviable patent-leather Jimmy Choo pumps. *Very Cleopatra-chic.*

"Probably not. Sandra's only been to Eureka Grove once before." Jenny looked toward the doors. "She headed for the powder room after the thunder struck. Must be some kind of storm out there."

"Yeah, Calvin said it was pouring."

"Well, I won't keep you," Jenny said. "Thanks again, Cece. Enjoy the night."

By this time, Cece had lost sight of Joe, so she headed back over toward the table.

"You and Bess should think about getting on *Dancing with the Stars*," Cece heard a deep voice from behind her say.

"Oh, yeah! We'd win that mirror ball trophy, hands down," Cece laughed, turning around to see Joe, who was wearing a perfectly dimpled grin along with his uniform. "I thought I saw you earlier. Doing your job, I see."

"Someone has to keep this rowdy crowd under control," he said, shrugging his broad shoulders.

Cece put her hand near her mouth, suddenly sure that a piece of lettuce had lodged between her teeth. "Yeah," she tried to say without moving her lips. "So, how long do you have to stay tonight?" Cece asked, trying to regain composure. She told herself she was being silly, surprised at her visceral reaction to his close proximity.

"I'm supposed to be able to get back in the squad car by 10, so not too bad. I have about an hour to go. Kind of nice to be in here where it's warm and dry."

Joe's jaw muscle clenched, then unclenched. Cece remembered he used to do that when he had something to say but didn't know how to say it.

"You look really beautiful tonight, Cece. And, hey, who said you need shoes, right?" Joe said, looking down at Cece's bare feet.

Before Cece could respond, the music came back on full force, exploding through the giant speakers causing an audible group gasp. "Well, I know everyone's relieved that's over," Joe said, practically shouting. "Better get back to my patrol. See you later, Cece."

As quickly as she had found him, she lost him again, and the crowd thickened with guests making their way back onto the dance floor. Cece noticed her grandmother nearby.

"How ya holdin' up there, Nana?"

"Oh, darling. I'm having a fine time watching everyone dance the night away in their finery. You know it's very hard not to be happy when you're dancing." She turned to wave at someone saying her name, then turned back to Cece. "You know people-watching is one of my many talents. Didn't I see you talking to Joe Barksdale over there? I wondered if maybe those old embers still had a little spark in them."

Cece rolled her eyes. "He's seeing Hailey from the hair salon, Nana. We were just being polite."

"Oh. Is that what it's called?" she said, nodding her perfectly coiffed head. "Uh-huh."

"Sorry to interrupt you two," Calvin said, appearing at Cece's side, "but I need a smoke pretty bad, and I was just wondering if one of you could point me to the closest door that goes outside. I'd rather not walk through the ballroom looking like this."

"We always have time for the man who saved the night," Nana said.

"Yeah, Calvin. You're a lifesaver. And in this weather, too. There's an exit over there," Cece said, pointing to a door in the very back of the room. "That's where the wait staff take their breaks. I think it's a loading dock."

"Got it. Thanks, Cece." Calvin turned to Nana. "Duchess, I'll see you Monday morning, right?"

"That's right, Calvin. Bright and early. And I don't need to tell you what those cigarettes will do to you, do I, my dear? They'll—"

"You don't need to tell me, but you still do anyway, Duchess, and I know, they'll rot my lungs out. I'm trying to quit. Just not tonight."

Calvin left just as Bess and Manny passed them on their way to the dance floor, with Bess leading the way. Both had big smiles on their faces.

"I thought I could keep up with this one on the dance floor," Manny said, tilting his head toward Bess, "but once again, I was wrong."

"Oh, he's a phenom. And he's totally lying. Listen, I'm going to have to stop soon for a bathroom break. I may need you to go with me, Cece, because it may take the two of us to get these Spanx back on."

"Get out of here, you two. It'll all be winding down soon, so y'all need to make hay while the sun shines," Cece said, pointing to the dance floor. Manny stared at Cece, trying to make sense of what hay and sunshine had to do with him and Bess dancing. Finally, he shrugged his shoulders and followed Bess to the floor.

With one hand rubbing her neck, Nana turned to Cece. "Darling, I'm not long for this world. I think I'll start saying my goodbyes, but first I have to sit down for a minute. You go do your thing, and I'll see you later."

"Okay, Nana," Cece said, kissing her soft cheek. "Love you."

Cece, still carrying her shoes, made her way across the room to check in with Lorna, who had been dutifully steering folks toward the silent auction tables situated around the room.

"How's the auction going?" Cece asked.

"Really well." Lorna smiled, pressing her reading glasses up on her nose as she looked down at her auction sheet. "Might be some record numbers tomorrow. I better head over now to announce we only have ten minutes left to bid. That should put us over the finish line."

"I guess I better hurry and take a look at all the goodies before they're gone!" Cece said, sitting down in a nearby chair and reluctantly strapping her sandals back on. She felt scattered and off. It was like somebody had pulled the spring and launched a ball into the pinball machine of her head. At that moment, Cece decided to talk to a doctor the following week and try to figure out what was making her feel this way. But for now, she figured she'd look over the auction table, then head to the bathroom to splash water on her face. It seemed to work in the movies, so maybe it would for her.

As Nana made her way back to her table, Dr. Simkins trapped her into listening to him expound on the latest crisis in the Royal Family, talking as if it were his own. Nana tapped her foot, only half-listening, and instead thinking about Cece. She couldn't shake the feeling that something was off.

The auction sheets were due to be picked up soon, and Cece wanted to see them before they were gone. She hadn't been able to see Nana's finished dollhouse beforehand, and this was her chance before some delighted child or collector got to take it home. She ran her fingers along the table's edge as she looked at the auction lineup, which included everything from a birdhouse made from a hollowed-out gourd to an all-expense-paid weekend getaway to New York.

Cece finally came to their dollhouses, placed beside each other at the end of a long table. Nana's rose majestically from the tabletop: a stately three-floor Georgian house with a hipped roof and sash windows, and next to it, Cece's two-room log cabin. She had to giggle at the contrast, glad that it hadn't been a contest.

Cece walked behind the table in order to see the interior of Nana's dollhouse, which, given her attention to detail, always promised to be even better than the exterior. In an instant, her previously fuzzy-feeling head cleared into hyper-focus. Filling her mind's eye, and crowding everything else out, was a scene of a staircase with the distinct scent of something stale and molded. And then, as quickly as it came, it was gone.

Cece lowered herself into a nearby chair to recover. She scanned the area around her, the experience so vivid she thought surely someone must have noticed. *I have got to figure out what is going on,* Cece thought, *because something is definitely very wrong.* She noticed that a few folks were leaving, and it looked as if the ball was beginning to wind down when Calvin came running toward Cece from where he'd gone out to smoke.

"Cece, come quick. Something's happened to Ms. Newport."

"What do you mean something's happened?"

Calvin was pulling Cece up by her elbow, breathless and soaking wet again. "I don't know. I don't know. Can you just come out there with me? Bring your phone. *Hurry!*"

Cece raced to catch up with him as he pushed open the door, and she followed right behind. It was semi-dark out on the loading dock. The exterior lights were dimmed by rain and fog, with only occasional flashes from headlights leaving the parking lot.

Cece saw the familiar blue velvet skirt first. Calvin was already kneeling beside her on the ground. "Oh, my God, it's Jenny," Cece said, as her eyes followed the light to see Jenny's still body sprawled in the dark corner of the concrete pad. She knelt opposite Calvin and felt for Jenny's pulse.

"Maybe she just passed out and fell. Can you call someone? I left mine in the car," Calvin said, talking so fast his words ran together. "I didn't even see her down there at first, and then I freaked out and ran back in for you. Maybe she just got dehydrated."

"Oh, Calvin. I don't think she passed out," Cece said, pulling her skirt out from underneath her knees. The red puddle that had formed under Jenny's head was now spreading onto the concrete and began to bloom up from the hem of Cece's dress. "She's dead."

7

Police Chief Reynolds stood on the stoop with his feet apart, holding his hat to his chest. Joe and another officer stood on either side of him, and all eyes were fixed on the body laid out on the concrete.

"Jenny Newport?" The chief already knew but had to ask anyway for confirmation.

Cece could hear her heart thumping in her chest as she held tight to Calvin's hand. Her mouth was dry, and she couldn't make herself give voice to words.

"Yes, sir," said Calvin, nodding and squeezing Cece's hand as hard as she was his.

"Have you touched anything?" the chief asked, pointedly looking at Calvin.

"No, sir. I'd come out for a smoke and—"

"No need to explain now," the chief continued, cutting Calvin off. "She's been hit in the back of the head. Cranial fracture. Blunt object." As he carefully knelt beside Jenny's body the chief recited to the other officer who was taking notes. "We'll need statements from both of you. Later though. Procedure."

Cece was beginning to shiver. It was the kind of shiver that came not only from temperature, although she felt more numb than cold now, but from her own internal thermometer's register of shock and fear. Cece had known the chief since he was a new member of the department, and she was in high school. Nana had taught one of his kids. Cece couldn't believe they were together in this situation.

The double doors opened from the ballroom and two EMTs with medical kits went right to Jenny's side. They were followed by an older woman with a yellow rain slicker that had *CORONER* in black letters on the back. She was accompanied by a young man holding a metal box with a handle.

Cece could hear Nana's voice from the other side of the door. She sounded frantic, but she couldn't make out what she was saying.

"Listen," Joe said. "Ya'll can go back inside and have a seat. It'll take us a while out here. I hear Ms. Chagall in there, and we've got that exit blocked. I'm sure she's worried about you, Cece. You can warm up in there, too."

Cece forced out a "Thank you" as Joe opened the door for them, and Cece headed straight into Nana's arms. Nana held her tight, but in that moment Cece could feel the vibrating alarm bells going off inside her grandmother. Nana had seen enough death and heartbreak. Cece didn't want to deliver the news of another one.

"I'm so sorry, Cece. I know she's gone," Nana whispered in her ear. "And I know you called 911 as soon as you found her," she said, pulling gently back from the hug. "I'm sure you'll have to stay here and talk to the police. Do you want me to stay here with you?" Nana asked, her hand making comforting circles on Cece's back.

"No, Nana. I'm okay," Cece said, still unsure if she really was. "Calvin'll be here. Joe's here. I'll be fine. Where's Buck? And Jenny's sister-in-law? Are they okay?"

"Bess took them to a private place in the hotel after they were notified. I think they left soon after that, but I'm not sure," Nana said, pulling her keys from her purse.

By this time the ballroom was empty except for the cleanup crew and the sounds of clattering plates and glasses. The police had already taken some statements and alerted the staff that they would need to talk to them at a later date. It was close to 11 now, and the police were finishing with photos and gathering any evidence.

"I want you to spend tonight in my house, please," Nana continued. "It'll just make me feel better for both of us."

"Sure. I agree. I'll grab a few things from the cottage and come over as soon as I'm done here."

"Okay, darlin'. I'll be listening for you to come in. Call me if you need anything."

"I will, Nana," Cece said, aware for the first time that her legs were shaking. She took a seat in the nearest chair for fear her knees might go out from underneath her. She watched Nana's straight spine leave the ballroom before dropping her head into her hands.

Calvin came and sat beside her. "Wonder when they'll talk to us?"

"I don't know. I just can't believe this is happening. I don't understand."

"I don't either, Cece. Thanks for calling 911. I just panicked; I couldn't find my phone, and I was afraid…."

"You don't have to say anything. We both did what we had to do." Cece knew Calvin was prone to leaving his phone lying around. He did it all the time at Nana's house. She also knew he grew some "plant medicine" at his house on the edge of town. He did his best to have as little interaction with police as possible.

Finally, Joe came in and said he would talk to them separately and that it wouldn't take long. He told them to stay in town in case other questions came up. Cece had never seen Joe "on duty" in this professional sense, and it seemed to her that, just as she was crumbling, he was growing stronger.

"Why don't we do Cece first so she can get home to her grandmother? Does that work?"

"Yeah. That's fine," Calvin said, patting Cece's back as she stood up.

Joe led Cece to a table in the far corner of the ballroom. As they sat down, she noticed the stark contrast of the glaring florescent lights on the ballroom ceiling compared with the warm glow of only candlelight and chandeliers from before.

"First, I am so sorry, Cece. I know how important Jenny's been to you. And I just need to ask a few questions. My first one is, did you see anything besides the body when you went outside with Calvin?"

"No." Cece shook her head slowly, retracing her steps in her mind. "No. Nothing. It was pouring rain and really dark. I didn't even see her at first until Calvin showed me."

"How did Calvin seem when he came to get you in the ballroom?"

"He seemed frantic. He said he didn't even see her there at first, but when he did I think he freaked out, and then he realized he didn't have his phone. He ran back in to get the first person he knew who had a phone."

"Okay. One last question for tonight, Cece. Do you know of anyone that might have wanted to harm Jenny Newport?"

"No," she answered immediately. "I mean, I can't imagine."

"Okay. That's all for right now. If you think of anything, anything at all, let me know. I'd like to walk you to your car, if you don't mind?" Joe asked, his voice still measured and impersonal.

Suddenly, Cece realized that whoever had done this to Jenny was still out there. The word "murder" began taking shape in her mind. She knew from past experience that in shocking situations, like this one now, her mind buzzed with white noise and canceled everything out but her heartbeat. In New York, crime had been a given, as much a part of everyday life as her subway stops. She was continually aware of her own safety. But here, in Eureka Grove, crime had never entered her mind. "Where's Bess?" Cece asked, not answering his question and now functioning on autopilot.

"She and her friend met with us, and then she had to go meet with the Mercy Hospital folks and talk to the inn wait-staff."

"Okay. Yeah," Cece said, remembering his offer. "That'd be great. That'd be great," she repeated, "if you'd walk me to the car. My legs are a little wobbly."

The glittering gaiety of the ballroom was gone. It was as if the thunder that blew the sound system had been a forewarning of things to come, a call to pay attention in the quiet while they'd had it. Cece wondered if her "episode" with Nana's dollhouse might be somehow related to the events of the night. There was no reason to think that; rather it was something Cece felt. The rain had settled into a steady drizzle creating a misty haze in the parking lot lights, while the wind had picked up and gusts of dead leaves lifted and scattered on the wet asphalt.

Joe put his hand on Cece's shoulder as she climbed into her Jeep, "You sure you'll be okay?"

"Yeah. I'm going to stay with Nana tonight, so May and I will be fine over there."

"Okay. Call me if you remember anything," Joe said, shutting her door.

Once she was inside the damp chill of her car, Cece felt the full weight of the night on her shoulders. The windshield wipers thumped background music to her thoughts: of Joe, of Jenny, and of her own strange, flaring mind-body signals. *Nothing makes sense.* Cece had not come back home only to have her life make less sense than it did before. Aloud, and alone in her car, Cece said, "I will figure this out. I'll try and remember any details about Jenny for Joe. I'll get my peculiars checked out at the doctor's office. I have to do it for my own peace of mind, and I will do it for Jenny. I'll do it for Buck. I'll do it so Dad won't worry. But most of all, I'll do it for me. It's about time I put on my big-girl panties and figured out my life."

8

Nana sat with both elbows on the kitchen table, hands kneading the back of her neck, and her cellphone in front of her set on speaker. The early morning light filtered in through her back window, and she had a perfect view of her overflowing raised herb gardens in the yard. The house was quiet, and Cece was fast asleep upstairs with May curled up beside her.

"She's comin' up next week, and I think you should come on up with her, and we all can talk," said her sister, Hazel.

"I know we need to, Hazel, but I just don't want to add to all she's got going on right now. You know Cece's the one who found Jenny? That's a lot to process, and she's still coming to terms with moving home. I just think she might need some more time."

"We can wait then. You're around her a lot more than me and have a better sense-feeling. I'm just worried about y'all bein' in town with some criminal on the loose, with Cece goin' through her peculiars and all. I don't know, Anna Beth. They got any idea who done it?" Hazel asked.

"Not yet. Not that I know of, but I wouldn't know, anyway. It's still early though." Nana said, continuing to talk as she got up to pour herself another hot cup of coffee. "I'm worried about Calvin. He can't help but look suspicious, even though I don't know anyone with a softer heart. Did you remember Jenny and her brother, Edmond, grew up in this house? Now both of them are gone."

"Oh, that's right," Hazel said. "I'd forgotten about her brother. What happened to him, anyway?"

"He got killed in a car crash down where they lived in Florida. He ran off the road and went into a canal. I'm pretty sure that's what Jenny told me." Nana took a long sip of coffee. "Now that we're talking about it, though, I remember that Jenny was never satisfied with the accident report. I'd forgotten that until now." Nana heard a distinct snapping sound on Hazel's end. "I'd know that sound anywhere. You're snappin' pole beans, aren't you?"

They both laughed and then Hazel's voice became serious. "Anna Beth, I've been thinkin' on this. What if Cece's peculiars, that's been happenin' more often and gettin' stronger, have something to do with what happened at that charity dance? Neither of us knew what was happenin' to us until we got thrown in the middle with it, and we didn't have any idea about what our power could do."

Nana nodded her head, thinking back, with worry beginning to crease her brow. "I hadn't thought of that. You're right, Hazel. I'll plan on coming with her to your house this week."

"Hope we can wait that long. You two be careful. Keep yourselves locked in good at night, now," Hazel said.

"We will. Promise. Love you."

"Love you, too."

After they hung up, both sisters sat for a while, thinking and looking at the same framed photo they each had on their kitchen wall. It was of their mother and grandmother, one of the few taken with just the two of them. Mother and daughter were both smiling and sitting beside each other on the porch in mint-green clamshell metal chairs outside the house where they once had all lived, and where Hazel lived now.

Both sisters knew this photo was taken before everything had changed. Despite being miles apart, they each bit down on their bottom lips, closed their eyes, and gently rocked back and forth in their chairs. They both were keenly aware that the sooner they got to Cece, the better, as they remembered just how dangerous power can be.

* * *

"Come on in, Buck," Cece said, opening the door, balancing on one leg, while the other kept May from running out.

"I'm sorry to bother you, Cece. I was in the neighborhood and thought this might be easier than playing phone tag. Do you have a minute?"

Buck's eyes were bloodshot, and Cece guessed he hadn't slept and was probably still wearing the clothes he'd changed into after the ball. The effects of fresh trauma and grief had already deepened the lines on his face.

"This is fine, and yes, I've got time," she said, closing the door behind him. "I stayed with Nana last night, so I'm just now getting over here. I'm so sorry about Jenny, Buck. I don't even know what to say. Please, have a seat," she said, pointing to the armchair. "Can I get you some water?"

"No thanks. I'm good. I'm sorry to drop in like this, and I won't be long." Buck's eyes took in Cece's cottage. "Jenny thought the world of you, Cece. She's—I mean, she *was*—so glad you were back." He took long pause, clasping and unclasping his hands repeatedly. "Anyway, I know she spent some time with you getting the dress pinned just two days ago, and then you're the one who called 911." Buck fidgeted in his seat. "I guess I'm just struggling with putting things together right now. You know Jenny kept her business stuff pretty close to her chest. She had some high-powered clients that wanted her to dig up information for them, even after she retired. And I know she had enemies on the town council." Buck seemed to be sorting things out as he spoke, giving each sentence a moment of thought.

"I've racked my brain, Buck, and I can't say I noticed anything out of the ordinary when she came over. Have you asked Sandra if she'd noticed anything unusual, or Marla at The Ivy?" Cece asked. "They hang out a lot."

"Unfortunately, Sandra has gone AWOL."

"What? What do you mean?"

"Well, she locked herself up in her room over at the inn. I guess she's really upset, and it's all too much for her. You know she lost her husband a couple of years ago. Anyway, she does weird shit like that. I'm sure she'll come around. But are you sure Jenny didn't say anything about a client or about the council?" Buck's foot tapped the floor.

"No. I'm afraid not, Buck," Cece answered. "We talked about the ball, Bess and the decorations, that kind of stuff. We laughed about her dad tellin' them he hid their inheritance, and before she left she told me how glad she was I was back in town." Cece started to tear up, then changed course. "But I'll keep thinking it through and see if I can remember anything."

"Yeah, okay, I'll do the same. I need to ask you one more thing. You know Calvin pretty well, don't you?"

"I do, yes, he's worked as a handyman for Nana for years now." Cece felt herself becoming defensive. "I can assure you he didn't have anything to do with any of this. He just happened to be at the wrong place at the wrong time."

"No, no, I didn't think he did," Buck said, putting his hand out. "In fact, he's done some work on our house before. That's not why I asked. I wondered how much he knew about computers."

"He knows a lot. I'm pretty sure he can take one apart and put it back together. Why do you ask?"

"I wanted to ask him about Jenny's computer. I think there could be some things on there that might help us figure out who's behind this. I wondered if he could take a look at it before the police get hold of it."

"I don't know, Buck," Cece answered, feeling uncomfortable. "But I guess I can ask him for you."

"I'd sure appreciate that," he said, standing up. "Let me know what he says."

Cece opened the door for him, remembering doing the same thing for Jenny just a couple of days ago. "I will. I'll call him. Take care of yourself."

"You do the same. Thanks, Cece," Buck said, and as Cece closed the door behind him, she wondered what might be hiding on Jenny's computer, and why Buck needed to see it before the police did.

* * *

May jumped in the back of Cece's Jeep, and they headed out to the trailhead. The rolling hills had a fresh blanket of wet leaves as she navigated the curving roads leading toward Mud Hollow Trail. Cece knew she needed some time away to process all that had happened, and a hike was the best way to do it.

She saw she'd missed a call from Joe while she was talking to Buck earlier. It was unnerving for her to be having contact with Joe in this new context. When she was being questioned by Joe after the ball, she felt needlessly guilty of something. For Cece, it was odd seeing Joe in uniform, a symbol of power and authority, which made her feel like she should confess all the bad things she'd ever done. That was one thing Cece liked most about escaping to a big city: her secrets stayed safe in a sea of anonymity.

She also wasn't crazy about how the balance seemed to have shifted between her and Joe now that he was a police officer. He was more dismissive and aggressive than she remembered him, and felt more like a boss than a friend. She understood that he had to be a certain way in his professional role, but she couldn't help remembering his sensitivity and how she had always felt listened to and seen when they'd been together in high school. She was also aware of how much people can change as the years go by. She knew she had. Cece had to remind herself that they were nothing more than friends, so she shouldn't waste time thinking about it, but that was a lot easier said than done.

She turned into the trailhead parking lot and was glad to see it almost empty. There were just a couple of cars and an old station wagon. The wagon had wood-veneer sides, and a bumper full of stickers like "Hike Naked. It'll Add Color to Your Cheeks" and "Wander Woman." Despite wanting to be alone, Cece hoped she might run into whoever owned that one.

The trail was muddy but navigable, and some of the trees were just starting to turn. The maples, birch, and beech trees tended to turn first, especially those in the higher elevations. It wouldn't be long now, depending on rainfall and temperature, before color spread through the branches, making it look like a red and yellow wave had washed over the valley. Cece gulped in the fresh air, letting it fill and expand her interior walls as if it were cleansing her with each exhale.

Cece had gotten so used to city life—to the hurry, the excitement, and the days that blended into night—that she'd almost forgotten how to surrender to the time of the natural world. Here, at home, time was counted in seasons, sunrises, and moon phases. Cece's Aunt Granny

Hazel planted "by the signs" to this day. She would organize her garden planting based on the moon phase and the Zodiac signs. Nana said if you questioned Hazel, she was always quick to say, "As the Good Book says in Ecclesiastes, to everything there is a season…a time to plant and a time to pluck up what is planted, and I ain't arguin' with God." There was a lot of wisdom in marking time more thoughtfully, and that wisdom had held true in the ways of her ancestors.

Before now, Cece had always downplayed or tried to hide her Southern roots. She realized she'd gone north to escape, trying to erase who she was and where she was from. She'd learned that as much as she'd tried to leave her problems behind, they always managed to hitch a ride and find her. Her feelings of not living up to the expectations of others, of never fitting in, and her peculiars, all showed up no matter how far she went to escape them.

Now, as she listened to the birdsong conversations between trees, she had to acknowledge that, all that time she had been away, it had felt as if there was something quietly pulling her back, and now that she was back, the pull was still there, if slightly different in its feel. Cece hoped her purpose would reveal itself if she tried to find answers and make sense of what was happening around her.

As the sun shifted in the sky toward its daily endgame, May slowed their walk down to a stroll, her old hips done for the day. Cece gave her water and lifted her gently into the back seat. She knew she should return Joe's call, but that would have to wait. There was another very important call she needed to make first.

* * *

"Is that you, Tennessee?" the familiar, scratchy voice asked through the ancient landline telephone.

"Yes, it is, Aunt Granny! How'd you know it was me?" Cece asked.

"Just a feelin'. How'n the world are you, baby girl? Been a month of Sundays since I heard from you," she said with a husky chuckle.

Cece could picture her Aunt Granny out in back of her wood-frame house, the light "haint blue" paint peeling off the sides and the wide front porch missing a few boards. It was the house Aunt Granny Hazel and Nana had grown up in, about half an hour outside Eureka Grove, and further up in the mountains. Cece imagined her out back, hearing the phone ring and making her way into the house either from the clothesline or the garden. Cece rarely saw her sit down and could hear her saying "God didn't put us here to lay around like a rug."

Cece had spent many summers with her Aunt Granny and had learned a lot about what God did and didn't put folks here to do. She also knew her Aunt Granny would be wearing her usual simple cotton dress above a pair of thick socks and worn-out work boots, her white hair in two braids down her back.

"It hadn't been that long, Aunt Granny," Cece said, teasing her. "Didn't I call you last week, when you were telling me about killing that snake under the porch with the shovel?"

"I guess you did. Had to hang that snake on the fence to call up rain," Aunt Granny conceded, "but it's still been too long between talking for my liking. Your Nana takin' good care of you? How're you feelin' after all that at the ball?"

"Who told you about that?" Cece asked, since Aunt Granny was pretty cut off from everything. She didn't have a cellphone or a computer, only an old console TV.

Aunt Granny paused. "Well, your Nana, 'course. I'm so sorry about that for you'uns."

"I'm doing okay. Still can't believe it. But I want to know how you're doing, Aunt Granny."

"I'm gettin' around like an old stud horse with sore hooves. But I brung in all the squash and chopped me a little firewood."

"Aunt Granny!" Cece said, shaking her head. "We told you not to chop firewood anymore. That's what Old Man Perkins is for."

"Aww, he's been comin' 'round regular. I reckon I need to do it ever' now and then to prove I still can."

Cece knew it was of no use to argue. "Whatever happened to Ms. Willis?" Cece asked. "You said you were heading down to her place last time we talked because she said she needed you right away."

"I'd done forgot about ole Verna. You'da thought her head cold was the Second Comin' as much fuss as she was makin'. I brought her some of my boneset tea directly, and that did her good right off."

"I'm glad you could help her. Aunt Granny, I'm planning on a visit to Charity Hill next week if that still suits you."

"That suits me just fine. I better start gettin' ready now, though," Aunt Granny said, and they both laughed, remembering Nana's favorite story about Hazel, about how it took a full week to get her ready for Nana and Sam's wedding. "I'm just teasin'. You know I love nothing more than a visit from you'uns. I just need to ask one more thing. Tell me how your peculiars are doing."

"It's been pretty bad, Aunt Granny. I'm not gonna lie." Cece nodded her head. "Yeah, they're definitely different than they used to be."

"I had a feelin'. We'll talk on that when you come. How's that sound?"

"That'd be good. In fact, that would be really good. You always know how to make me feel better. And please don't chop anymore firewood, okay? I love you."

"Love you, darlin'."

* * *

Cece had just nestled into her favorite armchair in her cottage when Joe called.

"Hey, Joe. What's up?"

"Hey, Cece. Did you get my call from earlier?"

"Yeah. I'm sorry. I took May on a hike up Mud Hollow Trail. I needed to clear my head after last night."

"I understand. It was a long, terrible night. Listen, Cece, I'm calling for a couple of reasons. First, I need to let you know that we brought Calvin Trivet and Beryl Bridges in for questioning. Second, I think we're going to need you to come to the station. Just to go over what happened again and see if we might've missed anything or if you've remembered something."

"Yikes," Cece said, letting the new information sink in. "Joe, I have to tell you our family's known Calvin a long time, and he wouldn't hurt a fly. As a matter of fact, I think he's Buddhist, and he literally doesn't kill anything, including flies. Calvin didn't even know where that exit door was until I told him, and he was beside himself when he ran in to get me."

"We just have to start somewhere, Cece. It makes sense to start with who discovered the body."

"Yeah, I guess you're right. I knew about the feud between Beryl and Jenny on Town Council, but I didn't think it was murder-worthy. I guess there's always more to a story," Cece said, hand on her forehead.

"Exactly. The investigation is just beginning, and we're following a number of leads right now. We have to cover all the bases."

"Okay. When do you want me to come in, Joe?"

"Can you come by first thing in the morning?"

"Yep. I'll see you about 9, then."

Bending her legs in under her and pulling May by her side, Cece opened her laptop and typed in Beryl's name. She wanted to see if she could better understand what was going on and why the police would consider him a suspect. Some of the things she already knew, like Beryl had been on Town Council for three years, bought two hundred acres on the west side of town with the intent to build a waterpark, and that he needed Town Council approval for zoning. She knew he had not gotten it yet, and that Jenny was one of the council holdouts.

Some of the things she didn't know included Beryl's passion for big-game hunting, even serving for a time as president of the National Big Game Hunters Association. The internet had some sickening photos of Beryl beside his "trophy" elephant, with rifle in hand and proud smile on his face. This was a side of Beryl Cece knew nothing about. It wasn't like it came up in dance-studio waiting room conversation, or he wore camo pants. Seeing as he was a skilled killer and had a conflict with the victim, she began to see why the police might be interested.

But Cece's instincts still agreed with Nana, that he was basically harmless, despite his overall creepiness. On the other hand, she had learned through experience how certain people were good at pretending to be something other than who they really were. She texted Bess, telling her she needed to bend her ear. She wondered if Bess knew all this about

Beryl, but primarily Cece really needed to just lay everything out for her best friend. She knew Bess could help her break everything down so she could better see the big picture.

Images of Jenny kept playing through her mind, the empty gaze of Jenny's eyes, and the fabric of her dress pooling along with her blood beside Cece on the concrete. Cece needed a marathon of *The Great British Baking Show*, which she considered a warm bath for the nervous system. She clicked on Netflix and ran her hand back and forth through May's thick hair. She could feel the rise and fall of May's steady heartbeat like a metronome for calm and began to let herself relax.

The show had just finished the "Signature Bake" section when May's ears perked up and her head swiveled toward the door. Then both heard the distinct sound of Cece's outer screen door slam. Cece froze in place on the sofa, May began a low growl, and they both waited for a knock. Nothing. She waited to see if she heard anything, like wind in the trees, to explain the sound. Still nothing.

Finally, she gathered the courage to stand up and go to the window, where she used one finger to pull back a tiny corner of curtain to peek out while reaching the other hand to flick on the outside light switch. Light filled the front walkway to the cottage, and the only movement was a few leaves skittering across the ground.

Cece convinced herself it had to have been the wind. She was sure it was her imagination, given the events of the night before. Plus, she was exhausted. She and May settled into the bed, where Cece put on the "Bedtime Stories for Big People" app from her phone. She soon fell asleep, with May curled behind her knees, following the story narrator through a garden gate and into a field of flowers and songbirds.

9

At first, still foggy upon waking, it felt like an ordinary Monday morning. That was, until Cece remembered. News of Jenny's murder was on the local news and in the paper. Since Cece had to go by the police station, she chose something dressier than her usual leggings and oversized sweatshirt. She pulled on her best jeans, boots, and a chocolate sweater over a white tee.

Thinking about the strange door slam the night before, Cece looked all around the yard. She looked for anything out of the ordinary behind the boxwoods that lined the front of the cottage, and even walked the circumference of it, but didn't find a thing. She then walked all the way around Nana's house, stopping to enjoy the big pots of yellow, red, and orange mums Nana had put out on the steps up to her front porch. Still, Cece didn't see anything irregular.

Cece had convinced herself she would find something, like maybe a letter with words cut from magazines, warning her to "Stay away or else!" It might even have been typed on an old typewriter that was missing a letter. That's certainly how it might work if she were in an Agatha Christie book, although she had no idea why someone would want to send her such a letter. Cece scanned the yard again, as well as the yard of Mrs. Jingles next door. Nothing. She knew she was being paranoid. She knew she was good at spinning a story ahead of itself and creating an entire scenario that had little basis in reality. It was just how her brain worked.

An idea dawned on Cece that had been in front of her all along. *Mrs. Jingles.* Violet Jingles knew everything about everybody in Eureka Grove. She spent most of her time stalking the town on social media, or on her "Nextdoor" app, which was supposed to connect folks in the same neighborhood so they could share information. Mrs. Jingles had been

Nana's neighbor for as long as she could remember, and Cece decided it was time to pay her a visit. It was the neighborly thing to do. Plus, if anyone knew rumors that might help find Jenny's killer, it was her. She would add that to her "to-do" list.

* * *

Cece opened the double door to the police station with five minutes to spare.

"May I help you?" a young man with slicked-back hair and a diamond stud in one ear asked from behind the metal front desk.

"Yes. I'm Cece Chagall. I have an appointment with Officer Barksdale."

The man tapped buttons on his desk phone. All of his fingernails, except the pinky on each hand, were painted glossy black. Before she could finish telling him she liked his nails, Joe appeared from somewhere in the back.

"Thanks for coming, Cece. Let's go to this open meeting room back here. Terrence, hold my calls, please."

Joe led Cece to a cubicle with three walls of windows off the main lobby area.

"Can I get you anything, maybe some water?" he asked.

"No, thanks. I kinda just want to get this over with," Cece said, both hands in the pockets of her sweater.

"I understand. Thanks for coming in, and this shouldn't take long. Please, have a seat." Joe gestured to the metal folding chair by the table. All the furniture looked standard-issue, and the beige-painted walls held only bulletin boards.

"I understand that you saw Ms. Newport the day before the crime occurred?" Joe asked, assuming a more formal tone than Cece had heard before, prompting her to sit up straighter.

"That's right. She came by the cottage so I could pin her dress so it could be hemmed before the ball."

"What time was that? Do you remember?" Joe asked, pulling the pencil that was tucked behind his ear.

"Umm, let's see. It was in the morning, maybe around 8? It was before I took May out for a walk and saw you." Joe jotted notes on a little red steno pad as she spoke.

"Yes. Good. And did you talk about anything in particular? Did she say anything that you think might be relevant to what happened?"

In the moment, she chose not to tell Joe that Buck had asked her the exact same questions.

"No. We talked about the ball, of course, and what all she had going on. She asked me how I was doing now that I was home. We talked about her not having any luck at raffles and how they never found her dad's box." Cece knew Joe understood what box she was talking about. "And stuff like that. Oh, and I got a call from a student's mom while she was there, too."

"Who called you while she was there?" Joe asked.

"It was Mrs. Callahan, the mom to one of my students. Ashley's mom."

"Ashley Callahan. The little girl that's in all those Instagram videos?"

"Yep. Afraid so."

"I see. Okay. And did she know Jenny was there at that time?"

"Yeah, I think I mentioned what I was doing when she called. I wanted to get off the phone so I could finish."

"Okay. And then, at the ball, did you see Jenny again?"

"Yes, I saw her talking to Beryl Bridges at the bar, and then she stopped me when I was walking by her table, and we talked then."

Joe continued scribbling. "And did you notice anything unusual about either of the times you saw her?"

"I think she and Beryl were having a heated conversation. I don't think that's anything new. And when I was at the table, we were just talking about the ball. Buck said something like, 'Jenny was about to wear him out dancing.'" Cece felt her eyes well up, remembering Buck's smile, his arm slung casually around Jenny's shoulders.

"I see. Okay." Joe scooted his chair forward and pushed a box of Kleenex toward her. "How about when you followed Calvin outside? Did you notice anything then? Any details? What was Calvin doing?"

Cece dabbed her eyes. "I didn't see Jenny at all at first. I didn't even really know what he'd brought me out there to see. It's a big space, a loading dock. She was laying on the opposite side from where we were, in the opposite corner, and it was even darker over there. A bulb was out or something, so we were standing under the only light. I remember the rain was still really coming down."

"I see. Good. Those are details we need to have."

"So what's going on? Have y'all found out anything yet?" Cece asked, clearing her throat.

"I've updated you about Beryl Bridges and Calvin Trivet. I can't really talk about the investigation, but we are following a number of leads. We'll get the information out to the public as fast as we can." Joe tapped his pencil on the pad. "How's your grandmother doing?"

Cece didn't know that he thought of her as "the public" now. "She's okay. She's been pretty quiet." And then, without thinking, Cece said, "I'll see what I can find out, too."

"Cece, that's our job, not yours. You just stick to dollhouses and ballerinas," Joe said abruptly as he pushed his chair back. "Got it?"

"Of course. Yes," she said, hating feeling like she was being "put in her place." Why couldn't she just say what she was thinking? "I just meant everyone involved in this is important to me, so I'll see if I can remember anything else," Cece said, overexplaining herself, as usual.

Cece didn't like the feeling of being patronized, and clenched her fists to resist the urge to bat her eyelashes and say, "Just like it was your one job to police the ball, and how did that go?"

Joe stood up, prompting Cece to stand as well. "Thanks for coming in, Cece. You helped a lot. Remember, more details might come to you later, so be sure and give me a call, even if you think it's nothing."

"Sure. I'm glad to help. And I'll let you know."

"This is just weird, isn't it?" Joe said, stopping mid-stride for the door and running his hand through his close-cut yet impossibly thick, dark hair.

"Well, yeah. It sure is," Cece said, glad to hear some humanity and a little of the old Joe in his voice.

"I mean, we haven't talked much in years, and then you move back to town one day, and now I'm bringing you in to ask about a possible murder." Joe gestured around the station. "It's just not what I…, I mean, it's just a surprise, I guess."

"I could do without any more surprises," Cece said, averting Joe's direct gaze.

"Yeah, I bet. Listen, I'm really sorry about all this," he said, opening the office door and leading her to the front of the station. "Keep in touch and have a good day," Joe said, with a nod of his head, having flicked his internal switch back to police mode.

* * *

On Bess's kitchen counter, sugar cookies in various sizes and shapes of leaves, acorns, and coffee mugs sat atop wax paper. She had just finished piping on varying designs in dark red, gold, and hunter-green icing. Bess prided herself on her single culinary skill, and Marla was happy to sell her iced cookies at The Iris. Bess found baking therapeutic, once she'd mastered the consistency of the icing after practicing her way through countless gloppy failures.

Bess's phone lit up with a text from Cece:

Be there in 5.

They hadn't talked but a minute since the ball, and Bess knew they had a lot to catch up on.

As Bess pulled the latest batch from the oven, she smiled, remembering Cece's righteous indignation back in high school when Claudine Rappaport stole a bunch of candy from the school store. Then, Claudine tried to blame it on poor Aaron Colley by stuffing the candy into his duffel bag when she knew she was about to get busted. Cece was determined to exonerate Aaron. She wouldn't stop until she got the school video footage, which she did, proving it was Claudine. Bess knew Cece liked justice to be served, and she expected Cece to lean in on trying to figure out what happened with Jenny. But murder is a little more complicated and danger-ous endeavor than stealing candy.

When Cece barreled through Bess's front door, she upended the life-size cardboard cut-out of Dolly Parton standing right inside the door. "Oh, sorry, Dolly," she said, placing her upright. Cece never failed to be surprised by Dolly, thinking Bess had someone else over. "O-M-G, it smells like sugar heaven in here!" Cece pulled off her jean jacket and gave her best friend a hug.

"Quite the weekend, huh, sister?" Bess said.

Cece plopped down in Bess's purple armchair. "You've got that right," she said. Bess's apartment had a retro-vibe feel to it, with most of the furniture and décor coming from secondhand stores. With Bess's great eye, it somehow looked all put together.

"So, *spill it*. I've got the day off and I'm all yours." Bess wiped her hands on a dishcloth, set a timer, and came to join Cece in the matching chair across from her.

"I'll cut to the chase. I'm not here to talk about what happened to Jenny, believe it or not." Bess raised her eyebrows as Cece continued, "As you know, I've had these 'peculiars,' as Aunt Granny calls them, when my synesthesia seems to kick into high gear." Cece tucked one foot underneath her on the chair. "But they've really ramped up recently, and to be honest, I'm a little worried about myself. They've never really bothered me until now."

Bess leaned closer. Cece rarely talked about her synesthesia, and Bess knew it wasn't easy for her. "What exactly do you mean by 'ramped up?'"

"So, I've had three in a row, and each stronger and stranger than the last."

"Go on," Bess said, never taking her eyes from Cece's.

"Once at the studio, when I was locking the door behind me...," Cece hesitated. "This is going to sound super weird."

"Keep going," Bess encouraged her.

"It was like the key got bigger, like the size of that cabinet door," Cece said, pointing into Bess's kitchen and watching for Bess's disbelief, but there was none.

"What happened next?" Bess asked matter-of-factly.

"Then I smelled sage, and it was so strong it made my eyes water. The next one was when I was trying to get the dollhouse done for the auction. I'm putting some mini books on a shelf inside the house when I get hit with a strong scent, but this time it's different, like heavy perfume. I jerked the tweezers and knocked over the shelf and all the books." Cece paused, lost in thought.

"And what's the third one?"

"For our last 'Tales from *Alice's Adventures in Wonderland*' on today's program," Cece joked, "I was looking at all the auction items at the ball just before Calvin came running in to get me. I got to where our dollhouses were at the end of the table, and I was looking inside the first floor of Nana's house. The staircase became bigger and super sharp in my vision, and I had another smell explosion. This time it was more like stale air and mothballs." Cece let out a big sigh. "So, there you have it, the never-ending circus in Cece's brain."

"Wow. I'm so sorry. I know that must've scared you," Bess said, in just the way Cece needed to hear it. "Have you talked to anyone about them? Like your therapist, or your dad?" Bess asked, just as her cookie timer dinged in the kitchen.

They both got up, Bess to the oven, and Cece to the metal and red vinyl chair at the kitchen table. "Not these recent ones. Of course, they know all about the old ones. They've been coming more frequently since I got back to Tennessee, but lately, well, it's just been really bad. Dad thought I needed another MRI, and I haven't even told him about these new ones."

"What about Nana and Aunt Granny? Do they know?" Bess asked, pulling the cookies from the oven and putting them out to cool before sitting down again with Cece.

"Yeah, a little. I'm supposed to go see Aunt Granny up in Charity Hill next week. I know she'll want to talk about it, and she's always insightful about these things. So, what do you think I should do?"

"The first thing that comes to mind is maybe you should try looking at what's happening in a different way, more like a dream maybe. Think about what you've seen, felt, or smelled, and see if those things could mean anything more than they seem. Maybe they relate to something in real life. Just like dreams that seem bizarre or related to nothing, but we're supposed to be using them, working things out from our daily life." Bess's eyes shifted to her bookcase, where she had books with titles on their spines about subjects like astrology and dream interpretation. "And don't you dare roll your eyes, Cece Chagall."

Cece looked at the books. "I'm not. I promise. In fact, I would sort of be glad if I could relate them to real life in some way. Then I wouldn't feel so out of control."

"That doesn't mean I don't think you should talk to your doctor; I just think it's something you should consider."

"Okay. I will. Thanks, Bess. I'll think about that. And I'll make a doctor's appointment, too. Enough of that, my friend. I think I've been previously crowned the official cookie tester, and I'm ready to get to work." Bess lifted the cooling rack and held it out to Cece, who grabbed a cookie from it and bit it, yelping, "Hot! Oh, hot!" as she still, somehow, valiantly, and perhaps unwisely, took a second bite.

* * *

Cece picked up Calvin after he finished work and they headed over to Jenny and Buck's house, which was a large, townhouse-style condominium in an old subdivision.

Cece couldn't help but be suspicious as to why Buck wanted Calvin to get into Jenny's computer. *Is there information about him that might be incriminating, and he wants to erase it before the police see it? And then what if he gets Calvin and me in there, and we see something we shouldn't, and he has no choice but to get rid of us using the fireplace poker?*

Cece reminded herself to slow down. After all, this wasn't a Lifetime Original Movie. Not yet, at least.

"I'm still nervous about this, Cece. I'm not going to guarantee I can do anything, or I may not even want to do anything, depending on the vibe I get from Buck," Calvin said, stroking a growing-in goatee. "I've got enough to deal with as it is."

"I get it. If it gets uncomfortable, we'll just leave," Cece said, imagining the iron poker coming down on her head and squeezing her eyes shut for the impact.

Buck opened the door and stepped back to let them in. Right away Cece was smacked by the lingering scent of Jenny's perfume permeating the room. It flooded her mind with a wave of memories that almost took her breath away.

"Come on in. Thanks for coming." Buck shut the door behind them. "Would you like some water? Afraid that's all I've got for now."

If Buck was going to use the fireplace poker on them later, he was sure putting on a good show. He looked terrible, and while he had changed clothes since Cece had seen him last, it was as if his whole body and spirit had deflated like a balloon. There was no trace of the animated, happy man she'd talked to at the ball.

Calvin jumped in first. "No, I'm good. Hey, I'm not sure I can help you, Buck. Maybe you can tell us what I'm looking for? That would help me."

"Sure. Please, have a seat," he said, pointing to the crisp linen-covered sofa and matching high-back chair. "I need to run some of this by someone, anyway, before it all goes to the police. I guess what's bothering me is I'm really not sure Beryl Bridges is their man, and I'm afraid the police think he is, and are on their way to an arrest. I know…, I mean, I knew Jenny," Buck said, running his hand along the side of his unshaven jaw. "And even though she and Beryl had a major disagreement about that water-park development, they seemed to disagree while still being able to hold a regular conversation. Know what I mean? It wasn't like they hated each other. I think they both respected that the other had a strong opinion. Does that make sense?"

Calvin and Cece nodded their heads in unison.

"Anyway," Buck continued, "my mind's been going a mile a minute. I know she worked privately doing some surveillance for a few old business contacts, but also for some locals. That makes me wonder if someone she was supposed to be getting information on found out and wanted to stop her. I think a look into Jenny's computer might help us at least see an email exchange or something. There's something else that keeps bugging me, too," Buck continued. "It has to do with Jenny's brother, Ed. You know he died in a car accident a couple of years ago. He supposedly veered off the road and went into a canal. Jenny always questioned that accident. She said she knew her brother, and he was almost over-cautious. He kept his phone off when driving and fussed about everyone having on their seat belts. She said she sometimes even had to tell him to go faster just so he'd be going the speed limit. It never made sense to her that he'd run off the road unless it had been because of a medical issue, and the autopsy confirmed there was none."

"Yikes. So you think they could be related? Are you sure you don't want the police in on this?" Cece asked.

"Of course. I already told them, in fact. It's just that I'd like to delay the police getting into this computer long enough to see if there's anything else in there. I'd like to know first, before the police know all of our business."

"So you want Calvin to see if he can hack into her account?"

"Yeah, I just think there might be something that will spark my memory or help give the police another direction to go in."

"What do you say, Calvin?" Cece asked.

"That's some story, man. Yeah. Yeah, let's see what I can do," Calvin said, standing up from the sofa. "But I don't have much time, so maybe you can show me this computer?"

"Yes, yes," Buck said, "of course. It's right down the hall on the right. That's our office."

* * *

Cece drove Calvin back to Nana's house where he had parked his old sky-blue Chevy pickup with a camper over the truck bed that he'd built himself. The only thing unusual Calvin was able to access on Jenny's computer was an invoice meant for Jackie Simkins, Professor Yerger Simkins' wife, for surveillance. "I wonder what that invoice was for?" Cece said to Calvin.

"I don't know, and I do not want to know. I'm leaving it all to the police," Calvin said, pushing one hand away from his body like he was pushing away bad luck.

"Well, I do, and I bet I can find out," Cece said. "I wonder if Dad's heard anything over at the college about him."

"I don't know, Cece, but maybe you should just lay low for now. Whoever did this is still out there somewhere."

"I'm just going to pick around a bit. Nothing serious," Cece said before leaving Calvin at his truck and heading back to her cottage.

10

Angel was waiting for Cece at the studio doors when she got there, her hair a mass of expertly woven braids perched on top of her head. Cece taught the youngest dancers today, the four-to-six-year-olds, and couldn't do it without Angel's help dealing with all the untied shoes and potty breaks during class. And the students loved Angel. This was one of Cece's favorite classes to teach because she got to roll around on the floor, pretend to leap like a frog, and throw scarves in the air. She loved the joy of movement in children before self-criticism and judgment took over.

"Need some help, Miss Cece?" Angel asked as Cece started to unload the Jeep.

"I got it. Thanks, though," she said, hoisting bags from the back seat. "How's school going so far this year?"

"Oh, pretty good, I guess," Angel replied in her mellow, soft voice.

Cece knew Angel worked hard to keep her grades up, frequently bringing her schoolbooks to dance so she could study while waiting for her older sister to pick her up. She had just started ninth grade, which meant she'd moved into high school this year. "I was thinking, Angel, maybe this is the summer you should go to a big dance camp. I mean, I know you've been to the regional ones around here, but I think we should give the big ones a shot."

"Really?" Angel said, her voice gaining power and rising with excitement. "Like which ones?"

Cece smiled at her reaction. "I was thinking maybe the Atlanta Ballet, or maybe go really big, like the American Ballet Theater or Alvin Ailey?"

"Wow!" She broke into a broad smile. "Do you think I'd even have a chance?"

"I wouldn't bring it up if I didn't think so. Plus, we never know until we try." Cece decided this was not the time to tell her own stories about New York or her M&M costume. "I'll look into the audition dates and guidelines. Most are right after Christmas, but we can be working on your audition pieces now. Why don't you be thinking about it, too? Maybe you could listen to some music and find a few pieces we might choose from. And you can look up the audition requirements, too. That'd help me a lot."

"Oh my gosh. I'd love that," she said, her otherwise serious face lighting up from within. Then her face dropped. "But I don't know how I'd ever pay for that. I'm sure they're really expensive."

"Let's not worry about that right now. All of them offer scholarships, so we can try for those, or we can raise money. Maybe do both. We'll figure it out after they send your acceptance."

"Thanks, Miss Cece," Angel said, her smile returning.

Soon, all eight dancers in the first class of "Intro to Ballet and Tap" were seated in a circle on their vinyl "spots" on the floor. This is not to say they were quiet or still. They were all wiggling and whispering, with a heaping side of giggles.

They always started class by getting their "talkies out," which was Cece's way for them to talk and share, so hopefully they got it out of their system and wouldn't do it afterward. This was one of Cece's favorite parts of class because you never knew what might come out of their mouths. Even those who rarely said a word became inclined to share when their buddies did, and Cece had learned all sorts of private things about the young families in her community. She knew who'd been fired from a job, who'd gotten a new car, and whose mom thought Glenda at the bank wore too much makeup. "Okay, ladies and gentlemen. Let's see if anyone has talkies to share, and then we become dancers. Okay?" Cece asked as arms shot into the air like fireworks.

"My sister lost her first baby tooth," "I went to Deena's house to play," and "Belinda told me a secret" were a few of the first, mostly innocuous, ones. That was until little Carolyn Mason said, "My mommy went to a dance, and she said *somebody died!*"

Initially, that statement caused a few blank looks, and then Amanda Schafer's youngest daughter, Lexi's little sister, Lyric, piped up. "My mommy said she went to a dance, and somebody died, and *they deserved it*," she revealed with a satisfied grin.

Cece's eyebrows shot up and Angel's mouth dropped open as Cece tried to calmly explain that something bad did happen at the dance but that the grownups in the town were taking care of it, so the girls did not have to worry. "How about we all go on a magic carpet ride?" said Cece, master of the pivot. She grabbed the stack of carpet samples in the corner, and soon they all were riding their magic carpets to exotic places like Disney World and Dollywood.

Next came the collective percussion of twenty tap shoes moving at once, which reminded Cece of her seventh-grade band concert. It was like you knew there was supposed to be a tempo or pattern in there, it was just that no one could find it.

After class was over, Cece fully expected Amanda to be late. Her ears were still ringing with what little Lyric had shared, and she didn't know where to begin to make a connection between Amanda Schafer and Jenny. *How did those two know each other, and why in the world would Amanda say such a thing? Of course, Lyric might've said it just to add on to what the little girl said before her,* but Cece knew that, more often than not, what these little ones shared was unfiltered and based on truth.

Not only did it seem that the news about Jenny was all anyone could talk about in the studio lobby, but they also all knew Cece was indirectly involved. Cece was never one to share her private life anyway, but she was not about to gossip about this horrible event.

This fact did not deter Delilah Browers, however, from going on and on about Beryl Bridges. She said she'd heard he had a domestic abuse charge in his past. Cece had never heard anything to suggest that, and knew this was how people's lives were destroyed. In a small town, one little rumor could sink you. "He ain't never seen a woman he didn't think oughta have his inspection sticker on," Cece overheard Delilah saying. "I bet Jenny Newport had enough sense to tell him where to go, and he didn't take kindly to that."

Amanda flung open the door. *Only ten minutes late today.* Cece purposely made her way over to Amanda.

"C'mon, Lyric. Hurry up." Amanda seemed in her usual hurry, scooping Lyric's shoes into her bag and helping her pull her pants up at the same time. She was halfway to the door when Cece stepped in beside her.

"Hey, Amanda. I still can't believe what happened at the ball, can you?"

"Oh. God, yes. Terrible," she said, close enough for Cece to smell the bubblegum of her layered-on pink lip gloss. "I heard you didn't see anything or anyone when you went out there, is that right?" she asked.

"Nope. Nothing. Did you see anything odd, yourself?"

"Besides Beryl and Jenny going at each other's throats at the bar? No." Amanda grabbed Lyric's hand and turned toward the door. "We have to run now. Steve's waiting for us." And they were gone.

* * *

"What a week!" Bess declared as she dropped into a chair at their usual table at The Iris. "It's been so busy at the inn, trying to deal with fallout from the ball. As you might guess, everyone's a little freaked out since the police haven't arrested anyone yet."

Cece took a sip of her coffee and pulled her thick cardigan tight around her. "Yeah, and even if they do, it might not be the right person. Wait 'til I tell you what I've learned." Cece proceeded to tell Bess all the details of her meetings with Buck and Joe, as well as what was said in the talkies at dance class.

"Poor Calvin," Bess added. "He must have been really nervous at Buck's since he's got to be the obvious suspect for the police." Bess dug down into her "What Would Dolly Do?" tote bag, pulled out a notepad and pen, and put them on the table. "Here, I know the way you sort things out is by writing it down. So just start making a list of what you know."

Cece looked surprised. "I thought you were against me getting involved in this."

"I know better than to try and fight it, Cece. As long as you don't impersonate a cop and go knocking on doors, I think you'll be okay."

Cece jumped right in. "Good. Let's do this. First, we have suspects number one and two, Buck and Calvin, who we both know are incapable of doing this. Next, we have Beryl Bridges, who witnesses saw arguing with Jenny at the ball, had a conflict with her on Town Council, and shoots big animals for fun." Cece listed with her fingers, then paused to catch up with herself on the notepad. "We have the Schafer's daughter telling the dance class her mom thought Jenny got what she deserved. We have Jackie Simpkins paying Jenny for something unknown, which brings me to the potential that Jenny knew too much about someone she'd been paid to get information on. Something else occurred to me, too. I wonder who all knew about this supposed 'hidden inheritance box' that Jenny's dad left for them. Someone might've wanted both the siblings out of the way so they could get all of it."

"True," Bess said, "but first, they never found any hidden box in the house, and Nana and Sam didn't either. And second, I imagine most of the town knows about it since it was never a secret."

"Oh, yeah. Good point," Cece said, biting her thumbnail.

"But you've already got quite the list. Where are you going to start?" Bess asked.

"I think I need to start with local sources, meaning people like Olivia here at the coffee shop. She was really good friends with Jenny and might have some insight. She also might know what Amanda Shafer's beef could be about. And then I thought I'd talk to our neighbor Mrs. Jingles, because she knows everything about everybody on social media, and, if the studio lobby is any indication, everyone is talking about it. You never know; one of those people might be our killer."

"What about Nick?" Bess asked while checking her phone. "I'm telling you; he's got a photographic memory. He'll remember verbatim every conversation he has with a guest at the inn, and exactly what they look like. He might be a really good resource."

"Great idea." Cece scribbled on the paper. "And then there's Beryl. I've read everything I could find online, and while it certainly makes him look bad, my gut says he's not our guy, and Buck and Nana agree. Buck also brought up the possibility of a connection between the siblings' deaths. I'm not sure where to go on that one."

"You could check with newspapers or police in Florida, or just ask Sandra, I guess."

"True. And finally, there's the unknown factor of Jenny's business clients. All we have is that invoice they found from your favorite professor's wife."

"Ah, yes," Bess said, raising both eyebrows. "The esteemed Dr. Simpkins must have some secrets. And don't forget he made that ridiculous fuss about being at the same table as Jenny. Maybe that's why, because his wife was about to find out about his secret life as a British garden gnome impersonator."

Cece laughed. "I meet Dad for lunch next week. I'll see if he knows anything." Cece tapped the pen on her cheek, thinking. "All of this feels like when I'm trying to figure out how to build a part of a dollhouse without the instruction book. I have to imagine the finished product, then move backwards to figure out what piece would fit where and how." Cece tore the paper off Bess's notepad and tucked it in her purse. "I better get home and walk May," she said, pushing her chair back. "Wait, I haven't even asked about Manny. What's up there?"

"Not much now. He's going to make a quick trip home soon. Said he had to help his parents, something about the fishing tours."

"Home to Florida?"

"Yep. I guess a date that includes a murder would send anyone running. But, he said he wants me to go down there with him when I can get a few days off, so all is not lost."

"I'm glad to hear it. He really seems like a nice guy." Cece reached her arms high and stretched. "You were right, Bess. Writing this all down and running it by you has helped a lot. I'm ready to see what I can find out."

"Okay, but please be careful, Cece. You can't act on every impulse. Be sure to keep the police in the loop. Did you give any more thought to what we talked about? About your synesthesia?"

"I promise to be careful. And actually, I've been giving it a lot of thought. I've written down all the details in my journal, and I think some more might be floating up as I write. I might even be making some con-nections to reality, like we hoped. I'm not sure I have enough to talk about it yet, but it's a start." She grabbed Bess around the shoulders for a quick hug before heading out the door with a little skip in her step because it felt good to be doing something.

II

Cece stood on Violet Jingles' lavender-painted porch, pulling the hood of her sweatshirt over her head. October was definitely breathing down the neck of September, ushering in a stiff wind with a shiver. Mrs. Jingles kept her front yard decorated for every season and holiday. Cece felt like she was on a Hollywood red carpet walking up to the front door, but instead of people, she was surrounded on both sides by a crowd of fall yard flags, containers of red and yellow plastic flowers, cement statues of saints, and tree branches heavy with various fall-related ornaments.

Her hands were full of containers holding Nana's pinto beans with chow-chow, with a side of skillet cornbread. Mrs. Jingles had lived alone next door to Nana and taught piano lessons for as long as Cece could remember, and Nana often sent food over.

"There she is!" Mrs. Jingles said, opening the tall front door. She was wearing a purple velour top and pants, accessorized by no less than ten necklaces of varying lengths and styles.

"Hello, Mrs. Jingles. Nana said this was your favorite," Cece said, handing the containers to Violet.

"That Nana of yours is just the sweetest somebody. She's right; it's my favorite," Mrs. Jingles said. "Come on in, Cece. Have a seat if you have time." She pointed to a dark red velvet Victorian-style sofa, all hard curves and discomfort. Mrs. Jingles' entire house was true to the home's Victorian architecture, which meant it was filled with dark colors and heavy furniture. Cece thought the only thing missing was dramatic organ music in the background.

"Thanks. I can't stay but a minute. How've you been?" Cece asked, taking a seat.

"I can't complain; I've still got enough piano students to keep me afloat, and they just warm my heart. I've been having a time with the arthritis in my fingers, though." Mrs. Jingles said, wiggling her fingers. "Sure don't look forward to winter, *no sir*. Then I got a ringin' in my ears, so I'm having a little dizziness now and then. Got the COVID a few months back and thought I would never get off that sofa." She pointed to where Cece sat. Cece couldn't imagine any scenario where that sofa would feel comfortable, let alone when sick.

"I'm so sorry. That sounds really tough. I hope you're feeling better soon. So, I guess you're up on the terrible news—"

"About poor Jenny Newport?" Mrs. Jingles interrupted. "Terrible. Just terrible. It's a matter'a time 'til they arrest that Beryl Bridges. I went to his house to teach his daughter a piano lesson once, and that place gave me the creeps," she said, pausing barely long enough to inhale. "He had all these stuffed wild animal heads with horns hanging on the walls. There were glass cabinets, too, that held fancy guns and knives. He even had swords. I heard he's been having money trouble. Doesn't surprise me a bit that he mighta done it."

"Oh, yikes. I didn't know that about his house. And, I had no idea he had any money trouble," Cece said, remembering he always paid the dance tuition on time.

"Well, that's what some of the folks in my Facebook group have been talking about," Mrs. Jingles said with authority.

"Do they have any other ideas about what might have happened to Jenny?" Cece asked, clearly desperate enough to look for answers from Violet's Facebook group.

"Well, most think it's Beryl, but some's thinking it had to do with Jenny's business, security and all. I don't really understand all that. I just hope the police hurry and get whoever it was. Now, where are my manners? You bring me food, and I don't offer you a thing. How about some sweet tea?"

"Oh, no thanks. I better get home and let May out."

"Of course. Well, you give your Nana a big hug for sending my favorites. And I'm keeping an extra eye out for all of us. We have to be more careful than ever now. I went outside with my BB gun the other night, thinkin' I heard something out back. Never could find it. I figured it was probably a critter in the trash."

"Was that last night, Mrs. Jingles?" Cece asked.

"Yes, I guess it was just last night," she said, nodding her head. "Why? Did you hear it, too?"

"I'm not sure we heard the same thing, but I thought I heard my screen door slam."

"Well, in that case, I'm going on full neighborhood watch. I'll tell all my Facebook friends to keep their eyes and ears open, too." Her face brightened as if she had won a prize.

"Nana and I will help keep an eye on things over here for you," Cece said, slowly backing down the porch steps. "Let me know if you hear anything else interesting."

"Oh, I will darlin'. You know I will." Mrs. Jingles said with a stern note in her voice and a twinkle in her eyes.

* * *

The next morning was overcast, with fog hovering over the town and blanketing the mountains. Cece had an appointment to get her hair trimmed and thought she'd stop by The Iris on her way for a coffee to-go.

Cece stepped into the warmth of the coffee shop, immediately greeted by Olivia, who was wearing cream-colored overalls sprinkled with a print of colorful fall leaves. "How're you doing, honey? I've been thinking about you. I know that had to have been a terrible shock for you to go out there and find Jenny, dead and all."

"Yeah, 'shock' is the best word for it, but I'm doing okay. How 'bout you?"

"I've just been trying to keep myself busy around here, so I don't have time to think about it. I've been interviewing to get some help, so I can get Ricky out of here. He's about on my last nerve. But hardly a minute goes by that I don't think about Jenny. I just can't quite believe it."

"Me, either. Jenny said she always looked forward to her weekly visit here because she got to talk to you and taste whatever had just come out of your oven."

Tears came to Olivia's eyes, and she cleared her throat. "She was the best kind of customer."

Cece and Olivia stood silent for a moment until Cece said, "Well, I'm glad you're gonna get some help here at the coffee shop. I'm sure it can't be easy to work with your husband—for any wife, I mean."

Olivia rolled her eyes. "Honey, he might not be my husband much longer if we don't get him out of here," she said, finishing with a wink. "It's going to feel odd around here without Jenny and Steve meeting right over there, same time every week," she said, pointing to the corner.

"Steve? Steve who?" Cece said, suddenly wide awake, even without having had her coffee yet.

"That new principal, Steve Shafer. It was about something work-related. She told me about it, but I can't remember, of course. They always had lots of what looked like blueprints spread out on the table."

"How long had they been meeting here?"

"Since late in the summer. It was before school started." Olivia looked out the front window at the grey, foggy day, shaking her head. "Just doesn't make sense. No sense at all. Well, I better quit yakking and take care of these people behind you," Olivia said, nodding at the people who'd just come in, now standing behind Cece. "I'll get you your coffee right over. And don't forget, God don't give us more than we can handle."

Cece had never liked that platitude. It made no sense to her since she thought she'd been given a lot more than she knew how to handle. She stared at the empty corner table, trying to imagine what Steve and Jenny were working on, and if that was the connection to Amanda.

Cece lingered over the historical photographs framed on the coffee shop walls. Their town had been established before Tennessee had even become a state. Her favorite photo was of Main Street covered in deep snow with a bull walking down the middle of it. It amazed her that even though a lot had changed, the basic footprint of the town was the same. *The same goes for people,* Cece thought. Even though people changed, the motives for their choices largely stayed the same. *Given the motives of love, betrayal, or money, we could all surprise ourselves with what we might do.* Cece shook her head at her own dark thoughts, took her coffee from Olivia, and turned to leave just as Joe came walking in the door.

"Fancy meeting you here," Joe said. "I remember when both of us thought coffee was something only our parents drank. Guess we've changed our tune since then, huh?"

"Yeah. I think late-night college study sessions did it for me. It felt like a requirement."

Joe laughed. "Yep, same for me. How've you been?" He paused. "Wait. I just saw you yesterday, didn't I? Sorry, I went camping last night and lost track of time."

"You went camping on a weeknight?" Cece asked, curious now, and glad to feel like she was talking to the "old Joe."

"Yeah. I do that sometimes. I head for the nearest park and pitch my tent. Sometimes it's the perfect medicine. And last night the stars were spectacular."

"Good for you. That must mean Hailey is a tent-pitching kind of girl?" Cece asked because she couldn't help herself.

"Uh, that would be a hard no." He shook his head as the shadow of thoughts passed over his face. "Just so you know, Cece, Hailey and I aren't together anymore."

"Oh. Well, Bess had told me… I mean, it's not my business any-way," Cece said, hoping the flush in her cheeks wasn't obvious.

"We dated for a little while, and it did not work out," Joe said, drawing out the last four words. "Now I'm trying to do the friend thing without muddying the waters. I did help her move some furniture the other day. Anyway, I just… I wanted to clear that up. So, you're teaching to-day?"

"Oh, yes, but first, speak of the devil, I'm getting my hair trimmed." Hailey worked at the salon, and Joe raised his eyebrows in sur-prise that Cece was going there, but there really was only one place to go in town. "Any news since way back yesterday on the Jenny case?" Cece asked.

"Actually, we've had a couple of interesting developments. But I can't really talk about them."

Cece let out an exasperated sigh. "I think I'd rather hear there's no news, than there is some, but I can't know about it." Cece swung her hair back over her shoulder and glanced at her watch, "Beauty calls! Sorry, I better not be late." With that, Cece turned and left.

"Okay. Guess I'll see you around, then," Joe said to Cece's back as she walked out the door, his face a frozen question mark.

Carlene was standing inside the door of Carlene's Cuts when Cece walked in. "Welcome in, Cece. You're looking pretty as ever," she said. Carlene owned the shop, was close to Nana's age, and wore her hair long and dyed jet-black. She had on dangling chandelier earrings and a bracelet of painted wooden beads.

Cece loved going to the beauty salon, even though no one called it that these days. There was just something more inviting about the words "beauty salon," and this particular beauty salon was always a beehive of motion, sounds, and scent.

There were six "stations" and a waiting area of upholstered folding chairs. They still had one of the old-fashioned "bonnet-style" hair dryers and a faded wallpaper border at the top of the walls that featured pastel drawings of Paris. There was a certain odd comfort in the hum of blow dryers and women's voices, coupled with the smells of shampoo and chemicals, that made Cece miss her small circle of friends in New York.

Carlene ushered her to her usual chair with Maddie. Both Carlene and Maddie had worked at the salon since before Cece left for college, which meant her life story was like a worn magazine on the table by the dryers, just waiting to be read or remembered. Since Nana went to the same shop, there were no chapters left out.

Maddie had washed and was trimming Cece's hair when Hailey, Joe's supposedly now previous girlfriend, appeared from the back. She stood across the salon from Cece and over by Carlene at the front desk, talking loudly enough for the whole salon to hear.

"And I told Joe I absolutely could not spend the night with him last night. He did everything but beg me. He's such a sweetheart, you know, so I finally said, 'Okay, okay, but I have to get up early," Hailey said, her voice animated, and with her hands up in surrender for dramatic emphasis.

Cece was uncomfortable, to say the least, especially since she'd just come from talking to Joe. It was clear one of them had to be lying. Cece couldn't help noticing Hailey's ample curves, peering down at her own flat chest and remembering when she had a pixie cut and got mistaken for a teenage boy at the firemen's pancake breakfast.

From the mirror in front of her chair, Cece watched Carlene slide her eyes back and forth between Hailey and her. Carlene knew Joe and Cece were a couple in high school, and Hailey obviously did, too. Hailey evidently needed to stake her claim. "Well, you know, men," Carlene said. "Now, who's up next for you, Hailey?" she asked, pointedly changing the subject and lifting her cat-eye reading glasses from the pearl chain around her neck to check the appointment book. Cece was relieved to get out of there as soon as possible.

* * *

At a little diner near Johns Town Community College, Cece slid into a booth early for her lunch date with her dad. Leo arrived soon after in jeans and a flannel shirt, looking a bit like the mountain version of Indiana Jones, and slid in across from her.

Leo was handsome, with an average build, and in his early 50s. He had a square jaw and a faded scar on his forehead from an old accident. His dark hair was silvering at the temples, and his skin was weathered from his pastime, since he was a boy, off searching for arrowheads. He had always loved American history, particularly stories about the earliest settlers of the land he came from. He was a marvelous storyteller, which made him a great teacher, and also innately curious, not just about history, but everything. He immediately peppered Cece with a dozen questions about the studio and Jenny's murder, and Cece gave him every detail.

"Okay, so now you've answered all the easy questions." He gave a gentle smile, "Now it's time to get down to the nitty-gritty. I want to know how it feels to be back home. It can't be easy going from your non-stop life in New York back to our little corner in the mountains." He hesitated, took a long drink of water, "I know Jenny meant a lot to you. She took good care of all of us after Mom died. She was devoted to your mom right to the end, and then, boy, she took care of our family with support and lots of casseroles. I understand that it must feel like a gut punch. I'm so sorry you had to see that."

Cece paused. She knew her dad would see through a pat response like "I'm fine" or "Doin' okay." To her surprise, tears sprang to her eyes. "I don't know which I feel more, sadness or anger." With her dad sitting across from her and Jenny on her mind, Cece couldn't help but think about when her mom died. "Remember all those shrimp rings and Mrs. Stouffer's casseroles we ate after Mom died?" she said with a tender smile, thinking back to how many stops and starts it took for her and her dad to find their way to a new normal. "I've been trying to make sense of Jenny's death, and I can't come up with anything."

Dad reached to put his hand on her forearm. "Baby, you can't make what's irrational into something rational. Hopefully, the police can catch who did it and give us some answers. You know the drug problem around these parts. More than likely someone was just out of their mind. Or, seems everyone's talking about Beryl Bridges. Could be right under our nose."

"I know. You may be right. I think I'm coping by digging into who could have wanted her dead."

"Have they arrested Bridges yet?" her dad asked.

"Not that I know of. Everyone's getting questioned now. I think the police think he did it, but I've talked to Buck, and he's not so sure. You know the nature of Jenny's business might have earned her some enemies. I think the police need to do a lot more digging."

"I'm sure they want to get it solved as fast as possible. I know you, and you're old enough to know that you can't fix this, right? No matter how bad you want to, sometimes it's best to leave the job to those who make a living doing it. Speaking of fixing things, how are your peculiars? You told me you were going to look into it. Have you done that yet?" her dad asked before taking another bite of his burger. Cece knew he was not going to let this go.

"Not yet, but it's on my to-do list. I promise," Cece said, taking a last bite of her sweet potato fries before they took her plate away.

"How about Nana and Aunt Granny?" her dad asked as he nodded thanks to the waitress as she took his dishes. "Have you talked to them about it?"

"Actually, I'm going to see Aunt Granny soon. And Nana wants to go with me, so we'll talk then."

"Good. The two of them can help you figure this out," he said, his face fixed and suddenly serious. "They know more than you think they do."

"I always listen to them, Dad," Cece said, not understanding why he would think otherwise. "Before I forget, I wanted to ask you about one of the other teachers here. Professor Simkins?"

"Oh, yes. Yerger in British Studies. He's a hard one to miss."

"Do you know anything about his personal life outside of the college?" Cece asked.

"I hardly know him *inside* the college. I really don't know him personally at all, only professionally."

"C'mon, Dad. This is a small college; you'd know if you'd heard anything about him."

"Well, maybe I have heard the students talking before."

"About what, Dad? You have to tell me. I think it might be important to Jenny's case."

"I can't imagine how. But I've heard he thinks of himself as a bit of a ladies' man."

"Yerger Simkins?" Cece asked with disbelief. "Yerger with the Napolean complex and a comb-over?"

"Yes, the very same. At least students say he seems to fancy himself as one by the way he talks." Leo uncrossed his legs. He wore boots not much unlike Aunt Granny's worn brown leather ones, old and beat-up.

"Has he had affairs? Please don't tell me he's had an affair with a student," Cece said, making a gagging sound.

"No. I don't know anything about that. And he may be all talk, as many are."

"Bess has him for a class this semester and says he's a creep. Do you know his wife?"

"Actually, yeah, kind of. Better than him. She works at the college library, and I see her there sometimes. Jackie seems to be a lovely person." her dad said, shrugging. He signed the credit card tab the waitress had left, and they both started to get up. "Let me know how your visit with your Aunt Granny goes. Give them both a big hug from me."

They walked out to their cars arm-in-arm, and Cece felt better than she had since the ball.

As Cece hit the highway for home, her thoughts were already racing ahead to Jenny's memorial service being held the next day. She had read enough crime mysteries and watched enough *Murder, She Wrote* to know that the service for the victim was prime viewing-ground for potential suspects. *It might be a stranger that shows up, unusual behavior, or something someone says,* Cece thought, determined to be on full alert.

Cece also wondered about Yerger and Jackie. She didn't know why he wouldn't want to sit at the table with Jenny and Buck at the dance. She thought about the invoice Calvin found on Jenny's computer and wondered if maybe Jenny knew something about Yerger she wasn't supposed to know, and if that something could be a reason for murder.

FIRE CIRCLE

A gust of wind pushed its way through the thick canopy of tree branches on the hillside behind Hazel's house, enough for the cold air to curl around the old women gathered by the fire. Cat leaned forward, elbows on knees, her long silver braids hanging low, and lifted her round, wrinkled face to the sky. She tipped her head back and sniffed the air, and as she turned her head to each side, she sniffed again. She then opened her mouth wide and stuck out her tongue as if to taste the wind.

"Hazel, rain's near. We better think of putting out the fire for the night."

"Yep," Hazel said, staring into the fire, her boots shifting the leaves.

"I know you are troubled by Cece, my friend. She will only come to know herself and her power when she has to, just like we did long ago. My family taught me to respect my place in the scheme of things and not to rush nature. We both know how hard that is, but we also know time is not ours to rush."

For a moment Hazel saw her friend as she must have looked when she was young, her smooth dark skin unlined by age, and her hair black like obsidian.

Cat continued, "It was out of necessity that we learned to read the skies, pay attention to the wind, and smell the comin' rain. We didn't seek it because we wanted to learn, but because *we had to*. The same will happen for Cece. The time is coming that she'll have no other choice. It will become necessary for her to act on what she already knows, but does not yet trust. She'll be okay, Hazel."

Cat reached her rough, age-stiffened hand out toward Hazel, and taking it, Hazel knew deep down that with these friends by her side, all would be well.

12

Nana sat in front of her laptop at the kitchen table, surrounded by pamphlets from historic inns around the world. Although Nana didn't work in an official capacity for the inn anymore, she had a reputation for her business savvy, and the general manager and department heads at the Eureka Grove Inn still wanted her input. Nana used this as an excuse to take her girlfriends on trips she said were for "evaluating operations" at different historic inns, and, if time permitted, they might also find time to see the sights, drink wine, and pick around at antique shops, and for Nana, time had a way of permitting.

Nana swept her hand across the table. "You see what I do to get my mind off Jenny's death. I just imagine myself in these other places," she said to Cece, who had just come in. They both wore simple black dresses and were ready for Jenny's memorial, which was to be held at City Park.

"Have you narrowed it down to where you want to go yet?" Cece asked.

"I was waiting for you to put in your two cents worth, since I hope you might come with me."

Although Nana traveled to a different inn almost every year, this was the first Cece had heard anything about her joining them. "Of course I will, but isn't the 'Brigade' going with you? And, who's going to run the studio while you're gone?" Nana's book club friends were her usual companions on these trips.

"I'll just bring you along as an honorary member," Nana said, smirking, as she picked up her car keys. "Darlin', somehow, someway, I managed to run the studio without you for forty-some years. Although I admit, it wasn't nearly as fun. Besides that, I can't think of anything better than having you join me. If you want to, of course."

Cece loved travel. "Oh, man. Thank you. Of course I will!" Cece said, her mind starting to spin with the destinations listed in bold letters on the brochures, like the *Cotswolds, Paris,* and picturesque *Vermont.* She imagined herself in an old manor-turned-inn, having tea in china cups painted with delicate flowers before walking the cobblestone streets. She might navigate traffic in Paris on a bicycle with flowers and baguettes in the front basket, or even hit the ski slopes in a long puffer jacket before having hot chocolate topped with fat marshmallows in front of a roaring fire.

"We better head out," Nana said, breaking Cece's travel fantasies. Nana picked up both of their jackets, handing one to Cece. "I'm sure there'll be a crowd, so we better get going."

Jenny's service had already filled the many rows of folding chairs set up at the park. Fittingly, it was an overcast day but not so cold as to be uncomfortable, and Cece and Nana found two seats together near the back. Cece scanned the rows for anything or anyone that looked suspicious or out of place. Nothing caught her eye except little Brennie Conover, sitting close to the front with her parents. She spied Cece and proceeded to wave, yelling, "Hi, Miss Cece!" across the rows.

They were seated near Nick Adams and his mom, which reminded Cece that she wanted to ask Nick some questions about the ball. She would have to track him down after the service. Cece thought no one looked suspicious, although she wasn't exactly sure what suspicious looked like. She also knew the ones to worry about the most were probably the ones that didn't look suspicious at all. After the service was over, and many had gathered by the gazebo, Cece threaded her way through the crowd toward Nick. "How are you, Nick? I haven't seen you since the ball."

Nick tossed his hair back from one side. "Oh, hey, Cece. Yes, what a terrible night. I thought the sound system was a big deal, and then this happened." He gestured toward the crowd.

"I know," Cece said. "Half the town must be here. Well, not really. That wouldn't make sense since that would be thousands, but a lot of people for sure." Nick smiled down at her. "Anyway, I know how observant you are and how you remember details. Bess is amazed at how you seem to know what the guests need before they do. So, I was just wondering if you saw anything unusual that night?"

"The police have asked me that, too. Like I told them, I was really preoccupied with the audio problem, but one thing I remembered after the ball was seeing Ms. Newport at the bar a couple of times."

"So, you think she might've had a lot to drink that night?"

"No. In fact, both times I saw her holding a bottle of water. The second time I saw her she was on a phone call, and soon after that she went outside by the same door you and Calvin used later, where you ended up finding her."

"Interesting. Did you notice anything else?"

"No. I can't think of anything. By the way, thanks again for calling Calvin for me. It seems so irrelevant now, but it sure helped me at the time."

"No problem. Glad to help. I guess I better head over to speak to Buck and the girls. Take care, Nick."

Cece caught up with Nana, and they moved toward where a line had formed to talk with Buck, Jenny's two grown daughters, and her sister-in-law, Sandra, standing inside the park gazebo.

Cece expressed her condolences, and when she got to Jenny's oldest daughter, Kara, she held Cece's hand with both of hers, just like her mom. "I think Mom thought of you like another daughter," she told Cece, whose eyes quickly filled with tears.

"She was the best. Just the best," was all Cece could get out.

Last in the line was Sandra, who Cece had never spoken to before. She had on a black silk suit and wore a dramatic charcoal hat with netting that came down over her face. Cece wondered if this was an outfit she just happened to pack for her trip from Florida or if she'd gotten it for the occasion.

"Hi. I'm Cece," she said, extending her hand. "Your sister-in-law meant a lot to me. She helped me through a really hard time in my life. I'm so sorry for your loss." Sandra barely grasped Cece's hand before letting go.

"Thanks. Is your grandmother here?" Sandra said, glancing at her watch, which Cece immediately noticed was a Rolex with tiny diamonds surrounding the watch face. Sandra was businesslike in her demeanor, her words clipped and brief.

"Yeah, she's somewhere in line behind me," Cece said. "I'm sure it's a comfort for your nieces to have you here. How long will you be staying?"

"I'm leaving tonight. Yes. It's tonight. Not long from now, actually," Sandra said, looking somewhere beyond Cece.

"Okay, well, I better keep moving. Again, I'm so sorry."

Cece and Nana were heading to the car, glad to see the overcast morning had given way to a cloudless blue sky, when they heard Joe's voice behind them. "Mrs. Chagall. Cece," he called, quickly catching up.

"Why, Mr. Joe Barksdale. It is lovely to see you, although I wish it were under different circumstances," Nana said.

"Me, too, ma'am," he said, leaning in to give Nana a quick peck on the cheek.

"Joe, I'm sure everyone is asking this, but is there anything new in the investigation?"

Joe's eyes cast downward, then back up at Nana. "I really can't say anything. I'm sorry. But I will say I think we're getting close. Really close."

"That's all I need to know, dear," Nana said as Joe opened the car door for her and helped her in.

"Hey, Cece," Joe said, walking around the car to her side. "I was thinking—I mean, you said you went hiking the other day, and I wondered if maybe you'd want to go on a short one on Sunday afternoon? I know a new trail I bet you've never been on. You can bring May, and I'll bring Truman."

"Umm, okay," Cece's brain instantly skipped over any hesitation based on him not giving her the information she wanted on the case. "Yeah, that sounds nice. Just text me the location of the trailhead, and we'll meet you there. Does 1 work?"

"Yep. Sounds great. See you then," Joe said, turning for his car.

Before Cece could get her seatbelt on, Nana was making an exaggerated throat-clearing sound, saying, "Ahem."

"Do you have an announcement, Nana?" Cece asked as Nana turned to face her, one eyebrow raised.

"No. Nothing. I'm not going to say a single word about you and your—what is it you call him? Oh, 'friend' Joe Barksdale." She moved a finger across to zip her lips. Nana knew how to lay it on when she wanted to.

* * *

When Cece walked in the door of her house, she kicked off her shoes, peeled off her black dress, and pulled one of Bess's cookies from the tin on the counter. She bent down to pet May, shared a piece of the cookie with her, and then went to the bedroom to pull some sweats out of the dirty clothes pile. Cece then helped herself to a second cookie in the kitchen and took her time, chewing each bite slowly while savoring the crispy edges and buttery soft inside of the cookie. She was thinking about Jenny and the service, how odd Sandra seemed, and how handsome Joe looked in his suit.

"Can't waste a moment we're given," she heard her mom's voice as clear as if she had been standing there beside her. Cece remembered exactly where she was when she said it. Cece had been complaining about having to go to Saturday dance practice, sitting cross-legged on the bed next to her mom, who was propped up on three pillows and covered with one of Aunt Granny's barn quilts. She was exhausted from her latest round of chemo. "Then skip it today, baby," her mom had said. "The world'll keep turning. You've been talking about wanting to help Aunt Granny with her garden. See if your daddy won't take you up there. I think time spent with any of the women on the Brown side of your family is never wasted."

"Really? I can skip?" Cece had asked in surprise.

"I'm not sayin' you need to make a habit of it; just use your good judgment."

"I *have* been wanting to help her plant those special tomatoes she's always talking about," Cece had said.

"There you go. Put on your jeans and do it. Can't waste a moment we're given, and for sure, you don't want to wish you'd done it but didn't. Go on and help Aunt Granny, then you can go to dance practice next time."

Cece felt her mom was the only one who suspected the truth, that dance was her talent, the part of her life that helped her fit in and feel normal, but maybe not her passion. Cece remembered how good it felt to get her hands into the earth, turning the dark soil over and mixing in the fertilizer, with Aunt Granny teaching her along the way. She wondered when she had stopped getting her hands dirty and why. Cece couldn't remember, but it was probably because she didn't have time for it. Like now, when she had a dollhouse to build for Mrs. Jingles, who had ordered it from her a month ago for her granddaughter. "Okay, May," Cece said, looking down. "I've put off this new build too long. Let's get it started."

The dollhouse pieces were carefully laid out on the table by letter and number according to directions. This design was a French Row House and had three floors with an attic room on top. Painting the pieces was always the first step, and Cece had already picked out the paint colors of cream and black. After socializing at the memorial service, she was more than ready to pull her introvert's turtle shell over her head and fall into her painting trance. She enjoyed the meditative repetition of the brushstrokes, because it was both soothing and gratifying at the same time.

Cece kept thinking about what Bess had said regarding her peculiars. As she moved the wooden pieces of the dollhouse around on the table, her mind wandered into that place where unimportant thoughts drifted to the bottom, leaving the space on top clear. It was in that moment that Cece brought the scattered parts together. Like a handful of marbles rolling out in different directions, only one caught her eye. Cece held the thought just long enough to finish the paint job on the house, but as soon as the brush had been swirled in the jar of water she grabbed her phone to call Bess, who picked up on the first ring.

"I've got it," Cece said before Bess could even say "hello."

"Hello to you, Sister. What exactly have you got? Besides the hots for good old Joe?"

"Cute. But, no," said Cece, reaching down to throw May's chew toy across the room. "It may not solve the murder, but it may help. I've got a hunch."

"Okay, you've always been pretty spot on with those. Let's hear it."

"I think the silver key is a clue. I don't know how, but it is." May dropped the chew toy at her feet, and Cece obediently threw it again.

"All right. Now, what are you going to do with this information?" Bess asked.

"I thought I might leave it on the EGPD 'tip line.' What do you think?"

"I think it will be shuffled through with dozens of other tips the police are probably getting. I doubt anyone else calling in a tip was at the scene of the crime but you. Why don't you just call Joe directly? You're more apt to get results that way, I think. It can't hurt, right?"

Cece took a sharp inhale and let it out slowly. "Okay. I'll call him."

"Another thing, Manny told me that when he was talking to Buck at the ball he learned Sandra lives in the town right next to his in Florida. I'd told him you'd been thinking about the murder and had a list with Sandra's name on it. He said he could dig around a little bit for us if we wanted him to. Just tell him what you want."

"Wow. That's great. When is he leaving? I need to get some details for him," Cece said, thinking while her finger made lines and spirals on the table like a pen.

"He's leaving Thursday, so you've only got a few days. I guess you've got your marching orders, sister, between calling Joe and getting info for Manny. You better get busy."

Cece had gotten a text from Buck while she was talking to Bess. He had invited her to a barbecue that night for family and a few friends. Cece thought it would be really good to spend some time with Jenny's daughters before they had to leave. She also knew it was the perfect chance to get the information she needed about Sandra to give to Manny before he left for Florida. Cece texted back:

Thanks for inviting me. I'll see you tonight.

She stood up to stretch, reaching her arms wide behind her. Cece decided to get the hard part over with first and picked up her phone to call Joe.

13

Cece walked into Jenny and Buck's house, a paper plate of deviled eggs in her hands. A small group of close friends and family had already gathered there, and she was a little embarrassed to add her puny plate of eggs to the almost full surface of the dining room table. Southerners excelled at this particular skill, and no matter the occasion, whether funeral or holiday, one would never leave any gathering hungry. There was an ample amount of barbecue in foil pans, along with multiple casseroles, many of which contained the same magic ingredient: a can of Campbell's cream of mushroom soup. As Cece was setting her plate down next to a heaping bowl of potato salad with pickle relish and celery, just gleaming with lumps of mayonnaise, a neighbor showed up at the door with a lit cigarette hanging out of the side of his mouth, and a bucket of Kentucky Fried Chicken in his arms. Cece overheard him apologizing, telling Buck he'd just gotten off his shift but wanted to be sure he brought something over. Buck assured him his KFC was just as welcome as all the other offerings.

Everyone had changed from their more formal memorial service attire, and Cece felt a somber energy running through their shared stories about Jenny, along with the relief of occasional laughter. She felt shards of her own memories resurface: when folks gathered at her house after her mom died, when the house was crowded, full of food and people, with Dad, Nana, and Cece standing in the middle of it all like deer in headlights. Those memories felt like puzzle pieces, part of a bigger picture Cece didn't have the headspace or desire to deal with right now. She spent time talking with each of Jenny's daughters, knowing from experience that just letting them talk about their mom would help.

Pastor Walls, the retired preacher of Valley Forge Free Will

Baptist, the church Jenny and Ed had grown up in, was called on to say the blessing before they ate. What started out as a blessing soon began to feel like a long-winded sermon. Just as Cece thought he was finished and would pick up her fork to take a bite, Pastor Walls would take a big breath, "Though I walk through the valley of the shadow of death, I shall fear no evil," he continued, his voice rising and falling, keeping a steady rhythm.

Cece's fork was almost to her mouth again when the end finally came, but then Rondell Barry launched into singing the hymn "His Eye Is on the Sparrow" in her breathy, tremulous voice. She stared at her potato salad with longing and prayed for strength.

Cece had always admired the unwavering faith of her Nana and Aunt Granny, but never shared it. She remembered having a glimmer when she was young, regularly attending church with them and going to Sunday School and Church Camp. But that was before her mom got cancer. Suddenly the potato salad she'd been longing for was difficult to swallow. She took a few bites anyway before setting her plate down to stretch her legs.

"Thanks for having me over, Buck," Cece said, coming outside to where Buck stood by the grill on the back porch. It was Cece's favorite time of day, twilight, and the sun had just disappeared beyond the trees, leaving behind a pastel glow. "It feels good to be surrounded by all things Jenny."

"Of course, Cece. I know what you mean. Hard to imagine getting rid of any of her stuff right now," Buck said, his face crossed in furrows that seemed to have appeared overnight. "I'm sorry Anna B. couldn't come, but I understand. It's been a long day for everyone."

"The good news is that you don't have to do anything with her things until you're ready. It's been really good to catch up with Kara and Nicole. Is Sandra still here?" Cece asked.

"Nope. She came by here to change and say goodbye, then left for the airport a little while ago. And frankly, Cece, I was glad. I don't know if it was grief, trauma, or what, but she was so agitated it was hard to be around her."

"Agitated? What do you mean?"

"Well, Jenny'd warned me about her, said she could be over-the-top about how things look. Appearances, you know. Or, as Sandra so tactfully put it, she 'finally got up here for a visit and this happens!' like Jenny's murder was such an inconvenience to her. And she said something about the special box left for Ed and Jenny by their dad. I'm here, you know, trying to get ready for all the visitors, and Sandra's just talking and talking, following me around while I'm trying to move tables and set up chairs. I'll tell you"—Buck shook his head—"sometimes she can be a lot. I didn't know what she was going on about, and then I remembered the gold box Jenny and Ed used to laugh about. They both said years ago that it was lost, and it probably didn't have anything in it anyway."

"Yikes. That's callous, and weird. Odd that she remembered it, too."

"Yep. I don't know; I told her she could change in our bedroom and have a look around if she wanted. She took me up on that, was in there for a while, and then seemed to want to get out of here as fast as she could. Uber was at the door before she'd even gotten down the stairs. She waved at Kara and Nicole, and then was gone."

Cece agreed with Buck, but didn't say anything. In her view Sandra had seemed distracted and short at the memorial too. "Bess said her date for the ball, Manny, was from a town near where Sandra lives," Cece said, hoping to prompt Buck.

"Yeah, nice fellow. His family's in Jupiter, and Sandra's in West Palm Beach. They're only about fifteen miles apart."

"They must be really wealthy to live in Palm Beach."

Buck half-chuckled. "She's certainly not hurting for money since Ed left her plenty, but the billionaires live on 'the island' of Palm Beach, over the bridge from where Sandra lives. She just acts like she lives there."

Cece nodded, easily detecting there was no love lost between Sandra and Buck. She still needed more specifics to give to Manny. "So does she live in one of those gated communities down there?"

"Yeah. She has a big house right on the Intracoastal. Just beautiful. View of the water, boat dock, the whole thing. It's called flamingo, or heron, something like that."

"Sounds like a fun place to visit."

"It used to be, when Ed was alive. We haven't been there since the accident."

Cece racked her brain, trying to think of a question to ask Buck that would give her something more specific to go on, but she didn't have to.

"Apparently she just sold Ed's old fishing boat and bought a brand-new Genesis 2000 Cabin Cruiser," Buck said, tipping back his beer.

"I didn't know you were a boat guy?" Cece looked surprised. She was also glad to have snagged a great clue to help Manny find Sandra.

"I'm not, or didn't used to be, but I loved going out on the water with Ed. I learned a lot about boats that way. He was a boat fanatic and was always telling me about the latest and best boats on the market, but he was way too frugal to spend that kind of money."

Jenny's daughter, Kara, came outside with a plate full of food and handed it to Buck.

"I'm not sure who you think is going to eat all that," he said, chuckling. "But thank you."

Kara smiled, pressing a stray blonde hair behind her ear. "You two come on back inside, it's getting cold out here."

"We'll be there in a minute," Buck said, watching her shut the door behind her. "Boy, she sure reminds me of her mother." He turned to look at Cece. "Before we go back inside, I need to tell you something I just found out before everyone got here."

"That doesn't sound good. What's going on?" Cece asked.

"The police searched Calvin's house and camper." He paused, rubbing back and forth on his jaw. "Cece, I'm afraid they found a piece of Jenny's jewelry in his toolbox. It was an heirloom, a locket from her grandmother."

Cece took a fast step back like she'd been slapped. "What? You're kidding me. That can't be true."

"Calvin swears he has no idea how it got there. The police are holding him at the station for now. I'm sure he'll be let go soon," Buck said. "I can't believe it either."

"I've got to talk to him." Cece tipped her head toward the door. "Let's get you inside, and I think I'll take off soon, Buck. Thanks for inviting me. I'm going to really miss Jenny. She was—" Cece's voice caught. "She was special in my life."

"I think she felt the same about you, honey."

Driving home, Cece let herself have a big, ugly cry that included gasping and pulling fast-food napkins from the glove compartment. She just needed to get to the cottage and to May, then she could figure out her next step.

Cece heard May barking from inside the cottage before she got to the door. She started talking to her as she got closer, but she didn't stop barking like she usually did when she heard Cece's voice. Cece unlocked the door and stepped inside, immediately feeling icy currents run from her fingertips up her arms. May was jumping on her, her bark now a high-pitched whining. The soft glow of the single lamp Cece left on for May created a wide circle of light, and at first Cece thought everything seemed okay.

She flipped the switch for the overhead light, and her breath caught in her throat. Cece instinctively scooped May into her arms and took a step back. She made a slow, deliberate pivot-turn back toward the open door, and ran.

14

Joe had seen the 911 call come in from Cece's address, and in less than ten minutes he was at the cottage. He arrived with his older partner, Morris, who was broad-shouldered with fading brown-to-grey hair and a deep, gravelly voice from years of cigar smoking. They immediately went in and searched inside Cece's cottage, and then around the yard surrounding both houses, checking all the windows and doors as they went. When they were finished Joe called Cece to give her the all-clear, so she could come out from Nana's house, where Cece and Nana had been inside checking all of Nana's doors and windows.

Joe and Morris were outside Nana's back door when they came out. Without saying a word Joe folded Cece in his arms. Both let go fast, and Cece swallowed hard. "The most important thing is that you and Mrs. Chagall are okay." Joe said, "and there were no signs of tampering at Mrs. Chagall's." He looked at Nana. "But that also might be because you have a motion-sensor light and Cece doesn't. We just don't know."

The four of them walked the few steps to Cece's cottage, stopping to stand inside Cece's living area. Being with Joe, Morris, and Nana, Cece felt the blood finally begin to rush back into her chilled body.

Morris was kneeling now and examining the door lock. "How old is this lock, do you guess?"

"I…I don't have any idea," Cece said, looking over at Nana, who was wrapped in her favorite ragged chenille robe and wearing ruby-red bedroom slippers.

"Oh, it's old. I'd bet it's as old as the cottage. We built this in '95, I think?" Nana answered.

"Yes, ma'am, Mrs. Chagall. That makes sense. Did you see any sign of forced entry when you arrived, Cece?" Morris asked, fiddling with the doorknob and lock.

"No, sir," Cece answered.

"These old locks are easily accessed with a credit card," Joe said. "Not much you could've done. Unless someone else has a key. Like maybe Calvin?"

"No. No, just me and Nana," said Cece, shaking her head again and looking over to Nana, who agreed.

"Okay, well, we need you to look around and tell us anything missing or that you notice as unusual. Anything at all," Joe said.

Cece began in her bedroom, where the wood floor was littered with the contents of everything under her bed, bedside table, and the floor of her small closet. Her bed had been pushed over a few feet and plastic storage containers, shoeboxes, and books had been pulled out from underneath and thrown to the side. The clothes in the closet were untouched, but the shoe rack and clothes hamper had been upturned with shoes and dirty clothes tossed aside. The scene was as strange as it was frightening.

Cece then checked her bathroom, which appeared untouched. The only really valuable thing she owned was her mother's wedding rings. They were in a porcelain dish inside a drawer where she'd left them.

Cece continued into the living room and kitchen, scanning the surfaces with methodical precision, trying to notice if anything was missing or even touched. In the living room, her loveseat and chair had been moved over a couple of feet, revealing a couple of candy wrappers and an old pen. The kitchen seemed untouched.

Cece put her hands on her hips, looking around. "First, why would anyone go for the cottage and not Nana's house?" She glanced at Nana, quickly adding, "Of course, I'm so glad nobody did. And it looks like they focused on the things on the floor and didn't mess with anything on the counters or in the drawers. It doesn't make sense."

"No, it doesn't, unless you are looking for something specific, and think the floor of your cottage is where it could be found," Joe offered, "or else someone just wanted to scare you."

"That makes even less sense," Cece said thoughtfully. "Unless someone dropped something accidentally or left it here. But it's not like

I've had a revolving door of company around here. I've had maybe five people total in the cottage since I moved in. And who would want to scare me?"

"I don't know. People do some pretty wild things." Morris shook his head. "Maybe whoever it is lost something?"

"I don't invite many people over, like I said, and if I did, and they left something behind, I'd let them know, or they could call me. Right?" Cece said, shaking her head. "I don't get this, and it totally creeps me out that someone's been in here."

Nana jumped in to say, "Of course it does. I'll call first thing to get new locks put in and some new lights installed. In the meantime, I think you and May should come for another sleepover."

"I think your Nana's right," Joe said. "That'll give us time to get a good look and take some pictures so you can put things back in place tomorrow. Ya'll can go on over there now, and we'll finish up here. We'll also check the yard and the neighborhood again. I'll text when we leave."

* * *

The scent of fresh coffee and Nana's cinnamon rolls woke Cece from a night of disjointed dreams amid fits of sleep and waking. She almost felt more tired now than when she went to bed.

"Good Morning, darlin'," Nana said, handing Cece a mug of steaming black coffee. "I guess I know better than to ask if you had a good night's sleep."

"Yeah, please don't," Cece said, shuffling over to the table wearing one of her grandmother's old, slick nylon robes with a quilted front. "I couldn't stop thinking about who'd been in the cottage, and then wondering who they knew, and just spinning out from there." She stopped to stifle a yawn, then dropped her head back, staring at the ceiling.

"Darling. All you'll do is churn butter going 'round and 'round about why someone broke into the cottage. Sometimes it never makes any sense," Nana said, sounding just like her son, as she pulled the cinnamon rolls from the oven. She spread the tops with Cece's favorite icing, made with cream cheese, confectioner's sugar, and vanilla. "I know it must just eat at you, but I think you'll just drive yourself crazy if you keep spinning it around." Nana brought the rolls to the table while Cece topped off their coffee. "You'll feel better after you get your place put back together. Let me know if I can do anything." Nana put the *Eureka Grove Gazette* on the table in front of Cece. "In the meantime, I thought you'd want to see this," she said, pointing at a headline at the bottom of the front page that read, "Local Businessman's Motives Questioned."

Cece pulled the paper in front of her. The article read, in part:

First Community Bank has filed suit against Beryl Bridges, town council member in Eureka Grove, over his proposed "Soaky Mountain Waterpark." FCB filed the suit in county court, claiming Bridges had borrowed five million dollars on a line of credit to build the water park. This aligns with county records showing a purchase of ten acres of land north of Eureka Grove. FCB claims Bridges falsified documents showing he had the necessary approvals and permits to complete construction of the park. The bank intends to enforce the liens it has on Bridges' construction business and personal assets, including his personal residence in Eureka Grove. Bridges did not respond to our request for comment.

"Yikes, so if Beryl didn't get approval for the waterpark, he was done for. I knew Beryl was pushing Jenny for zoning approval, but I didn't know he was risking everything he had," Cece said.

"Yes, it doesn't exactly paint the best picture of Beryl, does it?" Nana said, pulling the paper back to her side of the table.

"That's an understatement. Sounds like something that could drive someone to murder."

"You never know, Cece. We just never know what hides within a human heart."

Cece's phone pinged with a text from Joe:

Hey. You doing okay this morning? Still up for a hike? I'd understand if u r not.

Cece texted her reply:

Doing okay. Rattled. But I need a hike. Send me where to meet.

"Nana, May, and I are heading back to the cottage. I'm going to give it a deep clean and open up all the windows. Need to air out the icky break-in energy. Thanks for the sleepover, and I think I need one of these for the road," Cece said, taking a cinnamon roll and wrapping it in a napkin.

"Okay, darlin'. Love you," Nana said. Nana always gave Cece the space she needed, especially since she could throw a rock and hit Cece's door from hers. Despite their proximity, Cece never felt like Nana was keeping tabs on her, but now it felt like someone else *was*. Someone must've known she was out last night, either by watching her comings and goings or knowing her plans. Both ideas were equally disturbing.

Joe and Morris had left everything exactly as it was the night before. Cece scrubbed and vacuumed, working up a full sweat, trying to rid her house and her head of the remnants of what had happened while she was out. She gave May a couple of extra hugs as she worked, feeling lucky May was not hurt or lost by whoever'd been inside. By the time she finished getting her house back to normal it was almost noon, which gave her just enough time to eat something and take a shower before heading out to meet Joe. She pulled her hair into a high ponytail, corralled May on the leash, and headed to the trailhead.

May jumped from the car, heading straight to Joe's dog, Truman, where they enjoyed an intimate dog meet-and-greet. Truman was a happy-go-lucky medium-sized labrador retriever mix. Joe and Cece were a little more reserved, and definitely more awkward, in their greeting dance than their four-legged companions.

"I'm really sorry your place got broken into, Cece. I know it messes you up, but I'm glad you're okay and nothing was taken. I was afraid you wouldn't be up to coming today. I'm glad you did, though," Joe said, kneeling down to pet May. "I'm writing up the report this afternoon. I thought you might not want to talk about that today, but we can if you want to."

"No, I agree. Let's just leave the break-in and Jenny's case alone for today. Or at least I can try to do that. Besides, we have a few years to catch up on." Cece smiled, looking up into his face, which felt familiar and foreign at the same time. Cece knew that was due to the wide river of time that had passed since graduating high school. She wasn't sure she really knew the man, this policeman, he'd become. "You're right about this trail. It's a new one to me. How old is it, anyway?" she asked. The four of them began walking the trail, which was banked with fallen leaves like autumn confetti.

"It opened just a couple of years ago. Hikers had already worn the path here because you'll see it leads right up to what's called 'The Blue Hole,' where the river comes down the mountain. Even has a nice waterfall flowing into it. I'm really glad they allowed dogs on this one since most don't."

"It looks like these two appreciate it," Cece said as May and Truman led the way, both noses down.

Joe and Cece walked side by side, and the conversation felt easy and comfortable. It was as if they had picked up where they left off, except they wore older bodies, and each held a book of stories neither had read about the other.

Cece learned that Joe had one serious relationship a few years ago, but that she'd wanted to get married, and he didn't. Cece told Joe about her college boyfriend and one long-term romance in New York with a set-designer from Brooklyn. He'd wanted to move in together, and she didn't. Cece and Joe shared similar stories, which made it clear that commitment was a hurdle they both hadn't jumped yet.

They shared laughs, too—mostly about each other's dating nightmare stories, his of meeting a woman who asked if it was okay if she brought "friends" along, and they turned out to be her parents. Hers, of a first date where her date was talking about his big Italian family and let it slip that he was, "the only one still married."

The trail followed the river, and Cece instantly recognized The Blue Hole when they came to it. It was almost a perfect circle of clear water surrounded by smooth rocks. It was fed by cold river water dropped through the craggy stones like strings of sparkling beads, and both dogs hopped down to the edge and lapped thirstily.

"Looks like someone lost a sock," Joe said, holding up a freeze-dried-looking lone crew sock that had clearly been there awhile. "I hear this is a popular place for skinny-dipping." And the grin spreading across Joe's face as he said it was big enough to show his dimples. "Just what I've heard, of course," he said with a twinkle in his eyes as he lifted them to meet Cece's.

"Of course," Cece said, her arms crossed in front of her. "Officer Joe can't be doing something as rogue as that."

"Officer Joe might surprise you." He knelt to cup some water in his hand and locked eyes with Cece just long enough for her to feel as if the wake of a boat had just crashed over her.

Cece imagined just such a scenario: the idea of spontaneously stripping off all their clothes and jumping into the cool water gave her a little break from weightier matters such as break-ins and murder. Maybe then, she thought, she'd earn her "Hike Naked" bumper sticker.

"I guess we better head back so we're home before dark," Joe said, his voice reeling a reluctant Cece back in from her faraway thoughts. "I don't want you to turn into a pumpkin." He whistled to bring Truman to his side, with May pumping her short legs fast to catch up.

Grey clouds stood in rows behind the treetops as the foursome made their way back down the trail. The conversation had remained light, not delving into the past or the future and staying squarely in the safe zone. They were almost to the gravel parking lot and the trailhead when Joe stopped.

"Hey, Cece," he said, looking down first at his boots and then up at her. "There's something I should probably tell you."

Cece hesitated before saying, "Okay."

"You know I told you I broke things off for good with Hailey," Joe paused, then went on, "Well, she's not taking it so well. In fact, she's showing a dark side that, honestly, scares me a little."

"Oh-kaaay," Cece repeated, wondering where this was going.

"You should know that she thinks you're the reason I broke up with her."

Cece flinched. "Me? I…I don't understand. We haven't—"

"I know. We haven't spent time together except on the case. Until now, I guess. But she knows about our past together, and she's got this idea in her head that I never got over you." Joe took a deep breath. "I know it sounds crazy. But she's also been acting irrationally, too."

"Like what?" Cece asked, a bad feeling circling inside her belly.

"She's been texting me nonstop. She's even called my fishing buddy, Larry, and Ari, my friend from work. I've done everything but get a restraining order, which I don't want to do. I know I can handle it, but I worry. Not about me, but you—"

"You don't think she'd do something to me, do you?"

"That's the thing. I don't know. I never thought she could do some of the stuff she's already done," Joe said, putting his hands in his pockets.

"Joe, you don't think she was the one who broke into my cottage, do you?"

"I don't," he said with a split-second hesitation, "but I can't be sure. Your intruder was looking for something very specific, it seems. I can't imagine anything Hailey would want, unless she thought she could find our high school prom picture, or something weird like that. I just want you to be careful, Cece. And I'm really sorry about all of this." Joe gave a tug on Truman's leash as he turned toward his truck.

"Well, like Aunt Granny says, we can't help what other people do or think. And I'm sure us being together like this doesn't help."

"No, I guess not. I don't want to provoke her, but I'm not going to live my life trying to stay on Hailey's good side. Especially now that I've seen just how bad the bad side can be. I just want you to tell me if you get any strange calls, or texts, or anything."

"I will. I'll definitely keep you posted. And I'm proud of us for not talking about Jenny's case. Although, I would like to hear how it's coming. But not today. Right? Not today?" Cece said, her resolve disappearing quickly.

"Actually, there is one thing I need to tell you now about the case,"

Joe said with a solemn look on his face.

Cece's heart dropped a little lower in her chest, imagining it had to do with Calvin, or that they found out something bad about Buck, or even Jenny.

"I took your tip about seeing the key seriously, Cece. I remember, even back in high school, when you'd have a hunch it was right more often than not. So, I sent Morris over to Buck's to search the house and grounds to see if he could find any locked compartment or hidden container that needed a key. He did find a ring of old keys tucked up in the back of a shelf in Jenny's closet, and he wants to try it on a locked trunk he found in the attic. I told him to wait so I could see if you wanted to join us to find out."

Cece's grim face turned into a smile. *Maybe this is it, the break we need, the break I need*, Cece thought excitedly. *Maybe the trunk holds a clue.* "Of course I'll come!" she replied. "When?"

"As soon as possible. How about first thing in the morning, like 8?"

"Yep. I'll be there," Cece said, trying not to seem as eager as she felt.

"Okay. I'll see you at Buck's then, and I'm really glad you came today." Joe opened the door for Truman to jump into his truck, then walked May and Cece to her Jeep parked beside him. "I know there's a lot going on, Cece, but I was thinking, maybe we can do this again?"

"Yeah. Maybe so. Thanks for asking us today."

"I'll be talking to you soon then, and I promise I'll do what it takes to find who killed Jenny, and to catch the person who broke into your place," Joe said, leaning in for a quick half-hug.

"Sounds good, Joe." Cece climbed into her Jeep after May, popped it into gear, and headed for home, her mind humming with a mix of excitement and dread. She didn't want to get her hopes up that her vision of the key might actually help the case, but she couldn't help it. At the same time, she'd been thrown off by the idea that Hailey could be dangerous. After hearing Hailey talk like she and Joe were still together at the beauty salon, and then Joe telling her this, she wasn't sure who was lying. Cece was inclined to think it was Hailey, but she'd been gone from

Eureka Grove a long time, and people can change. And sometimes, not for the better.

15

The next morning Joe and Morris pulled up in front of Buck's house first, with Cece soon behind. The sky was a dull grey over the blue-black of the mountains. Only a single ray of sun pierced through.

"Come on in," Buck said, a wane smile on his face, wearing a wrinkled shirt and looking ten years older. The house smelled faintly of burnt toast and dryer sheets.

"We won't take much of your time, Buck. I really appreciate you letting us check this out. Something just tells me the keys are significant," Cece said, leading the three inside.

"Fine with me," Buck said, pointing to a ring of tarnished keys on the kitchen table. "Although I don't have my hopes up. Jenny kept her things extremely organized and always kept family heirlooms safely put away. I imagine that's what's in there."

But Cece did have her hopes up. Cece prayed for something to exonerate Calvin. She couldn't stand that he was a suspect. But it was more than that. If one of those keys worked, and if there was something in there of significance to the case, Cece might know what the visions she'd been having were about. She might be able to unlock her own life mystery.

Buck pulled the drawstring and unfolded the ladder to the attic. "Have at it," he said, stepping back while the three of them climbed up.

The attic followed the roof line, and Morris led them to a dim back corner where a small, weathered trunk sat. It was made of dark, sturdy wood with tarnished brass hinges. Morris kneeled down by the lock and began to try each key. The next-to-last key fit and turned the lock, popping open the latch. Cece held her breath.

Inside, the trunk was lined with faded fabric and smelled of cedar.

It was not filled with any obvious clue, but instead held carefully folded handmade tablecloths, napkins, and stained baby clothes. Morris carefully pulled out each item, shaking it out and handing it to Joe to refold, until he got to the bottom. No letter. No note. No clue.

"What's that up against the lid?" Joe asked, pointing to a wooden piece attached to the curve in the lid. Cece's rollercoaster of emotions, having just free-fallen to the bottom, began a slow upward climb. She watched every move Morris made as he pried off a narrow box from the top of the trunk. Inside was an assortment of vintage political buttons and nothing else.

"Oh, well," Morris said, wiping the sweat on his forehead, his knees cracking as he stood up as far as he could. "Sorry about that, Miss Chagall."

"Call me Cece, please," she said, shaking her head. "No, I'm sorry for sending you guys to do this for nothing. I don't know what I was thinking." Cece blinked fast, keeping tears at bay.

"Listen, some leads go somewhere, but most don't," Joe said, trying to make her feel better before the final blow. "But I don't think I can afford to spend any more time on these searches unless we have something more substantial to go on."

Once outside, Joe and Morris headed back to work, and Cece started the car, intending to go to the dance studio. She didn't realize how much hope she'd put into the idea of the key until it was over. She felt crushed. Any progress she felt she'd made in getting her life back on track had disappeared, and now was just a ten-car pileup of failure. She'd failed at dance in New York; her good friend was murdered; another good friend was a prime suspect, and her ramped-up synesthesia was probably some terrible neurological disorder. And that was just the beginning of the list. What Cece really wanted to do, as rain fittingly began to pelt her windshield, was to curl up into a ball on her sofa and binge-watch *The Great British Baking Show*. Instead, she did what she knew she should do, and that was to call Bess.

"Sister, that sucks. I'm really sorry," Bess said from her office at the inn, after Cece filled her in on the events of the last couple of days. "I still one hundred percent believe you were right in telling Joe about the key. Maybe that didn't work, but who knows, maybe it was something else you saw or smelled? Don't give up on figuring that out. I think what you need is something to get your mind off all of this mess, and I know just the thing. Let me make a few calls, and I'll tell you where and when. Hang in there."

Cece pulled up at her cottage at twilight after teaching all afternoon, only to discover the yard lit up like a football field. Cece felt like a celebrity as all the new motion detector lights flashed like paparazzi as she walked to the cottage door. *Nana meant it when she said she was taking care of this,* Cece thought. Now, if anyone dared walk on the property, they would feel like they'd taken center stage at Radio City Music Hall.

Cece almost stepped on an aluminum tin, covered in plastic wrap and placed between the screen door and door. She knew immediately it had come from Dr. Morley, her curmudgeonly neighbor. Underneath all that bluster and bluff was a heart of gold and a master baker of the one and only cranberry hootycreek cookie. These delicious confections were made from oatmeal, cranberries, chocolate chips, pecans, and lots of sugar. Dr. Morley had delivered these cookies to Cece at different times through the many years he'd been Nana's neighbor, from when Cece's mom died, to when she graduated from college. He always left them at Nana's door with no note, but now that Cece was in the cottage, he left them there.

Little did Dr. Morley know those cookies were exactly the medicine Cece needed that night. She promptly heated milk for hot chocolate and indulged herself before giving in to her long day. She slid between crisp, clean sheets, covered up with Aunt Granny's quilt, and, with the warm fur of her favorite creature pressed to her thigh, let herself fall into a deep sleep.

* * *

Cece and Bess opened the heavy, dark wood double doors and walked inside. From the outside it looked like the entrance to a mountain cave, with an arched rock wall on each side and over the doors. Inside was a rock fireplace big enough for Cece to stand in, holding a low burning fire, and surrounded by innumerable flickering votive candles. They were met with a wall of mint and eucalyptus scent, along with the added odd hint of pumpkin and cinnamon. Suki and Brent, each dressed in identical grey lab coats with their names embroidered on the front and "Eureka Grove Inn and Spa" underneath, met Cece and Bess on arrival and handed each of them a flute of champagne.

The spa addition had been built less than ten years ago and was a subterranean wonder built into the side of a hill adjacent to the inn. Bess went there regularly for her mani-pedi, but Cece had only been a few times since it opened. "We're so glad you're here," Suki said to Cece. "Bess told us the two of you were coming for a Spa Day," Suki said, bouncing with each word. She had teeth too big for her mouth and shoulder-length blonde hair in corkscrew curls.

"First up, we have a Pumpkin-Orange Life-Affirming Massage," said Brent, holding a clipboard and pen, checking off as he went, "followed by the Warming Ginger Chakra Facial." Brent seemed overly excited about his job and had black hair that was lacquered in place like a Ken doll's painted hair.

Cece and Bess tried not to look at each other, knowing if they did, one or the other couldn't help but laugh at the names they gave their services.

"And after that, the Caramel Apple Pedicure. Let's get you two started with these," said Suki, handing them each a plush grey robe and slippers. "Come on out here when you're ready, and we'll get you started with your facials."

Once they were alone in the dressing room, Bess said, "Next time, I want the chocolate soufflé with fresh whip cream and organic strawberries facial." Cece laughed. "And I would like the squash casserole with mushroom soup and Ritz crackers pedicure. Seriously, this is exactly what I needed, Bess. It feels good to not have to think about more than what color toe polish to choose."

Soon they were whisked off for their treatments and later reunited for their pedicures in side-by-side chairs, where they both chose an appropriate seasonal bright orange color polish and laughed so hard at one point Cece had to keep from spitting out her organic green tea, which then came out her nose.

Afterward, they sat outside by the firepit, still in their robes and slippers, sipping their apple-pie chai tea and munching on a plate of cheese cubes and melon balls.

Cece lifted her feet up onto the edge of the firepit to warm them. "So what exciting things are going on at work?"

"Let's see," Bess said, placing a finger on her lips. "We've got the National Storytellers Festival organizers coming next week. They're a nice bunch; we've had them before. We're just glad they didn't get spooked by the murder and cancel. And did Joe tell you the police think the murder weapon might have come from the inn? They were spread out and looking around the other day."

"No, he didn't say a thing," said Cece, "and I wish that didn't get on my nerves, but it does, like he's some all-knowing guru that can't impart his wisdom but to a select few. But to be fair, we agreed before the hike not to talk about it. I guess everyone at the ball would've had access in the inn, so it'd be hard to narrow down what it was and who it came from, I would think. Except maybe for the guests who came to the ball and stayed at the inn."

"Exactly. Like the hospital CEO and lots of others," Bess said, flipping her head down to pull her hair into a fat bun on top of her head. "Joe said they needed to check all the boxes. I really think he's basically a good guy, Cece. You should give him a break. I don't think he'd lie about the Hailey thing. I was surprised they were ever a couple, honestly."

"She's really pretty, though, with a great figure," Cece tried to argue.

"Oh-kaaay, I guess, if you're into fake eyelashes as thick as my finger and tube tops on grown-ass women. I still think it was a lot less of a 'thing' than Hailey made it out to be."

"You're probably right. Joe's never given me any reason not to believe him, at least not back in the day."

"C'mon, let's get dressed and out of here, Sister. I see movie night at my place in our future."

At Bess's apartment they made popcorn and watched old black and white *Dracula* movies to get ready for their favorite holiday,

Halloween. "Thanks again, Bess," Cece said as she pulled on her jacket to leave. "I think I'm ready now to face the toddler stampede I teach tomorrow."

"Keep me posted if the little ones give any more clues. And be sure to let me know how Aunt Granny's doing. Tell her I'm coming with you next time, and be sure to give her a big hello from me."

"Will do, my friend. Will do."

Driving back to her cottage, Cece felt more relaxed than she had in ages, thanks to Bess. She knew Bess was always the best one to pull her out of the dark places she frequently found herself in. It really had less to do with all the spa pampering and more to do with the company she kept. But the massage certainly didn't hurt. Cece knew she was not one to give up easily, or else she would never have taken the job to be a dancing M&M candy in Times Square while waiting for her "real job." It was time to move on from the failed "key" incident.

She knew exactly what she was going to do next.

16

"You want to do what?" Buck asked Cece, looking at her as if she'd sprouted another head.

"I know how it sounds, Buck, but I'd like to come over and take a look at your shelves," Cece said, remembering how, before the ball, she had been surprised by a smell so strong she dropped her tweezers, knocking over the bookshelf in the dollhouse she was making for the auction. *Now I can't remember the scent at all. I really need to keep a little notebook with me at all times.*

"Okay, Cece, you know I'm open to just about anything to find Jenny's killer, but can I just ask, why my bookshelves? Is this another hunch, like the key?" Buck was sounding less than enthusiastic.

"Well, it is, yes," Cece admitted, "but I'm just checking something out this time. No police, no expectations, and mostly to make myself feel better. I promise I won't be there long."

"All right. Come on over. But no police."

"No police, just me. Promise."

Before Cece left for Buck's house, she sat outside on a bench at the park, taking in the few leaves that had decided to turn and trying to hone her birdcall ID skills. Cece thought it might help to practice "preparing her mind" before going over to Buck's. She wasn't quite sure what that meant, but she was trying to open herself up to the possibilities that her peculiars offered. She wanted to be more receptive, which meant she had to stop assuming she knew everything. She wanted to be able to stop dismissing the things that came up, but didn't make sense. Basically, she needed to get out of her own way.

She had seen Aunt Granny do it all her life. Usually she would say, "I've got some thinkin' I need to do," and would head outside. Cece would watch her from the kitchen window, walking as her arms would swing in arcs by her sides. She would make wide circles around her property. Cece had never thought much about it, but knew when she came back, she was either in a better mood or would say, "'Bout got that figured out." Cece was about twelve when she asked her what she was doing, and Aunt Granny had said, "Sometimes there are things I want to get figured out but can't get there by thinking. So it helps me if I walk and just let myself be a vessel to whatever needs to come through."

"What does that mean?" she had asked.

"Just means to get quiet inside your head and quit listenin' to all that chatterin'," Hazel had answered.

Cece had no idea how she did it, but it was enough to keep the idea in the back of her mind all these years. Now here she was, almost thirty, and it was finally dawning on her what that meant. Cece understood she, too, could benefit from a moment of free space in the nonstop thoughts, a pause that she found helped her think more clearly going forward. *Especially when I'm truly relying on instinct alone by going to Buck's with the preposterous notion of looking at his shelves.*

"So I need you to show me all your bookshelves," Cece told Buck, after the usual greetings at the front door. She was glad to see him showered and clean-shaven.

"Do you even know what you're looking for, Cece?" Buck asked.

"Not exactly," Cece answered, really meaning "not at all." *Trust your gut,* she told herself. "But I think I'll know it when I see it. I'm pretty sure it's a bookshelf, and not just any random shelf like in a kitchen cabinet."

"Okay, that narrows it down a little. Follow me." Buck sounded resigned and led Cece around the house, showing her a couple of bookcases, one in the living room and a smaller one in their bedroom, before showing her their shared office, where a bookcase covered an entire wall.

Cece began with the smaller bookcases in the bedroom, trying to listen to her intuition on how to go about this. She had often thought her synesthesia would be a lot easier to deal with if it came with directions, like a map or guidebook. But she was on her own, so she began by looking the shelf over in general, trying to notice anything odd or out of place. Then she pulled a few books, thumbed through the pages, held each by the binding, and gently shook it out. She only found an old piece of torn blank paper and a paperclip.

This is going to take forever, Cece thought. But she didn't stop, instead pulling each book, checking, shaking, and returning it to the shelf. By the time she made it to the office, all she had was a measly pile of torn paper bookmarks and a couple of old grocery receipts.

Cece stood in the doorway of Buck and Jenny's home office, surveying the daunting task of the floor-to-ceiling bookcases. Luckily it was not all books, and some shelves had framed family photos and decorative objects like pottery and trinkets they'd brought back from travels. Cece persevered, determined not to give up.

She couldn't help but second-guess herself, knowing how ridiculous this must look to Buck or how it would've looked to Joe—and to anyone, for that matter. She knelt down, beginning her systematic clue search on the bottom-most shelf.

Cece made it to the final row of shelves, and as her hand pulled down the last book from the top shelf, leaving only a large ceramic vase there, the same smell returned, as powerfully as at the auction, only this time Cece recognized it instantly. It was familiar and strong, both floral and spice. It was the scent Jenny had on when she was hemming her dress before the ball.

Cece plopped down to sit cross-legged on the floor, staring up at the top shelf, empty except for the heavy vase. She took a few deep breaths, repeating *I'm a vessel, I'm a vessel* to herself. The scent, so strong a moment ago, was now fading, but was replaced by the dank, earthy smell of a basement.

Okay, I think I've got something. Keep coming. Help me here, she thought, pausing, her vision becoming fuzzy, as it did sometimes if she stared at one thing for too long. Her seeing went from blurred to hyper-focused in an instant, all coming together to make sense, and then she knew.

"Yes. Yes, I do have something. And it's definitely not in this house," she said aloud to herself as she stood up and returned the books back to their row on the shelf. "And thanks to wherever it came from," she added, looking up.

"Did you call me?" Buck asked, peeking his head around the doorframe.

"No," Cece said, realizing he had heard her. "Nope, I didn't. But I am finished."

"Well, any luck finding what you didn't know you were looking for?"

"Maybe. I'm not sure yet. But yes, yes I did. Thanks, Buck," Cece said, hurriedly pulling her jacket on and throwing her backpack over one shoulder.

"Sure. Anytime," Buck said, nodding his head, not understanding a word she'd just said, as Cece brushed by him and went out the door.

* * *

"Ms. Gibson, Cece's at the front desk to see you."

Bess looked at her watch. "Cece? Okay, send her back to my office, please, Kendra."

Before Bess could finish standing up from her desk chair, Cece came racing into her office. "I've got to tell you something. Remember when I was working on the dollhouse, and I had a peculiar episode, and I told you it was about a shelf? Well, I went to Buck's to see if I could learn anything, and I think I did. and I think this time it really might mean something—"

"Whoa, Nellie. Hold on," Bess said to Cece, who had yet to stop and take a breath. Bess walked around from behind her desk. "Slow down, take a breath, and tell me what happened." Bess pointed to a heavy wooden arts-and-crafts style chair.

"I can't, Bess, I'm telling you. We might need to do something right away," Cece said. She couldn't stop moving, shifting her weight from one foot to the other.

"Okay, can you just give me something to go on here?" Bess remained standing, leaning back against the front of her desk. "I can't help you otherwise."

"I think I can help find the murder weapon," Cece said, "and I think it's somewhere here at the inn, like you said. I was going through the shelves at Buck's and that same scent I'd had before came back, and this time I recognized it as Jenny's. And I knew how my thinking had been all wrong before. It wasn't what *was* on the bookshelves that was important, but what *wasn't*."

"Okay. What?"

"There was a big vase on a top shelf, and I understood, I don't know how, that it wasn't about a book on a shelf at all. It was about the heavy object missing from the shelf. At Buck's house the feeling, the scent, was so strong it was like Jenny herself was pushing me to the inn. Bess, I think what was used to kill Jenny was stolen from a shelf here at the inn, and I think I can find where it is."

Bess was standing at attention now. "We have a whole inn full of different shelves, Cece. Is there any way you can narrow it down? I'm pretty sure the police asked about that, and the staff has checked for missing items."

"Did they find anything?" Cece said.

"I don't think so," Bess said, "but I know our staff is pretty thorough."

"What about the basement? Because that was the second smell. It smelled like Nana's basement. And what about the storage rooms? The ones way back in those hallways no one ever uses. I could feel it, Bess. It felt cool." Cece rubbed her arms as if feeling it again. "And was a dark, musty room with what looked like bookcases."

"I don't know, Cece," Bess said, shaking her head. "I doubt they went down there because those doors stay locked, but I can check." Bess went back around behind her desk and opened the top drawer, pulling out a jangling ring of keys and holding them up. "Sister, you're going to owe me. Now, let's go see what we can find out."

"Do you remember they had me do the inventory down here when I first started working at the inn back in high school? It wasn't hard to figure out they gave me that job because no one else wanted it," Bess said, trying to keep up with Cece, who was skipping the steep steps leading downward. "Cece?"

The basement was both echoing and claustrophobic at the same time. It was like a rabbit warren of interconnecting and dimly lit hallways of massive stone and brick designed in an unrecognizable pattern. Since the inn had been built during wartime, there were several rooms made with doors built to blend into their reinforced walls. Those were used either for wealthy locals of long ago to hide their valuables, or hide themselves, depending on circumstances, since the inn had been built between the World Wars. "This place gave me the creeps back then, and it still does," Bess said.

Cece shrugged. "Don't worry. Remember Nana said all the ghosts are friendly."

Bess shot Cece a look, then almost ran into her from behind when she stopped abruptly at the end of a long hallway. Bess put her hands on her hips and said, "Okay, my peculiar friend. I don't suppose you could tell me which door you want to try first?"

"How about that one in the back on the right?" Cece offered.

Bess took the saucer-sized keyring with at least twenty-five keys on it and brought the keys closer to her eyes in order to read the tiny, smeared writing on the labels until she finally found the right one. As Cece hovered behind her, Bess slid in the key and turned the knob. She pushed open the door into a small room filled with stacks of boxes covered with dust and smelling of mildew.

"Yikes. This stuff looks like it's older than the two of us put together."

"Because it is," Bess said. "Anything in here ringing your bells?"

Cece shook her head. "Nope. I definitely saw shelves, not boxes. Do you have any idea which of these doors might have a room with shelves in it?" Cece was once again aware of how odd her obsession with shelves must sound. "Look! This was a case of 'Eureka's Tasteless Tonic,' manufactured by Bedford and Sons, Knoxville, 1915." Cece was wiping the dust off a box top.

"Too bad they didn't leave us a bottle," Bess cracked.

"Apparently, if they had, we could have tasted 'mountain magic guaranteed to prevent malaria.'"

"We've got enough of that dealing with *your* mountain magic.

Now, let's get out of here. Remember, I do have a real job outside of this ghostbusters gig you've gotten me into."

"Oh, yeah. Sorry about that," Cece said as she headed out the door and back into the hallway. "Is it just me, or are these ceilings high in some places and low in others?"

"It's how it was built. Half of the basement is built into the hill, you know. So, where to now, Madame?"

Cece led them back to where they began and stopped, her gaze scanning around them like a radar. "Where does that go?" she asked, pointing to her right.

"That's a dogleg. It goes right then left, bending in the middle."

"Come on," Cece said, running her fingers along the cool surface of the rock walls as she moved forward. She stopped and pointed at another door.

"How in the world would the murderer have found this room exactly?" Bess wondered out loud.

"I don't know, but let's get in it," Cece said, her urgency returning.

Bess once again looked through the keys, squinting at the labels. She looked up at Cece. "I can't find this one," Bess said while Cece rocked from one foot to the other.

"Please look through one more time," Cece said as she placed her hand on the doorknob, then looked back at Bess. "Never mind. It's unlocked."

17

Cece almost fell into the room, with Bess right behind her. Bess flicked the switch for the lone lightbulb suspended from the ceiling. Inside, an unusual assortment of objects covered the surfaces of the three dark wooden shelves that lined the walls. The objects included a number of mildewed leather-bound books and the water-stained, ruffled pages of a calfskin-covered Bible. There was also a collection of irregular tarnished silver, crystal thick with dust, and stacked on top of each other lay portraits in gilded frames.

"What…," Cece began to say, turning her head to take it all in.

"I know what this is," Bess said, clapping her hands together. "I learned about this back when I worked down here. It's from when German diplomats were detained at the inn during the war. They were forced to give up their valuables, and they stored some of them in here."

Cece was half listening, still carefully studying the contents of each shelf.

"There!" Cece blurted out. "Up there!" She pointed to an upper shelf. "Between the silver pitcher and that row of books."

Bess followed Cece's finger to the empty space open between the silver and the books on the dark wood of the shelf, where a clear imprint of a circle remained surrounded by grime.

"Something was clearly there, but now it's gone," Cece said. "Do you have any idea what it was?"

Bess tipped her head back, thinking. "Not off the top of my head. But certain employees got the 'extended' tour of the hotel that includes this basement, and I know someone who would absolutely remember what was on that shelf. Nick. I'll text him right now."

Within fifteen minutes Nick appeared in the doorway of the

storage room where Cece and Bess stood talking. They were both semi-frozen in place, afraid to move or touch anything. "Hey," Nick said, tossing his hair back, revealing his other eye. "What are y'all doing down here, anyway? Whenever they send me down here I always think someone's going to accidentally lock the door at the top of the steps, and I'll get trapped. That's a nightmare right there."

"I hadn't even thought of that, Nick, but now I will," Bess said, looking over at Cece. "Listen, we really need your memory skills. I know you haven't been down here much," Bess said, then pulled him by the elbow toward the shelf, pointing, "but we really need to see if you can remember anything about what used to be right up there."

Nick stared at the empty space. His blue eyes shifted first side to side, then up and down at the shelves. He stared for what seemed like minutes to Bess and Cece before he said, "It was a bust. It wasn't too big, and it was a woman's head. It was really smooth and white with a circular base."

"Yes!" Cece cried, "I knew it!" And she threw her arms around an unsuspecting Nick, who began to blush.

"Now hold on, sister," Bess said, hating to burst Cece's bubble. "We have to make a lot of assumptions to think that just because this thing is missing, then it must be the murder weapon."

"I know. You're right," said Cece, stepping back from Nick, who continued to blush. "It just feels good to have had at least this much proven right. And it still could be something important."

"Why don't we give Joe a call, let him in on what we found out, and take it from there? How does that sound? And Nick, I don't even have to go look on the inventory list. The minute you said what it was, I remembered it, too. I'm not sure what it was made of, but I seem to remember it had cracks in it." Bess led the three of them into the hall and back to the nearest staircase leading up to the main floor.

"I've got to get back. Hope I helped whatever you two private eyes are up to," Nick said, flashing a quick grin and turning to go.

"You were a huge help. Thank you again, Nick." They watched Nick race up the steps like his feet were on fire before Bess turned back to Cece. "What do you think about me calling Joe this time? Maybe hearing it from me will help bolster your case."

Cece paused and took a deep breath. She did a few deep knee bends and stretched side to side. "It really is totally far-fetched, isn't it? Maybe these more intense peculiars I'm having don't mean anything more than just what they are. Maybe I'm just making a fool of myself. Again."

Bess put her hands on both of Cece's shoulders. "Listen. First, like both of us like to say, you won't know unless you try, right? And we both know the things worth having usually take a lot more than one try." Bess dropped her arms and reached to pull her phone from her pocket. "Second, we all just need one person to believe in us, and I believe in you. Just like you believed that I would someday come out of my Goth phase, get rid of the piercings and black eyeshadow, and go on to do better things than wash dishes at Cracker Barrel."

Cece laughed as Bess called Joe.

Joe picked up right away, and Bess explained on speakerphone everything that had happened. When she finished Joe was silent, the only sound was the crackling of the police radio in the background.

"Are you still there?" Bess asked.

Cece chimed in, rushing her words. "I know it's a long shot, Joe, but I promise this one—"

"Wait, Cece," Joe said, interrupting her. "Hold on a minute. I need to let you two know that we sent out another team to search the crime area to be sure we hadn't missed something." Joe cleared his throat. "They found a couple of things. One was a pen with the logo of Beryl Bridges' construction company on it. The other was a fragment of what looks to be plaster, something that might come from a sculpture,"

"Or a bust!" Cece and Bess said at the same time.

"Or a bust," Joe confirmed.

"Yes!" Cece shouted, punching the air with her fist and then high-fiving Bess. Cece then silently danced around in a circle, pumping both arms in the air.

"Okay, you two," Joe said. "Yes, this is great information, and yes, I'm happy for you, Cece. But we still have a killer out there somewhere." Cece winced to hear the dismissive tone again. "We also still have to figure out why we found Jenny's locket in Calvin's toolbox. We're working on his history in the Cayman Islands right now," Joe continued. "And, now that we've found this pen at the crime scene, we might have concrete evidence against Bridges."

Cece whispered to Bess, "He certainly knows how to spoil a party." They both heard voices coming from Joe's patrol car speaker.

"I've got to go, but I'll send someone over to the inn, Bess, so you can show them what y'all found. I need you to also find that inventory list if you can. We need to confirm. And Cece?" Joe paused. "Great job. Now, *let us do our job*. Please. We're still working on your break-in, so maybe you can relax and let us take it from here, okay?"

"Okay, Joe," Cece said while shaking her head "no" to Bess.

"Thanks. Talk later." Joe hung up, and both Bess and Cece let out a loud "whoop" that bounced off one side of the stone wall of the hallway to the other.

Suddenly Bess stopped, put out her hands, and, with her most authoritative voice, said, "Okay. Back to work. I'm thrilled you got your validation. Now, I have to find the inventory list." Bess looked at her watch. "And I thought you said you had a private lesson with Angel this afternoon."

Cece threw her hand over her mouth. "Oh, no. I can't believe I forgot," she said, leaning in to plant a big kiss on Bess's cheek. "Now I'm starting to think that my peculiar episode with the key connected to the one with the shelf, because it wasn't about what was on the shelf or needing a key to unlock the door, but the exact opposite. Does that make any sense?" Cece said, trying to explain it to herself as much as to Bess.

"Yep. You mean the door was unlocked, so no key, and the bust is missing, so empty space. I get it. Maybe you're starting to get the hang of whatever is happening in there," Bess said, smiling and tapping her own forehead.

"Maybe I am. Anyway, let's go, boss," Cece said.

With that, Cece headed up the steps two at a time while Bess click-clacked in heels behind her, trying to keep up.

* * *

Cece pulled in at the studio just as Cassie was dropping off Angel. The afternoon sun felt especially bright to Cece after being in the dark basement of the inn. Cece parked and went over to the car just as Cassie rolled down her window.

"Miss Cece, I'm sorry about the other night. It was so busy at work I couldn't get out of there. Thanks for bringing this one home," Cassie said, tipping her head toward her sister, Angel, as she was getting out of the car.

"No problem, Cassie. I didn't mind at all. It's not like you ever do that. We were just worried about you."

"No, all's good with me. It's such chaos sometimes in that kitchen, I can't even get a phone call made." Cassie worked as a chef at one of Eureka Grove's nicer restaurants.

As Cassie pulled away, Cece put her arm around Angel, and they walked toward the studio double doors.

"Are you ready to break-in those new pointe shoes?" Cece asked.

"I think so. I already put 'em in the doorframe and slammed the door on them a few times at home like you showed me."

"Yep, that's the tried-and-true method for all of us bunheads," she said, smiling at Angel. "But the only real way to break them in is to get dancing. After you," Cece said, opening the door for Angel.

Inside the studio the "Broadway Jazz" class, taught by Jason, was already in session, and Cece and Angel headed to the other open studio room. They could hear each word of his booming voice—"What was that supposed to be, Miss Clark? How about ten more of those across the floor?"—over the startling volume of the soundtrack from the show *Hairspray*. Jason was tough, and not all students liked him because of that.

Angel sat on the bench against the wall, finishing the laborious process of putting on her pointe shoes, which involved wrapping her toes in lambs' wool before putting on the shoes, tying the ribbons, and putting rosin on the box of the shoe to keep from slipping. "Miss Cece, I found a video on YouTube I wanted you to look at and see if you thought I might do something like it for my audition," Angel said as she stood up, rolling through her feet and onto the toe box of first one shoe and then the other.

Cece had been so wrapped up in everything going on that she'd completely forgotten about Angel's audition dance. "Great. I can't wait to see it. Why don't I take a look after class?" Cece said, making a note on her phone to get started researching the various summer dance camp opportunities. "Let's go to the barre and begin with roll-throughs and relevés, two each side, eight relevés, in first, second, and fifth position, back and front."

Cece scrolled through the music on her phone to find the right track, which was connected to the speakers hung high in the corners of the room. She never did this without thinking of Nana, who told her about teaching with a record player and albums, and still owned both. She'd demonstrated to Cece how they used to have to put the needle of the record player down on the right track on the album by counting inward from the outer band. It made Cece appreciate being able to quickly scroll through a list on her phone and push a button to play her music of choice.

The sun had just dipped below the ridge, casting an amber tint on the changing hues of the trees, when Angel and Cece came out of the studio. Cassie was already waiting in the parking lot, leaning against the old Ford Escort she drove, and looking at her phone. Cece was struck by how much Cassie and Angel looked alike. Both tall and striking, they shared the same smooth, deep cinnamon skin and long eyelashes, highlighting their almond-shaped eyes.

Cassie looked up. "How was class?" she asked as Angel walked toward her.

"Painful," Angel chuckled quietly, "but good."

"Oh, that's right. New pointe shoes. I don't know why y'all go through all that. Makes my feet hurt just looking at yours, and I stand on mine all day," Cassie said, laughing.

Cece smiled, opening both arms wide, and said dramatically, "These are but the things we must endure for our art." Cassie just shook her head.

"Seriously. Angel, I promise to study your video before our next class so we can start putting together your audition choreography, okay?" Cece said.

"Thanks, Miss Cece."

Cece turned back toward her Jeep, digging out her phone from her purse to check for messages, which she always turned off when she was teaching. She had missed a call from her Dad; Bess had texted to say she was still looking for the inventory list, and Nana had texted reminding her about their trip to see Aunt Granny Hazel tomorrow. Cece had almost forgotten that one, too; she'd been so scattered lately. She looked forward to getting home, seeing May, putting her feet up, and having one of Mr. Morley's cookies.

Rushing to buckle in and get the car on and warmed up, Cece almost missed the folded piece of paper under one of her windshield wipers. She got back out and grabbed it, figuring it was another advertisement for the grand opening of a hookah lounge down the street. Cece wasn't even sure what a hookah lounge was.

Instead, she unfolded the paper to find three words in a small font on the center of the page. The note read simply, "Leave it alone."

* * *

Like a bathtub alligator, Cece's eyes were the only thing visible above the surface of her bubble-filled bathwater. She wasn't sure how long she'd been in there, but the water was decidedly cooler than when she started, and May lay asleep beside her on the bathroom rug. She'd already left Joe a message to tell him about the note and had double-checked the new door locks Nana had put in.

The note didn't worry her that much. She felt sure this was probably the act of a jealous ex-girlfriend, and the "it" in the note meant Joe. At the same time, while finally feeling like she'd gotten somewhere following through on her latest "sensory hits," it might be that what she'd been able to dig up had sounded the alarm for someone. And that someone could be a killer.

18

Cece balanced a pot of bright yellow mums on the floor mat between her feet as she and Nana drove out the next morning to see Hazel in Charity Hill. Nana always wanted to drive her crimson red Cadillac Escalade on these trips because she insisted she knew the roads better than anyone else. Nana prided herself on having always used the money she earned to buy her own car. "It was important," she told her husband, Sam, and then Cece, that "a woman has a few things all her own that she doesn't have to share or owe anyone for," and such was the case with her Escalade.

Nana and Cece chatted the whole drive there, keeping the conversation on the surface. Cece never mentioned the threatening note on her windshield, and Nana didn't bring up the murder case or Cece's peculiars. Instead, Nana brought Cece up to date on everyone in her "Book Brigade," which had just met the night before to talk about their latest book *Demon Copperhead* by Barbara Kingsolver, and Cece told Nana about Angel, explaining the more contemporary ballet moves they were adding to her audition dance.

The closer they got to Charity Hill, the more winding the road became, and the higher the forested hills rose on both sides. They passed various landmarks along the way, like the cluster of small brick buildings of Moody Bible College set back off the road, and the red metal roof of the farm and tractor supply store. They passed the white wooden steeple of the Charity Church of God of Jesus, and Cece noted the church sign today read, *Sin is like a Credit Card. Buy Now. Pay Later.* It was a Pentecostal church, and she had long been intrigued by the purported snake handling that went on inside, according to a friend she'd had in school named Abraham. She was fascinated by what it took to have that level of faith.

Cece always recognized Aunt Granny's house from a distance because there was an old sourwood tree in her front yard. In the fall the tree lit up with an uninhibited display of glossy crimson leaves, as it was today, and was like a red beacon signaling home. In the spring it became a mass of delicate white flowers that lured bees from all around to visit.

Cece remembered standing on Hazel's front porch in the summer, barefoot and with her eyes closed. She could feel the early sun on her face and would be listening to the tree, alive with the hum of a thousand bees. Aunt Granny would say the sourwood tree "must be holding a tent revival in there, and every bee in the county had to come." If Cece was ever afraid of getting stung, she would tell her to just hold her breath and they'd leave her alone. People loved the honey the bees made from that kind of tree and came from miles around to buy it at local stores.

Hazel was sitting in her favorite rocking chair on the front porch waiting for them as they slowed to make the turn onto the road leading to her house. Two wicker chairs, an old church pew, a couple of metal canisters, and an old-fashioned butter churn rounded out her front porch décor.

Hazel stood up to wave as Nana and Cece turned off the paved road and onto the dirt and gravel one heading up in the hollow. Hazel's house was the first one you came to, and they pulled in beside Hazel's old pickup truck, the color having faded from red to coral pink with the years.

Behind that was the old clothesline hung with Hazel's bedsheets. Further back was the shed, or "workshop," as Hazel called it. Inside, dried herbs hung from the ceiling and shelves were filled with amber bottles, mason jars, and small muslin bags. On the wooden countertop sat Hazel's mortar and pestle and a bottle of clear one-hundred-proof boot-legged liquor.

Tizzy, Hazel's cat, ran out from under the truck, hoping visitors might prompt Hazel to pay some attention to her. Nana and Cece took turns trying to hug Hazel. Unlike them, Hazel was not a hugger, never quite knowing what to do and stiffening and flailing her arms like flippers. "Now that's enough of that," she'd always say and quickly pull away to look at them. "Now, if y'all don't look pretty as June bugs. Come on in now. I got some tea, and I made someone's favorite cobbler." She smiled, looking at Cece.

Nana carried the cooler she pulled from the backseat, and Cece carried the mum, following Hazel inside through the back door.

"I'm gonna put this beauty on the front porch. It'll fancy it up a little," Hazel said, taking the mum from Cece.

The back door opened into a small storage room with a chest freezer on one side and a washer and dryer on the other. Nana unloaded the contents of the cooler. "I got you some of those tenderloin you like," she said to Hazel as she filled her freezer.

"Bless your heart. Thank you. I swear it's like Christmas every time y'all come. I open that freezer after you leave, and it's full of good surprises." Hazel was wearing her "uniform" of a cotton, button-up dress with work boots and her hair back in one white braid. She stood at the stove and poured out tea for each of them.

The women sat by the big front kitchen window in slat-back chairs at the round wooden table. Just as in Nana's kitchen, the black-and-white framed photo of Hazel and Nana's mother and grandmother hung low on the wall behind them. It was as if all five women had come together in that moment.

Cece scrunched her nose at her first sip of tea, which was clearly one of Aunt Granny's homemade concoctions. "What all is in here, Aunt Granny?" Cece asked, while forcibly swallowing the pungent, bitter liquid.

"I know it's right strong, but I made it special for you." She listed the ingredients while tapping a finger on the table for each. "Let's see, I've got you some Hawthorn leaf, passionflower, mullein, and goldenrod in this one."

Cece reached for the bottle of honey from across the table and poured a steady stream into her cup.

"Pass it over to me when you're finished," Nana said with a little cough.

"Okay, fair enough," Hazel said, lifting both hands in surrender. "Just tryin' to cure what ails you while I've got you here." She smiled and took a big gulp from her mug.

"Catch us up on what all's going on in Charity Hill," Nana said, stirring the honey into her tea.

"Law! There's always something to report when y'all come."

Nana noticed the deepening lines in her older sister's face. More than lines anymore, they were furrows that intersected and splintered like shattered glass. Still, her skin was soft, and her dark eyes were as clear as ever. Nana worried about her sister living out here alone. Hazel was strong as a horse, but Nana knew that strength didn't last forever.

"Let's see, now. You remember Tiny and Georgina Carr up the road, been there nigh fifty years I guess." Hazel said, and Nana nodded. "Georgina up and died right in the house while takin' a nap about a month ago. I tell you, grief stung Tiny like a hornet. We couldn't get him to come out the house for a month."

"Not a bad way to go—taking a nap," Nana volunteered.

"Nope. Not bad at all. I took him some cobbler." Hazel leaned her elbows on the table and clasped her fingers together. "And Dorthula's youngest, Sherri Lynn, is about to have her first baby."

"I remember her. We used to play together, didn't we?" Cece asked. "I remember she always had chewing gum."

"That's the one. She's swelled up like a toad frog. That baby should be here any day. Dorthula called me about some medicine for the swelling, it got so bad. I took over some stump water I'd saved from last Easter, and left their Bible opened to the book of Matthew. Seems she's doing right better now."

Cece eyed the wooden bookstand near the front door in the living room that held the family Bible. It had been in the family for generations, with each name carefully written in cursive by fountain pen on yellowed pages in the front. The backmost pages were reserved for names written only by the women in the family. One lengthy list contained the names of every baby in the area they had helped deliver. The other list was of all the ones they'd helped prepare for burial.

"I figure you'll be the first they'll call," Nana said, as Hazel refilled her cup. "How's the health clinic doing?"

"It's the best thing since sliced bread. They just celebrated twenty-five years here, cake and all. But so many around here still refuse to step a foot in there," Hazel said.

"Change is hard. I get it," Nana said, her fingers drawing invisible patterns on the smooth surface of the table while Hazel held the chair arm to help lower herself in the seat.

"I hope you're not chopping any more wood, Aunt Granny," Cece said, watching her get into the chair. "You aren't, are you?"

"Nope. Promise I've been letting Old Man Perkins do all the woodcutting around here. He even fixed that rotting board on the porch."

"Good," Cece said, looking around the inside of Hazel's house, which seemed untouched by time. Bess called it "The house that time forgot."

Hazel had the same sofa and chair, small TV on a stand, old upright piano in the corner, and thin, linen curtains on the windows that she'd always had. "Ain't no use in new if old'll do," Aunt Granny would say when anyone suggested replacing anything.

"Speaking of Old Man Perkins, what ever happened to the old Perkins place you used to never let me go anywhere near?" Cece teased Hazel, remembering how she could spend the whole day outside at Aunt Granny's if she came in to eat and wore the whistle Hazel gave her. The only warning she got was to steer clear of the old Perkins place up in the hollow.

Of course, Cece had heard all sorts of strange stories about the house from the other kids, about how it had once been a grand mountain estate until strange things started to happen there. The story that stayed and stuck was about a little girl from long ago named Pricey Perkins. They said she'd died in the house, and you could sometimes hear her singing if you were brave enough to get close. But Aunt Granny had filled Cece's head so full of images of falling ceilings, rusty nails, and broken glass that she never went near it, at least not until she was a teenager.

Hazel shook her head. "I heard someone's thinkin' of buying the property to build some kind of mountain vacation house. I'd rather kiss a rattlesnake than go near that place, but I sure don't want all that construction going on 'round here. I know Old Man Perkins is quiet as a church mouse about it. Hardly ever says a word about anything. Now, let's get on something more important," she said, directing her gaze straight at Nana before shifting to Cece. "I think you intended to talk on your peculiars. You told me on the phone they've been getting worse."

"Yep, worse and weirder. You know Dad's not the best to ask for details about when the synesthesia started and what it was like," Cece said, getting up and taking their cups from the table. "And since Mom's not here, I thought you two could maybe help me understand that part better before I go talk to the doctor about it."

As Cece turned to put the cups in the sink, Nana and Hazel shared a look. "Darlin'," Nana said, "I think your Aunt Granny and I can more than help you understand what's happening to you."

Outside the kitchen window, a dark flock of birds lifted from the crimson-filled tree branches and took flight.

19

Cece turned from the sink to look at them. "What do you mean? Do you know something you haven't told me?"

"Maybe I should get us more tea?" Nana suggested brightly.

"I've got a better idea," said Hazel, getting up with a groan to pull some old newspapers from a bin and spread them out on top of the table. She then took three plastic grocery bags full of green beans from the counter and gave one to each of them. Situating herself back in her chair, she said, "Now then. We can snap these green beans while the cobbler bakes, and y'all can take 'em home with you. You know what the Good Book says about 'idle hands'…"

"…makes the Devil's workshop!" Nana and Cece said together.

"Let's get back to what you two know about me that you've kept a secret," Cece said, refusing to be derailed.

"Darling, it's not that we've kept it a secret; it's just that we had to be sure you were ready," Nana said, her manicured hands snapping beans as fast and smooth as an expert knitter.

"I don't have some disease, do I? Something that's just now showing up?" Cece asked with a grimace.

"No, baby girl, you don't have a disease. It's nothing like that, I promise," Hazel said as she shifted her weight in the chair. "You know how the women on your dad's side of the family were known as 'granny women' around here a long time ago? We've talked a lot about that, huh?"

"Yeah. I know that. You two told me in the old days when the doctor couldn't get to people in the mountains, granny women delivered the babies and laid out the dead. They helped people heal using herbs, like y'all do. But I don't know what making tinctures and balms has to do with my synesthesia," Cece said, growing agitated in her frustration.

Nana leaned forward, taking a breath. "Well, along with the skills that have been passed down, many of us inherited other...." She paused, " . . . gifts, as well."

Cece straightened up in her chair, thinking these were the two women she loved and trusted most in the world, and she was beginning to worry about what was coming next. "What kinds of gifts are you talking about? Like my peculiars?"

Hazel snapped and sorted the beans, her eyes never leaving Cece's face. "Yep, like that. But we all inherited different ones from our foremothers; some are real quiet-like, and some knock you over the head."

"What about Mom? Did she have it?" Cece asked.

"No, only our side that I know of. But if you want my two cents, I think your daddy's gifts got buried under all that book learnin'."

"Hazel!" Nana shook her head. "I like to say Leo's gifts were strengthened by his education, not 'buried.'" She cut her eyes at Hazel. "He's an excellent historian, flintknapper, and storyteller."

"Okay, great. And so..." Cece said, holding both hands out, palms up. "I still don't know what any of this has to do with my three-ring-circus of a brain."

"Well, think back to what you told us you figured out recently working with your peculiars," Hazel said, "how once you let 'em percolate a while, sometimes things fall into place."

"Well, yeah, at least it felt like that, but I don't have any idea if what I've figured out is true, or if it can be trusted to help with the case, or anything," Cece said.

"What we're trying to say is that we know...." Nana looked at Hazel, then back at Cece, "If you keep working with your synesthesia, your abilities will get stronger. Bottom line is you'll have an ability to understand and see things other people can't."

Hazel broke in, unable to wait, "You might even be able to see things that ain't happened yet, or you might see into the past."

Cece reeled back in her chair, her eyes widening, "What? What are you talking about? Like some kind of psychic fortune-teller?"

"Cece." Hazel placed her calloused hand on top of Cece's, her voice low and steady. "What you've got is *a knowin'*. It's a powerful part of where you come from and who you are. Once you accept it, you'll understand it better. Our family's women just were born with better antennae, that's all. We pick up things other folks can't."

"But what if I don't want it? What if I don't want any more *weird* in my life?" Cece said, her voice faltering.

"You are neither strange nor weird," Nana said, her volume rising defiantly, "and you never have been. The fact is the more you work with your intense peculiars, the more you'll feel in control. The good news is you'll know what's happening now and how to deal with it, and your Aunt Granny and I will help you."

Cece pushed her chair back, stood up, and began pacing around the small kitchen. "How can I be sure it's going to get better? Why is this happening to me now?"

"Because it happened at different times for us, too. It's different for different people. Right, Hazel?" Nana said, as Hazel looked back and nodded.

"You and Aunt Granny can't have what I have. You would've told me, right?" Cece said, feeling as if the proverbial rug were gently being tugged right out from under her feet.

"No! No, I didn't mean we had the same gift as you," Nana said, as Hazel got up and disappeared into the storage room. "Ours are different from yours, and from each other's. Our abilities seem to come from the same roots of inner knowing Hazel was talking about it. And once those roots take hold, the gifts continue to grow and branch out in all directions."

Cece couldn't help but feel Nana was circling the answer without giving her a solid one. "What kind of directions, Nana?" she asked, just as Hazel came back into the kitchen with a container from the freezer.

"So, who wants some blueberry cobbler and homemade vanilla ice cream?" Hazel asked, holding up the ice cream.

"I do," Nana said, followed by the less enthusiastic "Me, too" from Cece.

Cece *didn't want* generalities about what had happened to them before and what was happening to her now. She wanted details. She wanted the nitty-gritty. *She wanted to scream.*

"Aunt Granny," she said, pulling three bowls from the upper

cabinet, "when did you find out about your gift, and what was it?"

Hazel had pulled the blueberry cobbler from the oven, which was bubbling underneath a crisp and buttery topping, and lifted it onto the counter.

"All right, baby girl." Hazel nodded her head. "You deserve to know our stories, so set yourself down and quit circling like you're churnin' butter, and I'll tell you," Hazel said, pulling out her chair. "You remember that little stone springhouse up across the road by the Graham's trailer?" She looked at Cece. "I was up 'ere playing with my bucket in the springhouse. I filled it up, turned around, and there was just the prettiest little girl standing there. I'd never seen her before in my life. She was quiet as a feather and had one leg shorter than the other, or so it seemed to me back then. We just talked, you know, like little girls do. When I went to empty the bucket, I turned back around, and she was gone. When I got home, I told Mama all about it, and that's when I learned." Hazel stuck a fork in the cobbler, saying as an aside, "Let's wait for this to cool down a bit first."

"Aunt Granny! C'mon! That's when you learned what?" Cece asked, her voice rising, pressing for an answer.

"Well, Mama went back of the house and came back with an old photo, asking me if that was the girl I saw," Hazel said nonchalantly, pulling an ice cream scoop from the drawer. "And I got excited because it was, but Mama told me that little girl had once lived down the road from us. She got the polio, and then died from a sickness soon after."

Cece took a sharp inhale, "So she was dead! You were talking to a dead person." Hazel nodded as Cece shook her head. "So, you've just seen dead people ever since?" Cece asked, elbow on the table, dropping her forehead in her hand.

"No, mine don't work like that. I don't know when it will happen."

Cece sat, head in hand, looking down at the table. "Okay, Nana, your turn. Hit me. Do you talk to dead people, too? What have you got?"

"Tennessee, the one thing you better learn right now is to respect the gift, because that's what it is: a gift. You can't be making fun of it," Nana said sternly.

Cece heard the firm reprimand in her grandmother's voice and lifted her head. "I'm sorry, Nana. I don't mean to. It's just a lot to take in is all. You don't have to tell me if you don't want to."

"It's not that I mind, but if we're going to help you through this, you're going to have to take it seriously." Nana's voice softened. "I know it's a lot. I know because I remember, and so does Hazel, what it felt like to be young and feel alone with your gift."

"You're going to have to have patience, too," Hazel chimed in. "It's taken this long for yours to float to the top for a reason. You're not going to get all your answers today, or even this year. Everything has a season. But I'm not here to be preaching. For now, that is," said Hazel, winking at Cece. "I'll let your Nana talk."

"Mine started when I was a little older than Hazel, about age twelve. I was rummaging through the junk drawer in the kitchen, you know, one like we all have with scissors and tape, keys, stuff like that. Well, I picked up an old bottle opener, of all things, and in my mind's eye, clear as day, was a big lady with dark hair sitting outside a tall building, crying. I told Mama about it, just like Hazel, and she told me she'd gotten that opener while out cruising Route 39 back in high school with an old friend that moved off to Knoxville right after they graduated. The more I described her, the more Mama knew it was her friend Shelly."

Cece was becoming more curious than freaked out now. "So, did you find out why she was crying?"

"Yeah, Mama looked her up and found out she'd just had some bad news. Never did tell me what, but it made sense in my mind. That's what it felt like to me at the time."

"So does this happen every time you look in a drawer and pull something out?" Cece asked, and Hazel began to chuckle.

"We used to call your Nana 'the junk drawer conjurer,'" she said, smiling over at Nana.

"To answer your question, Cece, no, it doesn't work like that. Mine's like Hazel's, and I don't know when it might happen. Your Papa Sam got used to it after a while. He'd say, 'Just let me know when it's happening, Anna B., and let me know if I can do anything to help,' and then he'd shake his head and smile," Nana said, her eyes fixed on something outside the window, and her thoughts swept back in time.

"Does everybody else in the family know about you two but me?" Cece asked, wondering what else she didn't know.

"No, darlin'," Nana said. "We stay humble to the gift. Yakking to everyone about it only leads to trouble. You'll meet others like you and learn from them. You've got us for now."

Cece finally had Nana talking and wasn't about to stop now. "What do you mean 'others like me'?"

"Other women whose foremothers are from these hills and mountains. Women who somehow got 'the knowing,' and then helped each other so they wouldn't feel so alone. It's like feeling your way into something that's waiting right there in the corner of your vision, but you can't quite see it."

"Yeah, that's exactly what it feels like," Cece said, nodding her head, and realizing the unfamiliar sensation she was having was relief. It dawned on her for the first time that she might not have to deal with this by herself.

"We call it 'the betwixt,'" Nana continued. "You've heard us talking about the veil between our world and another; well, 'betwixt' means you've got a foot in both. That's us sometimes." Nana pushed her chair from the table and stood up. "The part for you to focus on now is your own spirit. What I mean is that place that has nothing to do with what other people say or what you think you know. Like Good Witch Glinda said, you've had the power all along."

Hazel interjected, obviously thinking it was a good time for a Bible verse. "The Gospel of Thomas says if you bring forth that which you have within you, it will save you. If you do not, it will destroy you."

"Okay, so that's a little scary, Aunt Granny," Cece said.

"Alls I mean is it's your time, baby girl, and we've got you. So many times, our spirits been forced into staying quiet. Let yours out, and let it shine. No tellin' what you can do." Hazel lifted her eyes, continuing, "No telling what any of us can do."

"We can talk all the livelong day about this, can't we, Hazel?" Nana said. "But I think just opening the door is plenty for Cece today. Anyway, I think the cobbler's ready now. Ya'll stay put, and I'll get you some."

Cece sat motionless, imagining all this new information like pieces in front of her before building a dollhouse. It was only by putting it together that it would make sense.

Beside her, Nana and Aunt Granny sat and chatted about the weather and the status of Hazel's canning for the winter. They were both enjoying the warm cobbler with a big scoop of vanilla ice cream, while Cece's stomach felt like a garbage disposal. All three women welcomed a reprieve from the heavy conversation and were comfortable enough to allow for long silences at the table. Cece had learned from Hazel and Nana that it's okay not to talk, instead giving yourself a little time to soak up the energy of just being with each other.

After they finished, Hazel led them outside to tour her herb and vegetable gardens, or "patches," as she called them. Hazel loved nothing more than to stroll between rows, explaining the properties of each plant and what it might be used for. Cece already knew most of them, having grown up planting alongside Hazel, but she paid attention as if never having heard it before.

Hazel stood in the yard, feet apart, hands on her ample hips, looking up at the noon sun in a cloudless sky. "Comin' a cloud soon," she said. "I can smell it."

"We better be making our way back to town, Sister," Nana said to Hazel. "I'll be back up next week and bring you some more of those chocolate-covered cherries you like."

Hazel smiled, and a web of new wrinkles spread across her face. "You know I can't wait. And Cece, you call me anytime and ask me any question, okay? We're all in this together now. Remember you come from a long line of tough mountain women. If anybody asks you about your magic, or whatever they call it—and they will—you hold up your two strong hands. You touch your head, heart, and belly, and that's all they need to know. Like I always told you, your peculiars are your superpower. It was true back then, and it still is. The difference is now you get to learn how to use it."

Hazel waved until their car was out of sight before ambling up to her favorite rocking chair on the front porch. Winding around her feet was Tizzy, the cat Hazel had fed on the porch for years and made a bed under the glider. When the temperature dropped low enough, she let her come inside. Tizzy had shiny black fur with white paws and always jumped on Hazel's lap when she sat down.

"We got that done, Tizzy," Hazel said, filling her bowl with cat food pulled from a wooden box on the porch. She turned in time to see a handsome silver-haired gentleman on her front steps.

"Well, look who the cat drug in," Hazel laughed. "Come have a seat right here beside me." She walked over to her rocking chair and patted her hand on the arm of the chair next to hers. "Guess you saw she was here. What's it been? Ten years now? Anna B. still manages to tell some story with your name in it every single time I see her, Sam," Hazel said, watching the clouds begin to gather over the mountains.

Hazel rocked until the sun balanced on the curve of a mountaintop in the distance, ready to sink. She pushed herself up and out of the chair reluctantly, saying to no one in particular, "Better get movin' and get my chores done before weather comes."

She headed inside, the screen door slapping shut behind her.

20

Heading home, Cece wanted to ask a hundred questions and, at the same time, didn't want another morsel in her bursting head.

"You know, it hasn't been easy for your Aunt Granny," Nana began, speaking the thoughts already circling her mind. "With the choices she's made in her life, not to marry or have kids, and to live on her own." Cece watched Nana's face as she remembered. "They called her names. Said she rode her broomstick to school and made fun of her every which way. I've always felt guilty, like I didn't do enough to defend her."

"You were young, too," Cece offered. "I'm sure you did what you could."

"It never felt like enough, though, for all she's done for me. She's always walked her own road, and it's been one I admired, not paying any attention to how people thought she should be or how she should live her life. And it's not been an easy road, not at all. But her knowing runs deep. Just like yours, I think," Nana said as the distance between the sharp curves grew longer and the inclines less steep.

"But you two were so different. You wanted totally different things, didn't you?" Cece asked.

"Oh, yes. I couldn't wait to get out of the hollow and see the world. I tried to get Hazel to go with me, but that was something even a stick of dynamite couldn't make happen." Nana laughed.

Soon they were pulling into Nana's driveway. Nana said she was going to take a nap, and Cece headed to her cottage with a bag full of green beans and a lot to think about.

* * *

Lulled by the rhythm of steady rain, Cece overslept the next morning. When May couldn't wake her with a paw to her cheek, she resorted to walking over her belly.

Cece awoke with a start from a dream-filled sleep with a dog on top of her. Her dreams had been a jumble of images blurred on the edges: of fire, a thick book, a circle of old women, and row after row of empty shelves that seemed to go on forever.

Cece rolled out of bed, pulling on her sweatpants and T-shirt as she stumbled into the kitchen to make coffee. She'd told Bess she would go with her to some kind of special yoga class they were giving at the Inn that day, but Cece couldn't remember what time it started. She rubbed her eyes and poured water into her coffee pot, still half-asleep and functioning on autopilot. She was trying to remember the details when her phone buzzed with a text from Bess.

Meet me at the Carlisle Room at 9. 

It was followed by another text, this time from Joe:

Call me when u get a chance.

Cece was still reeling from the visit to Aunt Granny's, which had almost been enough to forget the break-in and the note on her windshield. Seeing the text from Joe brought her back like a gut punch. She decided to give herself a few more minutes for the fuzz to clear out of her head before she got dressed and called Joe back.

Cece sipped her coffee and ate a piece of cinnamon toast as she scrolled the want-ads on her laptop. Teaching dance was fulfilling in many ways, as was building dollhouses, but neither paid much, and Cece really wanted to be able to afford her own place. Plus, she wasn't even sure the dance dream was really hers to begin with. May, who had been sitting patiently at her feet, looked up at her and barked.

Cece leaned down to pet May's long black nose. "I know I'm out of it when you have to tell me to feed you, May." May looked back at her as if to say she was about to give up and do it herself.

Cece fed May and then walked her holding an umbrella since it was still sprinkling rain. After May was settled and Cece was on her way to the inn to meet Bess for the yoga class, she called Joe back on speakerphone.

Joe answered and said, "Hey, Cece. Thanks for calling me back."

"Sorry it took me a minute. I spent most of yesterday up at Aunt Granny's."

"Is she doing okay?" he asked politely.

"Oh yeah, doing great. She made us some of her blueberry cobbler and sent us home with a load of green beans from her garden. She keeps herself busy." Cece wanted to add, *And she's been talking to dead people, too.* "What's up?"

"I just wanted you to know that we confirmed with the inn that the fragment we found near the crime site did come from a head-and-shoulders sculpture, a bust. We also verified that a bust listed on the inventory is missing. We're working now to try and make a match between the two. I thought you'd want to know."

"Good deal! If you know what was used as the murder weapon, that should help a lot, right?" Cece asked, immediately aware of her submissive tone and kicking herself for it.

"It definitely helps, but we have a ways to go to determine if it actually was the murder weapon," Joe said.

Cece wondered why it seemed so hard for Joe to admit she provided a credible clue. It wasn't like she was questioning his abilities; she simply would have appreciated a little credit.

"Have you gotten any more notes on your windshield?"

"Nope. Nothing. I still think Hailey must've done it. Have you talked to her, anyway?" Cece thought it would make sense for him to ask her outright.

"Nope. Not lately. Just be careful, Cece, at least until we get this case wrapped up." Cece could hear Morris's growly voice in the background. "I've got to go now, but I'll be in touch," Joe said, hanging up.

"Well, look at you, looking all your best self and everything this morning," was Bess's greeting as Cece pulled her raincoat off in front of the yoga room at the inn. Cece looked down, not sure of what she had grabbed and put on, to see she was wearing indigo yoga pants with a black tank.

"I don't know about that, but I could say the same for you," Cece remarked with a laugh as Bess made a full-360 turn, showing off her outfit of multicolored yoga pants covered in what looked like paint splatters, complemented by a bright fuchsia tank.

"Oh, these old things I just bought yesterday?" Bess said, grinning. "And isn't this top the best? It's CYA, meaning it 'covers my assets.'"

Someone unlocked the double doors into the Carlisle Room and the small group that had gathered in front walked in.

"Hello, Cece. Hello, Bess," came a whispery voice from behind them with a distinct and genuine British accent. It was Keely Bodden, the yoga teacher and Calvin's longtime live-in girlfriend. She was from Grand Cayman Island, a native "Caymanian." In addition to her voice, her features were also delicate, and framed by thick, light brown hair sectioned into numerous narrow braids with shells woven in at the ends. "Hello, my friends," Keely said when Bess and Cece turned to see her. "Good to see you both. I'm so glad you came to my class." Keely was just a wisp in stature, but strong enough to balance her entire body weight on one arm. Bess and Cece had been to several of her classes elsewhere.

"Hey, Keely," Bess said, "we're really happy to have you teach this class for us today. Looks like we've got a good group of guests taking part, too. We're hoping to get something on the inn's regular schedule."

"I do hope they like the class," Keely said. Standing near her, Cece picked up a definite hint of patchouli and coconut.

"I love her classes," Bess said as she and Cece unrolled their yoga mats on the floor. "But I could take a thousand and never be able to do that," she said, watching as Keely warmed up by doing the splits like a Barbie doll, one after the other on both sides.

Cece tipped her head down so only Bess could hear. "You just come because she puts a lavender washcloth on your forehead at the end of class."

"I can neither confirm nor deny," Bess said, taking a seat when Keely struck her singing bowl, sending a vibrating chime through the room.

After class was over, Bess and Cece helped Keely carry her bags to the car.

"How's Calvin doing?" Bess asked, walking beside Keely.

"He is doing okay. He's not allowed to go anywhere, or at least not far, so we had to cancel our plan to go home to see my family. That was sad for both of us."

Cece caught up and joined them. "Listen, Keely, I'm so sorry about everything. I know they're going to find who killed Jenny and figure out this was all a huge mistake with Calvin."

"I hope so, Cece. He is not a dishonest man, and this has really bothered him. He is not himself."

Hearing this made Cece angry all over again. She couldn't imagine who or why someone would plant Jenny's necklace on Calvin. "Please tell him again we are pushing to get answers, and we won't stop until we do."

"I will, and he does appreciate your texts," Keely said, resignation in her voice. "We're just afraid the longer the case drags on, the more they will need an arrest, any arrest."

After they'd helped Keely, Bess walked with Cece to her car. "Joe told me you found that the bust was on the inventory list," Cece said, unlocking her car door.

"Yeah. The inn told Joe before they even told me, but that might've had something to do with Manny being in town," said Bess, unable to repress a big smile.

"Manny came into town, huh? Was that a surprise?"

"Sort of. I knew he was heading to Florida soon, and he said he wanted to see me before he left. Which reminds me, I told you he said he'd be glad to check out Sandra while he was down there, if you still wanted him to. He drove down yesterday and should be there by now. Do you want me to tell him anything?"

"Yes! After hearing Keely talk about Calvin, I'm ready to do something. I'm tired of sitting on my hands and waiting, while Joe tells me to 'leave it to them' and nothing happens. If there is something I can do, whether I use my peculiars or not, I'm ready," Cece said, her voice stronger and louder with each sentence. "Didn't Buck tell Manny where Sandra lived? Something about her town not being far from his?"

"Yeah, he said their towns were like ten miles apart in South Florida."

"When I talked to Buck, it was clear he didn't think too highly of Sandra. Tell Manny that Buck thought her gated neighborhood had some kind of bird name. He said she lives right on the water and has a brand-new boat," Cece said. "Will you be sure he has my number?"

"Will do," Bess said as she pulled a hooded jacket on over her yoga clothes. "I've got to go change and get back to work, but I still need an Aunt Granny update. Coffee date soon?"

"Sounds good," Cece said, unsure Bess was ready for the "Aunt Granny update" she was about to get.

* * *

"And one, and two, bend four, five, six, step, step, close." Nana spoke each word on the beat while demonstrating the steps. It was her favorite time of the week, teaching her Senior Swans ballet class. Ramona, who drove in as soon as she got off her shift at the Waffle Hut, called the group the "Island of Misfit Ballerinas." Women of every shape, size, and age made up Nana's regulars. And there was also Mr. Jerome, who had never missed a class since Nana had started it, and was always first to raise his hand when she asked for someone to lead.

There was no dress code, so some came in regular leotards with tights, some in yoga clothes, some in sweats, and some, like Myra, in a sparkly tutu. Students filled both sides of the free-standing ballet barres.

Nana always began class the same way, "Blair, what is your stage name for the evening?" Blair was over six feet tall and had played basketball in college. She had always wanted to take ballet, but her parents told her she was too clumsy and her legs were too long.

"My name tonight..." Blair paused, thinking, "is Giselle Raminokov," she said, quite pleased with herself, as she swept her arm out to the side with a flourish.

"Welcome, Madame Raminokov," Nana gave her a slight bow and moved down the line.

The class progressed from the barre to their center floor dance step combinations and finished with steps traveling across the floor. Nana was using music from the famous ballet *Swan Lake* that night. Mr. Jerome had informed Nana twice that he had been the prince in his dance school's production of *Swan Lake* forty years ago.

Although most were drenched in sweat by the end of class and would surely be sore the next day, they couldn't wait to come back the following week. As Blair told Nana after class, short of breath, "Because for one hour once a week, I don't think about paying bills or laundry. I am a dancer—Giselle Raminokov!"

Nana told everyone goodbye and pulled her long, puffy coat on over her dance clothes. She had just gotten in her car to head home when her phone vibrated, and Leo's name came onto the car's screen. "Hello, Son. Are you calling to see how Senior Swans went tonight?" she teased, knowing Leo never had her schedule straight, but that he had been especially worried about both her and Cece since the break-in.

"Hey Mom," he said, "of course I am. Did Myra wear her tutu tonight?"

"*You're a smooth one*, Leo Chagall. And, yes, tonight she wore her red one. To what do I owe the pleasure of your call?"

"I wanted to give you and Cece the heads-up on something I heard down at the *Gazette* tonight when I turned in my column. Carl, who covers the police beat, said they uncovered more information about Calvin and his ties to the Caymans. Turns out Calvin did boat repair for a company, including a charter that ran guests from Miami. Carl also said the police were working on a tip that tied him to Jenny's brother, Edmond. So, if they link those two, it appears Calvin might have a motive to have killed Jenny."

Despite Nana having cranked up the heat in her car, she shivered. "Oh, no. Leo, he's worked for me for years. He has never said or done anything that wasn't aboveboard. In fact, he's honest to a fault. I know things I'm quite sure I shouldn't know."

"I agree with you, but we have to consider that we don't know his life before he moved back here. It's possible he got involved with the wrong crowd or something and maybe owes some money. Hard to say. I just wanted you and Cece to keep being extra careful. You know what Dad would say, 'Don't make me come down there.'"

Nana laughed. "Yes, he certainly would have said that. But don't worry, darling, and stay right where you are. I have enough security lights up around the house now aliens could use it as a landing pad. I'm not taking any chances. I also refuse to believe I'm supposed to be afraid of Calvin, of all people."

"Okay, Mom. I'll call and check in tomorrow. Love you."

Nana had left a few lamps and overhead lights on in the house before she left in the afternoon, and she turned on a few more as she came inside, dropped her purse on the kitchen counter, and headed straight upstairs to get out of her dance clothes.

Feeling much better in her robe and slippers, Nana rummaged around in the fridge, pulling out an icy bottle of Coke and the blueberry cobbler Hazel had sent home with her. As she settled onto the sofa and clicked on the TV, she felt a familiar twinge of pain in her hip and hoisted herself back up to get her ice pack from the freezer. It seemed to Nana that old age seemed to have a little bell it was always ringing, like a spoiled child in his sickbed. Just as you had tended to one need, the bell rang again, and off you went.

She finally settled on an old Rock Hudson movie on the Classic Movies channel as Bliss jumped into her usual place on the cushion beside her. Nana knew her cold cobbler and coke wasn't the healthiest snack but also believed that the endurance race of age deserved any reward available, and so enjoyed every bite.

As she put her drink back on the side table, she glanced at the framed picture beside the lamp. It was of Sam and herself dancing at the inn's one-hundredth anniversary celebration. She remembered that champagne-colored, beaded dress she had splurged on for the occasion. Sam looked splendid in his black tux with his silver hair and blue eyes. She could tell by the sly grin on her face that he had probably just whispered a dirty joke in her ear.

In a way, she was grateful they hadn't known he would be gone before the year's end. They danced and laughed until late in the night, just as they had forty years before when they met. They had giggled at the mayor's speech, which they thought would never end, and been touched by all the former employees who came back for the occasion. Nana was well aware that sometimes it's what you don't know that saves you.

"I get what you're thinking, Samuel Chagall," Nana said aloud to the picture, "that if I tried to use my gifts, I might be able to help Cece and this whole murder case. Maybe I could find something that belonged to Jenny and be able to see a clue. Of course, I've thought about it." Nana took another bite of cobbler, considering the idea as she chewed. She wished she really could talk to Sam on the other side, like Hazel could talk to some. Talking to his framed photo would have to make do.

"But we both know from experience," Nana continued, "that I have to be careful and not just jump into the middle of something. When I've done that before, it didn't end well. I must get that message across to our Cece. With all this talk about gifts she must understand it's not all glitter and magic wands. Sometimes things came through that I didn't want to know, or that scared me. I must warn her that once the channel is open she will experience both sides of human nature. I have to teach her how to protect herself." Nana opened the drawer in the wooden coffee table and pulled out her pen and journal. Writing in her journal was how she both came to understand her gifts, and the legacy she wanted Cece to have someday. "I know, Sam. I know what you'd say. Get it all out. Write it down."

With that, Nana pulled a soft, warm blanket over her legs, clicked off the TV, and continued to write her story.

FIRE CIRCLE

Hazel built up the fire against the sharp October chill until sparks flew so high they seemed to join the stars in the night sky. She settled onto a tree stump behind Cat, her bent fingers combing through Cat's long grey hair. Hazel's hands weren't as nimble as they used to be, but they were still deft enough as she separated the hair, weaving and pulling Cat's long strands into braids. A silvery veil hung over the moon, and low clouds obscured the mountaintops to the east. "We all seem lost in thought tonight," Hazel said. "Fiona, I think it's a perfect time for one of your tunes."

Fiona reached behind the tree log she was sitting on and pulled out her fiddle, nestling it under her chin. She put the bow to the strings and played a haunting melody with lots of low, drawn-out notes. It was eerily fitting music for the surging fire casting shadows and shapes against the back of Hazel's house.

"How 'bout playing one of those jigs you like? Something a little more upbeat? I don't need any more of that mournful music," Hazel teased Fiona, whose auburn hair and fair skin shone in the firelight.

"I've got just the one," Fiona said, laughing and starting the beat by tapping the toe of her boot on the ground. Soon, Cat was clapping along, and Hazel was standing up, creating her own rendition of a jig with some marching in a circle and knee-bending. Not one to be left out, Sally then stood to join Hazel, lifting her long skirt and showing off some fancy footwork. Soon the women's laughter rang like music through the dense forest behind them.

"Now I'm 'bout worn out," Hazel said, lowering herself back onto the stump after giving it a full ten minutes, "but it sure does feel good," Hazel said to Fiona while trying to get her breath back. "Makes me forget my troubles listening to your fiddle."

"You've heard the same six songs from the homeland over and over all these years and never complained, which is good, 'cause that's all I ever learned." Fiona shrugged and went on, "Because my folks didn't think a woman playing was very seemly. My brother got lessons and secretly tried to teach me when he could."

"You should just make some up yourself. I have an idea you have a lot on your heart we'd like to hear," Cat said encouragingly. "And I'll wear my dew claw rattles next time to add another beat."

"I would like that. I do actually have a few songs of my own. Would you like to hear them sometime?"

"'Course we would," Sally piped up. "And I'll trade you a few bird calls I just learned. We'll have us a concert. And Hazel, I, for one, am glad you got your talk with Cece. She needed that time with you, and now both of you can move on to what comes next."

"If you know what comes next, I'd like you to share it 'cause I'm not sure I do," Hazel said, patting Sally's hand.

"I don't mean anything in particular, just that you both can move forward now. There's a lot of power that comes from getting clear on who you are and what you come from. She'll need some time to get used to that. Of course, she's got you and your sister, and you've got us."

Hazel took up a stick and stirred the dirt in front of them meditatively, like it was a pot of stew. "You're right, I know. It'll come in due time, due time," she said, her musing interrupted by the shrill scream of a bobcat piercing the mountain air from somewhere behind them.

"I think she wants us to leave so she can have our fire," Hazel said as the other three all stood up at the sound.

"Well, she can be my guest and have at it," said Cat, as she cupped her mouth with both hands and returned the bobcat's sharp, hoarse call, sending out the "all clear" signal to her feline sisters in the woods. All four of the women chuckled as they gathered their belongings and headed out into the night.

21

Manny called just as Cece had started mopping the floors at the dance studio. She leaned the mop against the wall and went to the small office where she and Nana worked on the books so she could sit down and focus.

"Hey, Cece, I just wanted to let you know what I found out from my dad while I was in Florida," Manny said, talking on his car's speakerphone as he headed north up Interstate 95 back to Tennessee. "It's a pretty small world down there when it comes to fishing and boats, and it just so happened someone contacted my dad awhile back about a boat that had been repossessed from one Sandra Newport in West Palm Beach for defaulting on a loan. Thought you might find that interesting."

"You're kidding! I thought she had loads of money. You're right, I do find that very interesting. I wonder if the Eureka police know? I owe you big for doing all this, Manny. I'll have to think of something to pay you and Bess back for all the help you've been."

"You don't need to worry about that; as long as Bess is happy, I'm happy," Manny said as Cece crossed her fingers in hopes Bess felt the same way. "Sorry, Cece, that's Bess calling in now, better go."

"Of course. Tell her I'll see her later. Bye."

Cece returned to her mopping duty, thinking about all the parts of the case floating in her thoughts, none of which seemed to make sense together. She couldn't figure out how the break-in to her cottage and the threatening note on her windshield were related to Jenny's murder. It was easy to pin those events on the jealous ex-girlfriend Hailey, but was that too easy, Cece wondered. If those incidents weren't Hailey asserting herself over Joe, that might mean they had to do with Jenny's death, but what could *she* have to do with any of that? Her heart ached again for the loss of her friend, and she felt frustrated that she hadn't been able to knit everything together, for Jenny's family, and for poor Calvin, too. She just couldn't imagine him guilty. Aunt Granny used to tell Cece that sometimes what you're looking for is right in front of you, and you still can't see it, so you need to be patient and wait, as it is trying to reveal itself. Cece was never great at being patient, and she couldn't shake the feeling that the answer was right there, hovering on the edges like the bees in Aunt Granny's tree.

Cece's plan was to go out and visit Calvin before meeting Bess for coffee. Calvin and Keely lived on the outskirts of town in a two-bedroom frame house with a chain link fence in the back that made a yard for their two black labrador retrievers. As Cece pulled into the gravel driveway, both big dogs rushed for the fence, barking, doing their job as the best alarm system around. Cece was surprised to see Calvin's grass needed mowing, and his garden was overgrown with weeds. *It isn't like him to let that go.* She could see Calvin in the carport, his head inside the camper he'd built on the back of his flatbed truck. "Hey Calvin," Cece said, hopping out of the Jeep, holding a bag with some tea from Nana and the last tomatoes and beans of the season from Aunt Granny's garden.

As Calvin walked toward Cece, she was struck by how thin he'd gotten and by the dark circles that had appeared under his eyes. "What've you got here?" Calvin asked, taking the bag from her. "Come on in, Keely's in there practicing the sitar."

"I thought I heard something," Cece said. "I've heard of those but never seen one. I didn't know she played."

"Come on in and take a look. She just started taking lessons." Calvin's voice sounded flat to Cece, like a song with one note. He led Cece in through the side door that opened into the kitchen, which was heavy with the smell of incense and wet dog.

"Hey Cece!" Keely's voice bounced out from the walls of their living room. "Come on in!"

Cece joined Keely, taking in the unique style of the room, with recycled saris made into richly colored curtains and the low table altar at the end of the room. It was filled with brass and pewter likenesses of Ganesh, Laksmi, and other Hindu deities Cece recognized but didn't know much about. Tiny lights framed the window borders, and plush velvet cushions on the floor replaced chairs. Cece recalled Calvin telling her Keely had lived and studied in India for a few years, and this room reflected that experience.

"You want to look before I put it up?" Keely asked Cece as she carefully lifted her instrument to lean against a stand.

"Sure. The sound was lovely," Cece said, moving in for a closer inspection. It looked like a guitar, but with a much longer neck and smaller body, somewhat resembling the end of an oar. The long strings gave it an ethereal, resonant sound. It was made from polished wood that was smooth to the touch. "It's beautiful Keely."

"Thanks Cece. Come on in and have a seat," Keely offered, leading them in to sit down at the kitchen table. "What have you got in the bags?" Keely asked.

"Well, this all comes from Nana and Aunt Granny."

"And I bet I know which is which," Calvin remarked from the kitchen sink where he was washing his hands.

"The tail-end of the green bean and tomato harvest from Hazel's garden, and the Duchess's magic tea mixture guaranteed to cure me. I've been lucky enough to get these before."

"You got it," Cece said as Calvin sat down between them.

There was a brief silence while each circled the elephant in the room. Calvin spoke up first. "I just got word a little while ago that the anonymous tip they got about me down in Miami turned out to go nowhere."

"Great! That's great news!" Cece said, surprised at the new information. "Any ideas on how the necklace got in your toolbox?"

"Nope. The police just said they were still questioning people that might've seen something that night."

"I still can't believe this is happening, Calvin, and that they haven't caught the guy yet," Cece said.

"You and me, *both*," he said, glancing at Keely. "I'm not sure how much longer Keely can stand me. This whole thing has made me…unwell."

Keely stood up, walked over to behind Calvin's chair, and leaned in close to his left ear as she wrapped both arms around him. "This too shall pass," she said with an almost unnerving calm that made you believe her.

"Tell your Nana I'm coming tomorrow to mow, if you don't mind," Calvin said, blushing a little as he looked at Cece. "I'll text her, too."

"Sure, I bet anything she'll have another project ready for you by the time you get there. But maybe it will be me giving you the message, because, you know, she still leaves the house when you mow. I guess it reminds her too much of Papa Sam."

"Those two were quite the pair, weren't they? Never saw the Duchess without the Duke, and vice-versa. I think the secret was all those jokes he used to tell her. She was never without a smile when he was around."

"That's because most of 'em were dirty," Cece cracked. "But no doubt they had a good thing going."

The three of them talked for a little longer before Cece had to go. As they walked her out to the car, Keely slipped a purple crystal into her hand. "That's amethyst, for your intuition. Keep it close," she whispered to Cece as she gave her hand a squeeze.

Cece turned the volume up on her '90s radio station and rolled her window down despite the cold air outside. She had wanted to see Calvin, but then, when she did, she felt helpless and didn't know what to say. *If I am supposed to have some kind of "gift," then where is it?* She couldn't even think of the right words to say to make Calvin feel better. *And if Aunt Granny and Nana have gifts, why can't they use theirs to help catch the killer? Can't Nana find something of Jenny's and learn something that might help? And as for Aunt Granny, if she can see dead people, why can't she just ask Jenny who did it?*

Cece was beginning to think a colossal trick was being played on her and at any moment someone would jump out and say, "Gotcha!" Cece turned the volume even higher on the radio, joining the Backstreet Boys for the chorus of their song, "I Want It That Way," at the top of her lungs and decidedly off-key. By the time she pulled into the parking lot of the coffee shop, she was feeling a lot better. Nothing worked like yell-singing alone in her car to make everything seem less cataclysmic.

* * *

Since October had officially arrived, Olivia had gone all out with the Halloween decorations. Black-branched trees with twinkling purple lights, pumpkins with battery-operated candles inside, and fuzzy spiders hanging from the ceiling were just the beginning of her extravaganza.

"Hey, Cece," Olivia called out in greeting from behind the counter. Cece spied Bess sitting over at their usual table in the corner and waved to her before getting in line for coffee. They always had the most delicious-sounding fall menu, very much like the spa menu at the inn, but these you could actually eat and drink. Cece couldn't decide between an apple butter, maple caramel, or oatmeal cookie latte, and she already knew she wanted a piece of Olivia's homemade carrot cake with cream cheese frosting. "What would you like today, Cece?" Olivia said. She was more bubbly than ever now that her husband Ricky had gotten a job at Paty Lumber Company, and she had on a particularly festive outfit of black overalls, a pumpkin hair clip, and orange high-tops.

"I haven't tried your maple caramel latte yet, and I'll have that with a slice of carrot cake."

"Excellent choices. I'll get that made, and then I want to tell you about something. I'll get these folks tended to and then come over to your table."

Cece paid and nodded her head, smiling because she hadn't known five minutes ago that Olivia's energy was exactly what she needed. *Sometimes,* she thought, *you just need to absorb the good vibes coming from someone else. Maybe that's how Olivia keeps people coming back to the shop, or maybe it's just the cream cheese frosting.*

She dropped her bag on the back of her chair and sat down with Bess, who had some kind of official-looking magazine in front of her. "You know what I was thinking, Cece?" Bess said, wearing new glasses with wide black frames.

"Since when do you wear glasses?" Cece said, taken aback by the sheer size of them.

"Oh, these things?" Bess said, adjusting them on her face. "They are what we call a 'fashion accessory,' serving no purpose other than looking good. Sort of like Manny!" Bess said, breaking into her full body, contagious laugh. She could really crack herself up, not even caring if anyone else got the joke at all.

"Sorry to interrupt. What were you starting to say?" Cece asked, giggling at Bess while she dug in her purse for her phone.

"I was thinking you might want to work at the bookstore with Shane. You read all those mystery books, and you write in your journal all the time. I just thought you might like it, and Shane told me they were hiring right now."

"I don't know, Bess. I was hoping to find somewhere that I could work my way up."

"Like a dance studio where you could teach and could someday own?"

"Yeah. There's that possibility, too." Cece knew she shouldn't cancel out the possibility. It felt like looking a gift horse in the mouth to even think about not keeping the studio going.

"Anyway, just a thought," Bess said. "So how is Calvin? And have you talked to Joe? And how was Aunt Granny? See what happens when we miss talking for a few days?"

"First, seeing Calvin just made me sad, and even more determined to help him get out of this mess. I called Joe on the way to the studio and told him what Manny had learned about Sandra's boat."

"Did Joe say if they already knew about any of that?" Bess asked, clicking her newly painted bronze fingernails on the table.

"You know how he is: 'We're working on all angles; we've got a lot we're following up on; Cece, we've got it,' things like that. Basically a non-answer, which probably means he didn't know about it but doesn't want to admit it."

Olivia, who was trying to untangle herself from the curtain of black spider ribbons hanging from the door to the kitchen, said, "So sorry to interrupt you two, but can I have a minute?" Startled, Bess and Cece looked behind them just as Olivia freed herself. "I may kill myself on all these decorations before we even get to Halloween."

"Please, have a seat," Bess said, offering a chair.

"Cece, I just wanted to let you know Ricky told me he remembered what Jenny was meeting about with Steve Shafer," Olivia said. "Steve was getting Jenny's advice on which new security system to put in at the high school. Ricky also said how one time after Jenny left, Steve told him his wife was getting jealous of his regular 'dates' with Jenny, but that Steve said he didn't intend to stop it. Can you believe that?"

"I'm not surprised," Bess added. "I heard he and Amanda got married before the ink was dry on the goodbye note he supposedly stuck on the fridge for his first wife to find. No tellin' what he's up to now."

"Thanks for finding out about why they were meeting, Olivia," Cece said. "I'd been meaning to ask if you'd remembered anything. On one hand, it's good that the meetings were legit, but on the other, not so good. Steve liked that it made Amanda jealous. Do either of you know her at all?" Cece asked, looking between Olivia and Bess.

Both shook their heads. "She keeps pretty much to herself from what I've heard. She's only been in here once that I can remember. Uh-oh," Olivia said, looking over at the line that had quickly formed at the counter, "I better go give my new help a hand." She hopped up and started away, but turned back as if she had another secret to share. "Don't forget, 'Every cloud has a silver lining.' See y'all later."

Cece had stuffed two huge forkfuls of cake into her mouth in the time it took Bess to turn back around to face her. In response to the look on Bess' face, Cece, with wide-eyed innocence, asked her, as best she could with her mouth full of cake, "Wha–? Wan' some?" she managed as she smirked and chewed dreamily.

"You and your metabolism. Don't even get me started. And what silver lining is Olivia talking about?" Bess rolled her eyes. "Now, back to your visit to Charity Hill. So, how's my favorite Granny Woman?" Bess asked.

Cece swallowed quickly and began, "Well, you might call it a visit for the ages." She paused, deciding in the moment exactly how she would explain it all, and said, "I think you better put your seat belt on and get ready for a wild ride."

"Ooooh, interesting," said Bess, wiggling down in her seat and rubbing her hands together in glee. "I am so ready, Sister, ready for whatever you have to tell me." Bess grinned, but Cece wasn't sure she was ready at all. She paused shoveling cake into her mouth and launched into a retelling of the day in the mountains. Cece had decided to tell some, but not all, that she had learned from the visit. She told Bess in general about "the gifts," omitting who did what and how it worked, since she was still learning herself.

"I knew it!" Bess said, slapping her knee, after Cece finished her long story. Bess's voice was loud enough for the couple next to them to turn, then lowering her voice, she continued, "I always knew something was up with you Chagall women. I could tell the three of you were 'extra.' Too bad you didn't know all this earlier; think of the fun we could've had in high school!"

Cece leaned back in her chair, shaking her head, "I did well to make it through the day back in high school. I wouldn't have been able to handle it back then. I'm not even sure I can now."

"What do you mean, Cece? You wanted answers, and now you're getting them. No telling what they haven't told you yet. Maybe you'll get to be in a coven, or like a sorority for witches, and you'll do things like have a secret handshake and wear each other's clothes."

Cece laughed. "I'd be more than happy if it just helps me figure out my peculiars, for now."

"Listen, Cece," Bess said, straightening up in her chair and leaning forward, "You've hated being different for as long as I've known you. This is your chance to use your peculiars to do who-knows-what brilliant things in the future. I know you can't go back and change the time in algebra you told Karen Morehead her voice sounded like French-fry grease because, well, that's a hard one, but now it's possible you can use your synesthesia in other ways that will make all the people that called you 'weird' eat their words. Wouldn't that be great?"

Cece had to admit, the idea was appealing, and she was thinking especially of Emma Turner from sixth grade. Emma would turn around just to stare at Cece in Mr. Beasley's class at Grant Elementary, and then whisper to her friend Joella Moore, who sat beside her. Joella would then turn around, too, and they would laugh together. It happened almost every day like clockwork, and just thinking about it made Cece burn with shame. *There could be an upside in this gift thing after all.* "You're right, it would, but, right now, this supposed 'gift' of mine feels like an abstract painting. I know it's supposed to mean something, but I have no idea what." Cece looked out the window, aware it seemed noticeably darker outside.

"I don't really know what I'm talking about either, but at least now you know where to get your questions answered," Bess said, picking up and checking her phone. "Ugh. I have to go back to work. Have you got anything going on for the weekend?"

"Nope. Just applying for jobs and working on a dollhouse. I might stop by the bookstore and see Shane. I'll ask about the job you mentioned while I'm there," Cece said, gathering her things. "I had a message from my old college boyfriend. You remember Ben? He said he might be coming through Knoxville soon."

"I thought he was married?" Bess said, putting her jacket on.

"He is. I'm sure he just wants to catch up, and it's just for coffee. Wish I'd brought my umbrella in," Cece said, noticing a steady rain had begun outside.

"Well, let me know if you want to go out or watch a movie. I have to work tonight but not the rest of the weekend. Hope this rain stops soon," Bess said, pulling her hood over her head.

"Me, too," said Cece, turning to leave and narrowly avoiding running into the cauldron display. "I'll text you later."

22

Nana wiped her forehead with her workout towel, adjusting the speed on the spin-bike. She was proud of herself for making it to the local gym twice a week these days, although she found riding a bike that didn't go anywhere *utterly boring*. Nevertheless, she propped their latest book club selection on the bike's device holder and kept at it.

"Greetings, Ms. Chagall," came a male voice with a British accent from behind her. Nana turned her head to see Yerger Simkins wearing a white terry cloth headband and knee socks. "Looks like we're in for a proper downpour," he said, hands on his hips, twisting side to side with his comb-over askew. "Have to keep the spine flexible, you know, very important as we age."

"Is that so?" Nana said, entertained by the fact that he was telling a former professional dancer the importance of the spine. She wanted to challenge him right then and there to see who could hold a plank the longest, but instead asked, "How is Jackie?"

Yerger's ingratiating smile slipped from his face. "Just dandy," he said curtly. Nana had seen her at the grocery store last week, and they had talked. Nana already knew Jackie had laid down the law to Yerger after some of his unsolicited flirtations had come to light. Nana had given Jackie a tincture for Yerger's tea, telling her that, if nothing else, slipping a little in his tea would help her feel better.

"She's gone to her sisters for a visit," he continued, bending to pull his sock down and scratch. Nana could see bumps, like a rash, that had spread all the way up his leg. She smiled.

"I'm sure her sister must be tickled to death to see her. Please give her my regards," Nana said, turning back toward her book. She was just beginning her cool down when her phone rang.

Nana answered saying, "Hey, Hazel. You okay? I'm just finishing up at the gym right now. Yes, us, too. We're having a gully washer down here. I may wait until this rain calms down a bit before going to my car. No, I haven't talked to Cece today. Have you? Uh-huh. Are you sure that 'bad feeling' you're having isn't just your arthritis? You know what happens when it rains." Nana nodded her head, her expression changing. "Well, I'll be sure to check on her before I go out tonight. She's probably going out with some of her friends, anyway. Uh-huh. I'll tell her. You're right, we should probably get with her this weekend. She'll need to know that part. Okay. Love you, too," Nana said, hanging up as she slowed to a stop on the bike.

Nana was thinking she needed to get home, shower, and get the birthday present wrapped for the dinner tonight. And, not one to ignore one of Hazel's "feelins," Nana also decided she would call Cece after she got home.

The relentless rain kept up through early afternoon, trailed by a new weather system from the west, bringing storms. Cece and Mabel hurried through the front door of the cottage after a quick walk. Immediately, as Mabel shook out her fur, and Cece, her umbrella, a jarring clap of thunder surprised them both.

"This is a good night to snuggle in, work on the dollhouse, and watch that *Murder, She Wrote* marathon we've been looking forward to," Cece said to Mabel, who seemed more interested in dinner than a Jessica Fletcher binge. She changed into her soft cotton pajamas, fixed herself a sandwich, and fed Mabel.

As she leaned against the kitchen counter, eating her sandwich, she surveyed the mix-and-match décor of the cottage, which somehow didn't have the same charm as Bess's did. This was probably because Cece had regarded the cottage as temporary ever since she moved in almost eight months ago. She never intended to stay long, realizing she had been living lease-to-lease for the better part of the last nine years.

Cece liked the antiques and tasteful linen-covered furniture of the cottage, but none of it was hers. It had all come from Nana. Even in New York most of her furniture had come from Goodwill, so when she left, she carried only a couple of suitcases and had shipped back boxes with what little else she owned. She imagined what it would be like to have her own house, where she could plant her own flowers and herbs, decorate in her own style, and where she might finally feel a true "sense of place."

This notion of "place" was central to her family, meaning pride and understanding of the people and land you come from, and all that came before you. It meant carrying this truth inside you no matter where you went, knowing that your heart would always spin a thread back to the land, people, and history of where you came from. Aunt Granny, Nana, her dad—they all had it.

Aunt Granny loved nothing more than to "walk the line," which meant walking the perimeter of her two-acre, mountainside property line. To her, it was more than just a measurement, it was part of who she was. She was wedded to every sugar maple and beech tree, every white-tailed deer and wild turkey, and the song of the river running just below her house was her song too. She knew the quick, whistled notes of the Carolina Wren and the whinny of a screech owl, the resin scent of pine after a rain, and the taste of pure, cold spring water.

Cece remembered how, like Nana, she couldn't wait to leave after college: the mountains made her feel claustrophobic, and her accent embarrassed her. She couldn't get enough of the newness of city life, the fast pace and fast food, and the wonder of living in a place where people of every color and language waited with you at the crosswalk. She had loved it.

And yet, after a while, Cece had felt a complicated stirring inside, one that she had successfully ignored until she couldn't anymore. It was not about her failures, or her mother's death, although she respected that as part of her story. It was more about an ineffable pull toward home, something Cece thought of more as a longing to have what Aunt Granny had, to be connected to the folkways, or way of life, of one place in the world.

For now, as Cece dream-scrolled through real-estate listings, she knew a lot of things had to change before buying a house, or even renting one, could even enter the realm of possibility for her. She needed another part-time job or to consider quitting the dance studio and getting a full-time job.

Cece put her phone down, feeling herself careening down into the black hole of social media, turned her TV on to the *Murder, She Wrote* marathon, and sat down at her dollhouse worktable. She'd started to pull the tape off where the glue had dried the corners of the walls together when her phone buzzed.

"Hi, Nana," Cece said, "I saw your house light up a while ago. I figured you'd just gotten home."

"Hi, darling. I'm just trying to get ready for Pink's birthday dinner over at the Char. I'm running late as it is. We don't like to stay out late, you know, especially with this weather," said Nana.

"Meaning past seven?" Cece teased. "How old is she anyway?" Cece asked.

"She's turning eighty. For her birthday last year she made us all go to a country bar with a jukebox, where she proceeded to ask every man in there for a dance." Nana paused. "Remember those birthday parties we had here when you were little? Lord, there would be twenty kids racing around the house, up and down the stairs, and out in the yard. It about did in your Papa Sam."

Cece could feel Nana smiling. "I do remember! One time Dad rigged up some kind of slip-and-slide using the slide of your old swingset. Remember that one? And then, remember that time we got in trouble for using cardboard to slide down your steps?"

"How can I forget? I thought I was going to have to jerk a knot in your tail, but your dad got there just in time. I need to get going, but your Aunt Granny made me promise to tell you she was having one of her 'bad feelins' and wanted you to be extra careful tonight. And just so you know, when Aunt Granny has a feelin', you listen."

"Since I'm in my pajamas working on a dollhouse at home, I don't think she has much to worry about," Cece said as she glued a window frame in place.

"You know your Aunt Granny. She just worries about you. You might give her a call, just to make her feel better."

"I will. Have fun tonight. Don't party too hard and be sure you call me if you need a ride home," Cece laughed.

"Very funny. Talk later."

Cece had separately made all three floors of the townhouse. She had painted the exterior a cream color, with all the window and door-frames painted black, along with all the exterior balconies. Now she had to place one on top of the other and put the staircases in. She got up to stretch, almost stepping on Mabel, who had not moved out from under her feet since the storm had begun.

After putting each floor of the dollhouse in place, Cece stepped back to admire her work. The staircases were all she had left to do for now, letting the glue dry overnight. She had just put her headlamp on when the lights flickered in the cottage. This was one time that Cece was glad to be wearing her otherwise ridiculous-looking accessory, unexpectedly preparing her for power outages. Regardless, she was grateful when they came back on and stayed on.

Even while working on her miniatures, Cece's head spun with suspects and clues like balls in a bingo wheel. She thought she really should get a little notebook like the one Jessica always had in *Murder, She Wrote*. Without much thought, Cece picked up the miniature people she always included in her dollhouse projects and gave them the names of the suspects in Jenny's murder.

When she was choreographing a dance for her classes, she often used objects, like clothespins, or Nana's empty pill bottles, to plot out patterns. By moving the miniature people around on the worktable Cece was creating her own crime scenarios, imagining different combinations of people and circumstances. For Cece it was a way for her to think through the complicated twists and turns of the murder case. Using the rooms of the house, she began to incorporate dollhouse furniture from the box under her table to set up possible crime scenes, even imagining a back porch like the stoop outside the ballroom where Jenny's body had been found. She would then play the tape of possible motives backward in her mind to open herself to the different possibilities.

But thinking about the case was not getting the dollhouse finished. Cece got back to work, bending over and tipping her head low, directing the light into the bottom floor of the dollhouse. She then carefully pushed the pre-stained miniature staircase into place.

As she began to pull her hands out of the house, colors started hitting her vision field like waves breaking on sand. One after the other, they came pounding in as Cece squeezed her eyes shut. When she opened them, she saw a realistic scene, all in miniature, quickly switching out for another scene when the next wave hit. She saw herself as a child at a birthday party; she saw the staircase at Nana's house; she saw the swirling blue fabric of Jenny's dress. Cece rubbed her eyes and shook her head. *This is it!* she thought. *Finally!* All the pieces came together at once, and she knew exactly what to do.

Completely ignoring Aunt Granny's advice, Cece went to her toolbox and grabbed her two biggest screwdrivers. She pulled her raincoat on over her pajamas and slipped on her tennis shoes. She knew where she needed to go and what she needed to do. Finally, pulling Nana's house key from the kitchen drawer, she told Mabel, "I'll be right back. You stay here," and she stepped into the dark, wet night.

* * *

Cece padded through the muddy backyard up to Nana's back door. The rain was steady now, casting a yellowed haze from the lights on the outside walls of the house. She went to put the key in the door, but the knob turned without it.

Cece thought it wasn't like her grandmother to leave it unlocked, especially recently, but tonight she had a job to do and didn't have time to worry about it. She walked into the back hallway, heading straight for the landing beside the staircase. Along the wall near the bottom step was a tall mahogany China cabinet with three drawers on the bottom and two etched-glass doors with shelves behind them.

Cece carefully unloaded Nana's "Desert Rose" wedding china with green leaves and pink flower-blossom borders, stacking them on the floor, along with the fragile stems of Nana's crystal. She then pushed as hard as she could with both hands and one shoulder to move the solidly built cabinet. Behind it, at hip height, was the door to the old dumbwaiter that, long ago, was used to carry food and dishes, or even firewood, between the floors when the house was first built. It worked manually, by a pulley and rope system.

The door to the dumbwaiter had been sealed shut years ago by Nana and Papa Sam after Cece and her friends had gotten in trouble at a birthday party for trying to cram themselves inside it. After that, they decided to seal the door permanently shut.

As Cece wedged the long screwdriver between the wall and the sealed door, the lights flickered again two times before going completely out. Cece had run out of her cottage so fast, she'd forgotten she was still wearing her headlamp. She clicked it on and continued to shift the screwdriver back and forth, trying to get it a little further in between the door and the wall.

Cece was gaining momentum, knowing at last that this hunch was the right one, and feeling victory at hand. With one final push, the door cracked halfway open. Cece felt a sudden flash of unease; the hairs on the back of her neck stood up and her body went on full high alert. It was then that she heard the unmistakable click of a gun cocking behind her.

"Step away from that, Cece," came Sandra's monotone, cold voice. "I've come too far for you to get in my way now."

Cece slowly turned around with her hands held high, her headlamp throwing light on Sandra's dead stare.

"I figured Mr. Newport's box of gold had to be somewhere around here. And you're nice enough to not only show me, but open the door for me," Sandra said in an eerie, singsong voice while tightening her grip on the gun.

"Think about what you're doing, Sandra. Don't do this." Cece's voice was pleading.

"I've done nothing but think about this. I'm finally going to get what I deserve, and your skinny ass is not going to stand in my way."

Suddenly the back door slammed open, and Joe came running inside with his gun drawn.

"Drop your weapon, Sandra," Joe demanded. "Now!"

Sandra whirled around, her eyes darting between Joe and Cece. At that moment, the lights came back on, and for a split second, blinded, Sandra hesitated. Cece took that moment to make a run at her but tripped, falling forward and headbutting Sandra with her saucer-sized headlamp, knocking her backward.

As Cece came crashing down on top of Sandra she reached for the gun, her hand colliding with Sandra's, and the gun fell from her grip, sliding across the polished wood floor. Joe grabbed the gun while Cece scrambled to get up. Joe grabbed Sandra by the wrist, flipped her onto her stomach, and secured her arms behind her back.

Joe stood up to his full height, pulling Sandra with him, as Morris and another officer appeared at the back door. He started to walk Sandra toward the door but stopped, turning to look at Cece.

"Good work, Cece. But next time, could you wait for backup?" His eyes met hers for an instant before he started to turn. "And maybe leave the headbutting move to Hulk Hogan. Morris, can you take a look at Cece's head?" Joe said, with the slightest trace of a smile beginning on his lips.

Cece could feel her heart thudding as she rubbed her forehead and tried to regain her equilibrium.

"You okay?" Morris asked, his growly voice suddenly beside her. "Let's get that head looked at." He pulled out an alcohol wipe and Band-Aid from his pocket. "Gotta make do in a pinch here."

For a big, bearlike man with even bigger hands and stale tobacco breath, he had a soft touch. "That should work until we get you checked out at the hospital."

"I'm fine, really. I don't need a hospital. It's just a little cut," Cece insisted as she spun around and walked over to the half-pried-open door of the dumbwaiter. She wanted to finish what she'd started with her screwdriver and find out if her peculiars had been of any use here.

"How about using this?" Morris said, holding a crowbar and giving her a rare smile. Cece murmured a faint "thanks," and with one last shove and pull of the crowbar, the door finally swung open.

Morris, and now two more officers, gathered around as Nana appeared from the back door, heading straight for Cece. "Are you okay?" she asked, pulling Cece in for a firm embrace.

"Yes, Nana. I'm fine. Maybe a little numb, but okay," Cece said, with a shiver inside of Nana's warm hug.

"Let's go in the kitchen so you can sit down, and I'll get you something to drink," Nana volunteered.

"Wait a minute, Nana. I have to see what's in that box first!" Cece pointed to the now-open dumbwaiter. The officers had ripped the remainder of the plywood off, which revealed a worn cardboard box with crumbling packing tape on it and the word "shelves" written in thick black marker.

"That looks like Sam's handwriting. That must be one of our old moving boxes," Nana said, walking closer.

"Excuse me, ma'am," Morris said to Nana. "If you don't mind, I'll get it out of there." With gloved hands, Morris lifted the cardboard box out of the dumbwaiter and onto the floor. Opening the top, he first brought out a scratched red glass ashtray and three old cigar boxes. Then, he lifted out a wooden box about the size of a loaf of bread with a curved lid and a decorative brass padlock with a key already in it. The box had been painted gold.

23

"Are you thinking what I'm thinking?" Nana turned to Cece, taking her hand.

"This has to be Jenny's dad's gold box. The one he told them was their inheritance. This was what Sandra has been after all along. But how did it get in there?"

"My guess is your Papa Sam must've found it, not knowing what it was, and threw it in with some things of ours in that old packing box. He must've used it to fill the space when he sealed up the dumbwaiter. He probably thought it was all junk, and I know he wanted to make it as tough as possible for you to get in there again."

"Is this s'posed to be valuable?" Morris asked, lifting the gold-painted box from the floor and placing it on the small round table in the foyer.

"We think so. Can we open it?" Cece asked him.

"By all means," Morris said, handing them each a pair of gloves as he moved aside, and Nana and Cece stepped in.

They quickly pulled on their gloves, Cece's hands shaking as she did so. Nana turned the key to pop open the lock. Cece looked at Nana, then lifted the lid. Inside was a yellowing white envelope. In scraggly cursive on the outside of the envelope it read: *To my children, Edmund and Jenny. With care and attention, this will change your life. Love, Dad.*

Cece again looked at Nana, and she nodded. The glue on the flap of the envelope was long gone, so Cece easily pulled out the contents, which looked to be ten pages of legal paper filled with Mr. Newport's writing. There was no cash, no stocks or bonds, only the words of a father to his children.

Nana was peering over Cece's shoulder, her reading glasses perched on the end of her nose. "It looks like it says, 'Words to live by,' and then he's written something like a list on the rest of the pages."

"I see the first one on the list is, 'Always be patient with those who love you.' Oh, I feel bad even looking at it. Especially since the people it was meant for are gone," Cece said, folding the pages and placing them back in the envelope.

"We'll call Buck and see what he wants to do. It might be nice for Jenny's girls to have. But right now, I want you to come sit down in the kitchen."

"So she did all that for a letter that wasn't even for her?" Morris asked incredulously.

"No, Sandra did all that because she thought the box was full of money," Nana said.

"Ahh, yes" Morris nodded. "Money. Of course. That makes more sense."

"Wait a minute, Nana. I think I see something else in the bottom of that box," Cece said. "It looks like a book."

As Nana peered into the box, a look of surprise and recognition registered on her face. In an instant, she linked her elbow in Cece's. "You better come have a seat. You've had quite the night, and you've done everything you can now. Even though I wish it hadn't happened in this way, you did catch Jenny's murderer, Cece. You don't need to worry about anything else," she said, steering Cece into the kitchen, not stopping until she had Cece seated in the kitchen chair. "Besides, I need to have a look at your forehead."

"But Nana, I wanted to see what else was in there. It looked like a massive antique book with gold patterns on the cover. Maybe that's the valuable thing!"

"Darling, I'll keep it safe, I promise. But that never belonged to the Newports. Samuel Chagall is going to hear from me later, I can tell you. Now let me get a look at your head," Nana said, peeling off the latex gloves and tipping Cece's head back. "It's not a bad cut, but I need to clean and put on some antibiotic ointment."

"And I will have some leftover spaghetti heating up in the microwave for you in a minute," Nana said as she finished cleaning Cece's wound and returned her first-aid kit to the cabinet.

"I'm not hungry, Nana. I just want to take a shower and go to bed. Joe said he'd be calling first thing tomorrow morning. I'm hoping he'll clear the scene so we can see the book at the bottom of the box. It looked like an antique, and pretty cool."

"Of course, darling," Nana said, her eyes resting briefly on the photo of her mother and grandmother hanging on the kitchen wall. It was both an antique and a very cool book, indeed, and one that Nana hadn't intended for Cece to find in that way. In fact, she thought it was lost, herself.

"Take this just in case you get hungry," Nana said, handing Cece the leftover spaghetti, "and you go get some rest. I imagine we'll both get better sleep now that this is all over."

"I sure hope so," Cece said as Nana pulled her in for one last hug.

After Cece left, the police had gone, and Nana was sure the house was empty, so she went back to the cardboard box. Morris had checked with Joe, and they had given her permission to touch it and its contents since the box belonged to her, and Sandra had never touched it. She put both hands inside, slid her palms underneath the book, and lifted it out. She gingerly placed it on the kitchen table as a poof of dust billowed from between the pages. Nana didn't open it, instead running her fingers along the gold embossed words and patterns on the thick leather cover.

Nana stood in the center of her kitchen, gazing at the moon between the clouds now that the rain had stopped. She picked up the bottle of water on the table and lifted it up, as if for a toast, toward the photo of her mother and grandmother on the wall, chanting the words she knew so well:

Sisters gather in spirit, and spirit is power.
Protect her, protect her in desperate hours.

She then lifted the bottle higher and said, "Thank you for helping keep our Cece safe."

She upended and emptied the bottle with one gulp, set it down with a hollow thud, and went to lock up for bed.

* * *

Nana outdid herself the next morning, making a grand breakfast of eggs, bacon, cheesy grits, and fruit salad. The kitchen smelled heavenly, but after the excitement of the previous evening, Nana felt strangely slow and unable to bounce back like she used to.

When she'd gotten the call at the restaurant last night that the police were on the way to her house, she knew it was Cece and that Hazel had been right. It had been so long since she and Hazel had faced such a situation that she'd almost forgotten what to do, but she was able to remember enough to invoke protection before she left for the birthday party. Nana now understood why the book had suddenly shown up after all this time.

"Nana, you didn't need to do all this just for me," Cece said, touching a finger to her bandaged head. Cece was proud of herself for putting on jeans and a boxy mock turtleneck, when she didn't feel like getting dressed at all, and still didn't feel clean after taking two showers in the last twelve hours. She couldn't seem to scrub enough to get rid of the layers of fear on her skin.

"Well, it helps to take my mind off things if I'm cooking," Nana said, tightening her apron over her new "Good Trouble" T-shirt.

Cece sat at the table rolling her neck from shoulder to shoulder. She hadn't been able to run or workout at all in the last few days, and felt stiff as a starched shirt. "Need any help, Nana?" Cece asked, just as there came a persistent knocking on the back door. Cece looked back questioningly at Nana as she went to answer it.

"Hey, good morning," said Joe, standing outside the door wearing gym shorts, a hoodie, and holding a red notebook.

"Oh. Joe!" Cece said, trying to hide her surprise and failing, while giving herself an inner high-five for deciding to get out of bed and get dressed. "I didn't know you were coming by. Come on in."

"How's your head this morning?" Joe asked, stepping inside and following Cece into the kitchen.

"Brilliant as ever," she said, shrugging her shoulders.

Joe reached his hand up, his fingers gently tracing the line of the bandage on her forehead. "Looks like you'll be back in the wrestling ring before you know it," Joe said, dimples blooming along with his smile.

"Very funny," Cece said, calling into the kitchen, "Nana, Joe's here," adding, "I'm sure glad you just happen to have enough food for an army in there."

"Good morning, Ms. Chagall," Joe said, leaning in to give her a kiss on the cheek.

"Mornin', Joe," Nana said. "Cece, darling, I thought it might help if we could get Joe to explain things for both of us in person instead of making him repeat himself."

"Actually, I asked your Nana last night if I could come over this morning," Joe inserted. "I wanted to brief you on the case, and I really wanted to be sure you both were okay."

"I say we have a seat and get down to business. How about some fresh coffee, Joe? Cream? Sugar?" Nana said.

"Yes, ma'am, I'd love some coffee, and just black is good." Joe laid his red notebook on the table, sat down, and opened it. "Sandra confessed last night to killing Jenny, and the first thing you should know is that Sandra Newport wasn't really Sandra Newport. We started digging into her past right after the murder and quickly discovered she had a different identity before she married Edmond. In fact, she'd had a string of aliases she created while she conned wealthy men, then disappeared with their money."

"So she had Ed completely fooled?" Nana asked, pouring coffee into three mugs.

"For a while, at least. Having been burned in his first marriage, we think Ed was becoming suspicious."

"I thought Sandra was supposed to have had a ton of money after Ed died. Did she spend all of it?" Cece asked.

"Yeah, that's what it looks like. Not only that, but she was also in serious debt and clearly looking for any way out. Buck told us Jenny and Ed made remarks all the time about their 'golden inheritance.' They would talk about what they'd buy with the money or where they would go when they found it. Buck said everyone around here knew they were joking, but apparently Sandra took them seriously and became determined to find it. She thought it was the answer to her problems. We started putting it all together then."

"I guess it was Sandra who stole Jenny's necklace and put it in Calvin's toolbox at the ball?" Nana asked. "And called in the tip about him having ties in Florida?"

"Yep, we searched the house and found a substantial amount of incriminating evidence, including a burner phone and a few 'Bridges Construction' pens, like the one found in the shrubbery by the loading dock," Joe said as he devoured the plate of eggs Nana had fixed for him only after soaking them in ketchup.

"So how did she get the bust from the basement at the inn? And what happened to it?" Cece asked.

"Turns out she got a new employee at the front desk at the inn to give her a tour of the basement rooms. Apparently Sandra made sure one of the rooms remained unlocked, so after she killed Jenny she could hide the stolen bust until she could return, put it in a trash bag, and throw it in a dumpster."

Nana shook her head. "Lord have mercy, that means we need to get a new security system put in the basement of the inn, and another one here at the house and cottage."

"I guess the old one was that bell over the back door? And, by the way, I had to grab that bell in one hand so it wouldn't ring when I ran in the house last night, and I might have accidentally broken it?" Joe grinned. "Anyway, after we made the connection of Sandra to your house, one of our officers found her empty car parked down your street. By the time I got here I figured Sandra had already gotten inside the house. What we didn't bank on was Cece." Joe turned to face Cece, who had a mouth full of fruit salad. "We didn't bank on Cece or her martial arts skills."

Cece swallowed hard, pointing her fork toward Joe, "I thought you said I was Hulk Hogan?"

"True," Joe said, "maybe Hulk Hogan *and* Bruce Lee." Joe closed his red notebook. "Even though Jenny Newport's murder case is closed, we have enough evidence against Sandra to reopen the investigation into

Edmond's car accident. We've already talked to the Palm Beach County Police about that one. No matter what, she'll be put away for a long time."

"Has anybody told Sandra it was just a letter in a wooden box in the dumbwaiter?" Nana asked, now beginning to pick up dishes and stack them in the sink.

"Oh, yeah. Morris couldn't wait to deliver the news to her in her cell." Joe stood up to help Nana with the dishes. "He said she let loose with a string of words so bad even he hadn't heard some of them."

Soon, Joe was at the sink rinsing the dishes while Nana was putting them in the dishwasher, and Cece was making a plate for Joe to take home, per Nana's instructions. The three were quiet and lost in thought until the punch-kick of the Snoop Dogg song ringtone of Nana's phone broke the silence.

"Good morning, Hazel. I was just about to call you," Nana said, lobbing a look Cece's way. "How're you feelin' this morning?"

"I was all up in a swivet ever' bit of last night over Cece," Hazel said, so loudly they could hear the agitation in her voice. "You may as well lay it out for me. I already know it's bad."

"I'm sorry; I really should've called you last night, but Cece's right here, and she can tell you everything that happened. You talk to her, and we can talk later," Nana said, handing the phone over to Cece.

"Hey, Aunt Granny," Cece said, walking into the living room and sitting down on the sofa. She knew Aunt Granny would want to know everything, and just hearing her voice made Cece feel better.

"I guess I better get to the office and start on the pile of paperwork I have to do," Joe said, handing the last dish to Nana. "But tell Cece I'll be calling her later to get some more details. I still haven't heard what prompted her to come over here last night, if it was something she heard or maybe saw," Joe said as he picked up his notebook.

"It's not what you'd think, but I'll let her explain all that," Nana offered.

"Well, with Cece, it rarely is. Never a dull moment, for sure," Joe said, flashing a toothpaste-ad smile.

"Yeah, Cece doesn't have room in her planner for such things as dull moments," Nana joked.

"Thank you so much for that incredible breakfast, Ms. C. I don't think I've eaten since yesterday."

"Take this home with you," Nana said, handing Joe a foil-covered plate, "and you can eat it later. I guess you know . . .." Nana paused, her voice catching in her throat. "I guess you know I can never thank you enough for saving our Cece. Lord knows what that woman would've done had you not gotten there when you did."

"You're welcome. It's my job. And Cece really saved herself, you know."

"I guess we all have to save ourselves in the end, but what matters is the help we get along the way," Nana said, patting Joe's back as she walked him to the door and waving as he got into his patrol car.

Cece came out of the living room holding Nana's phone, just as Nana came back inside.

"Joe said to tell you he had to get back to work and he'd call you later. How'd it go with your Aunt Granny?" Nana asked, putting her phone in her pants pocket.

"Oh, you know, she wished she had warned me, but knows I wouldn't have listened, and I told her that while I wouldn't do it again, I did learn something I've needed to know for a long time."

"And what might that be?" Nana asked, holding onto the kitchen counter and swinging one leg back and forth to loosen up her hip.

"I learned to trust my peculiars, or synesthesia, or intuition, or whatever I'm supposed to call it. I can see that you and Aunt Granny are right; the more I pay attention to putting the pieces together, the sooner the whole story eventually appears."

"That's my girl," Nana said, pulling Cece in for a side hug, then turning to look for the amber bottle of hip tincture. "It often comes back to stories, whether it's one we hear or one we tell ourselves. Sandra's story was about getting what she deserved, and it looks like, in the end, she will. You're starting to see the power that comes with believing your peculiars are a strength and not a weakness."

"Yeah," Cece said, nodding her head, "I guess I am." Cece turned to look at the front hallway, "You said you'd keep that book I saw in the dumbwaiter last night. Can I look at it now?"

"Oh, yes. About that book, Cece," Nana said, pulling out a kitchen chair, "why don't you have a seat here, and we can look through it together."

24

"Sister, don't you scare me like that ever again, okay?" Bess said, standing outside the door of The Iris. After a long embrace, she stepped back to look Cece over, head to toe. "And I think you're going to rock that Harry Potter scar you've got there," she said, looking at Cece's forehead and smiling. Cece had already filled Bess in on all the details of the night before on the phone, including the "headlamp as weapon" part.

"I'm just glad it's over. Now, let's go inside; I'm freezing," Cece said, opening the door for both of them, and they quickly tucked themselves into a corner table to catch up.

Bess reached into her Dolly tote bag and set a compact package wrapped in bright paper and tied with a wide satin ribbon on top of the table.

"What's this?" Cece asked, pulling off her jacket.

"A little something to celebrate you still being alive," Bess said. "I figure there's really no better reason to give a gift. Go ahead, open it."

Cece peeled the paper off to find a paperback book with worn edges. Cece turned it over, examining it, and noticed the miniature diorama on the cover. "Hmm. *The Nutshell Studies of Unexplained Death.* I've never heard of it, but it looks like it might have something to do with miniatures?" Cece looked at Bess, eyebrows raised.

"Yes! I'd never heard of it, either, but Shane found it and ordered it for me to give you. It's not a new book, as you can see, and it's not about just any old miniatures. These were made by a woman named Frances Glessner Lee back in the 1940s. She wanted to replicate actual crime scenes and teach people how to collect the right evidence. Have you ever heard of her?" Bess asked.

"No, I can't say that I have," Cece said, flipping through the pages. "But it looks right up my alley. Thank you, my friend." She nodded thanks to the young woman who brought coffee and cinnamon rolls to their table.

"It's more than interesting, Cece!" Bess insisted, her eyes sparkling with excitement. "It's what you can do, except you can be the modern-day version. Did you know they use these dioramas to train investigators around the country, *even now?*"

"No, I didn't," Cece said, "and I don't believe I've ever seen you this excited about miniatures before, or maybe about anything. Tell me some more about this Frances lady."

"Well, not only did she create these detailed miniature scenes, but she brought attention to the isolation of women, and uncovered all the violence that was being overlooked back then. So, it was a lot more than just teaching them about how to find clues to a crime. Just think about what you could do with your miniatures and your peculiars put together!" Bess seemed to be positively beaming now.

"Bess, I love you for believing in me, but I have no police training, or anything like that. I was a dance major, for heaven's sake. Everything I know I learned on *Murder, She Wrote*, and I'm pretty sure that won't work on a resume. How am I supposed to start something like this?"

"Frances didn't have any training either, and I know you, Cece. You can create your own job, just like she did," Bess said, licking the cinnamon off her finger.

Cece grinned at her friend across the table. "I have to admit, it's intriguing. Especially the part about educating on the realities of crimes against women. You know better than anybody how bad it is around here." Cece chewed on her thumbnail. "I'd have to figure out just exactly what I could offer, and I'd have to keep fine-tuning these peculiars."

"There's my girl. You just need that little notebook and pen you've been talking about, and you can start taking notes as you read the book." Bess leaned over and peered into her tote, pulling out a newspaper. "That reminds me, have you seen your dad's column in today's paper?"

"No, but he told me what he was working on. Is that it?" Cece asked.

"Yeah, you can have it," she said, holding it out to her, "and I'm really glad you're okay. We've got lots of shows to binge-watch and boxwine to drink, and my crystal ball says we have many more adventures ahead."

The Eureka Grove Gazette

BACKROADS

by Leo Chagall

All That Glitters

October 2024: Eureka Grove recently lost two longtime community members, Jenny and Edmund Newport, to tragedy. But behind the salacious headlines about murder and greed, you'll find the real story of a father's devotion to his children.

I had the pleasure of talking to some of the Newport family friends, and the story heard most often was about the "box of gold" that their father Jimmy had supposedly put away in a safe spot for when Jenny and Ed grew up.

You see, Jimmy told the kids that their inheritance was contained in this hidden box, but they had never truly believed their dad's tale, and they didn't think much about it until after his passing, when the house was put up for sale. They searched all the nooks and crannies but were unable to locate the mysterious box, and it became somewhat of a joke between the siblings. They would tease each other and laugh about what they would buy or the trips they would take when the box was discovered. They even told the new owner of the house she could have a cut if she ever found it.

Their father, Jimmy Newport, according to his friends, was a man of few words and loved nothing more than a good joke, but what mattered most to him was his children. He coached their sports teams and boasted of their successes to anyone who would listen. So when news became public that the elusive box had been found, no one who knew him was surprised to learn it was filled not with money but words of wisdom.

Jimmy had left his children the words he felt would best guide them through life, passing down a list of aphorisms that included:

"In the end, we will remember not the words of our enemies, but the silence of our friends."
Martin Luther King, Jr.

"Brevity is the soul of wit."
Hamlet by William Shakespeare

"Resentment is like drinking poison and then hoping it will kill your enemies."
Nelson Mandela

These are but a few of the many words of wisdom Jimmy had written in his faded cursive on notebook paper and precisely folded to fit into a gold-painted box.

Unfortunately, in an unbelievable turn of events, the notion of a box filled with inheritance money had been taken literally by a criminal whose greed drove her to murder.

For this criminal, the aphorism "All that glitters is not gold" was apt in that there was never any money to begin with.

But if we are able to look past the tragedy, we learn that what we truly inherit from our family members has nothing to do with giving us money, everything to do with giving us love, and sometimes, if we're lucky, they carefully save some for us for after they're gone. As Tennyson wrote, "Love is the only gold."

Fire Circle

Twilight bathed the hills and ridges in muted ribbons of scarlet and gold as the women gathered for their annual All-Hallows' Eve ceremony. The trees were peaking, waving their bright leaves for the many tourists who traveled far just for the show. Hazel had piled kindling beside logs Sally had already cross-stacked for the fire. Cat brought the sage, tobacco, and sweetgrass to offer the ancestors, along with a clay bowl for smudging, Sally brought her sweetening jar, and Fiona had composed an original fiddle song she would be playing for them later.

"What time is Cece supposed to get here?" asked Cat, holding her herbs in a bundle and tying them together at the ends as she walked clockwise around the fire. "She should be coming up here anytime," Hazel said, peering down toward the road.

"How do I look?" Fiona asked, patting down her glossy hair, lifting her skirt above her ankles, and turning around.

Hazel chuckled. "She can't see you, Fiona. What difference does it make?"

"But she might," Fiona said. "Tonight is the one night she might be able to see us. Or it might just be one of us. I want to look good in case I get to meet her."

Hazel had to grin at Fiona's earnestness. "You are beautiful, as always," Hazel reassured her.

Just as dusk gave into darkness, Cece's Jeep turned off the paved road, headlights bouncing up the gravel.

"Here she comes, everyone. Get ready!" Sally said, straightening her skirt.

Cece parked by Hazel's truck and began the walk up behind the house toward the little fire. Hazel often talked about her "fire circles," but

Cece had never actually been to one. She felt honored to have been invited.

On top of the knoll behind Hazel's house lay the family cemetery. Hazel and Nana tried to keep it up, but weeds and brush still surrounded the gravestones. The graveyard was a mix of leaning, lichen-covered headstones and flat, fieldstone markers, some dating back to the early 1800s. There were stones etched with only one word, such as "Infant" or "Father," and some telling open-ended tales of the dead, like "Hattie Brown, 1871–1940, Finally at Peace." The low rock wall that once surrounded the cemetery had collapsed long ago and been replaced by an austere chain-link fence. Hazel's fire circle lay halfway between the cemetery fence and the family house.

"Get on up here," said Hazel, using her walking stick to push herself up from her tree-stump seat. "I've been waitin' for you."

"It's really beautiful and a little bit spooky up here, Aunt Granny," Cece said, going in for a half-hug. "I see why you like it, though," she said, closing her eyes, tipping her head back, and taking a long in-breath. "This is the best air in the world. But it's so loud. The tree frogs and owls are knockin' it out of the park tonight."

"It's not so much that it's loud, baby girl; it's just we're never quiet," Hazel said. "I got you your very own tree stump to sit on," Hazel smiled, pointing to the one across from hers.

"Thanks, Aunt Granny, you didn't need to go to all that trouble," Cece said and winked as she took the seat and put her palms up by the fire. She soaked in the layered sounds of the forest, the background chorus of crickets and creek adding to the melody of owl and frog.

"Well?" Cece said finally, turning to look at Hazel.

"Well, what?"

"Are we just going to sit here, or are you going to introduce me to your friends?"

Author's Note

Appalachia is a land of the liminal. With one of the oldest mountain ranges in the world, the veil between past and present, seen and unseen, is porous and malleable. It is a melting pot of diverse cultures, including Native American, African American, and Scots-Irish, among others, and from early on was deemed "a strange land and a peculiar people" (Williams, 2002).

The people of this area mixed traditional Christian concepts and folk magic with a deep respect for the natural world. They did so in order to provide meaning and find the personal power necessary to survive centuries of colonialism and marginalization. Instead of being "primitive and backward," theirs was a holistic worldview that broke down barriers between the material and spiritual world to find harmony and balance.

It is from this strong, rich broth that the Granny Woman comes from. These older women served as midwives and healers, prepared the dead for burial, and passed down ancestral wisdom. Her learned skillset drew from the combined knowledge of her multicultural ancestors.

Before the early 1900s these communities were isolated and difficult for a doctor to reach, and even if they could, many residents distrusted them. Because of this the Granny Woman became an integral part of their mountain community.

Frequently, Granny Women were seen as being "outside the norm" because of the power they held, along with their knowledge of the natural world, which was exclusively reserved for men of that time period. She also might have been unmarried or childless, again outside the cultural norm of the times and therefore the subject of ridicule and ill-will. For these reasons, they were sometimes referred to as "Granny Witches."

Despite these obstacles, Granny Women continued to provide the often unpaid labor that kept communities alive.

It is from this history, and that of summers spent with my mother's family in Carter and Washington Counties of East Tennessee, that this book was born. My own Great-Aunt Hazel was a lot like "Aunt Granny Hazel" in the book, and my grandmother shares similarities with "Nana." It has been great fun revisiting those memories.

I believe the world is full of modern-day Granny Women who serve their communities with resilience and fortitude in a myriad of ways, bucking the norm every day. I also believe we depend upon our Fire Circles, or whatever we choose to call our friend groups, that teach, nourish, and support us. Our Fire Circles seem necessary now more than ever. I've been lucky enough to have both in my life.

I bet you know a modern-day Granny Woman. You might even be one yourself.

I bet you are part of a Fire Circle that has made an invaluable contribution to your life and the person you are today.

If so, I'd love to hear from you. I invite you to be a part of my Fire Circle. Thank you for giving my words a cozy corner in your imagination. You can reach me at

bewildernesswriting.com or
ellis@bewildernesswriting.com

Ellis Elliott
Juno Beach, FL

April 2025

Acknowledgments

This book could not have been written without the support and encouragement of many folks I hold dear and in great regard.

My gratitude extends first to my foremothers on both sides of my family, from the mountains of East Tennessee to the farmland of North Carolina. These were my original Granny Women. Their fortitude and resilience remain humbling and inspiring.

To my herbal consultant and friend, Meg Madden, from The Elderberry herb shop in Charlottesville, VA.

To my friends/cheerleaders/first readers: Laura Beer, Kathleen Henricksen, Amy Gatewood, and Christie Bates, I am indebted to your gifting me with your generous time and effort with my manuscript. To my friend Lisa Braner, for the gift of her insights and for taking the time to write for the book cover.

To my friends/editors/publishers, Dianne Pearce, and her husband, David Yurkovich, for their keen skills and unwavering support throughout the process.

To my brother, Bill, who always answered when I called to ask a multitude of family-related questions, like "Do you remember where Aunt Hazel kept the Bible?" I am also thankful for his excellent memory and for being our unheralded family historian.

To my family, especially my dear husband and always first reader, Tim, who patiently listened to me ramble about plot twists and characters with only an occasional push of the "uh-huh" button. His belief in me is enough to bridge the gaps when I can't quite get there myself.

EE

Meet the Author

ELLIS ELLIOTT is a facilitator of the online writing group Bewilderness Writing. She also teaches writing and ballet in an after-school arts education program. Ellis holds an MFA from Queens University. She is a contributing writer for the *Southern Review of Books,* and serves as an editor/workshop instructor for *The Dewdrop* contemplative journal.

She is the author of the 2023 poetry chapbook, *Break in the Field* (Old Scratch Press), which KIRKUS calls "A deeply felt collection of candid verse." Her work can also be found in numerous publications, including *Signal Mountain Review, Plainsongs Poetry Magazine/Award Poem, Euphony Journal*, and the *Women of Appalachia Project Anthology*. Ellis has a blended family consisting of six grown sons. She resides in West Palm Beach, Florida, with her husband, Tim, and a feisty dog named Mabel.

From the Library of the Modern Granny Witch

Ballard, H. B. (2023). *Roots, Branches, & Spirits: The Folkways and Witchery of Appalachia*. Llewelyn Publications. (Or any of H. Byron Ballard's books)

Chadde, S. (2020). *Medicinal Plants of Appalachia: A Field Guide to Traditional Medicinal Plants of the Appalachian Region*. Orchard Innovations.

Foxwood, O. (2021). *Mountain Conjure and Southern Root Work*. Weiser Books.

Howell, P. K. (2006). *Medicinal Plants of the Southern Appalachians*. Botanologos Books.

Hutchison, K. "Granny Witches, Mountain Shamans, Haunts, Witches, and Jesus: The Complex Spiritual Consciousness of Appalachia" M.A. Thesis, Shepherd University.

Kimmerer, R. W. (2013). *Braiding Sweetgrass: Indigenous Wisdom, Scientific Knowledge, and the Teachings of Plants*. Milkweed Press.

Lily, A. (2023). *Appalachian Witchcraft for Beginners: The History, Remedies, and Spells of a Rich Folk Magic Tradition*. Rockridge Press.

Maier, K. (2021). Energetic *Herbalism: A Guide to Sacred Plant Traditions Integrating Elements of Vitalism, Ayurveda, and Chinese Medicine*. Chelsea Green Publishing.

Meiklejohn-Free, B. (2022). *Scottish Witchcraft: A Complete Guide to Folklore, Spells, and Magikal Tools*. Llewelyn Publications.

Richards, J. (2019). *Backwoods Witchcraft: Conjure & Folk Magic from Appalachia*. Weiser Books.

Wigginton, E. (1972). *The Foxfire Book Series*. Random House, New York.

Williams, J. A. (2002). *Appalachia: A History.* University of North Carolina Press.

Break in the Field

An original poetry collection
by Ellis Elliott

"Elliott explores responsibility and dependence in this debut poetry collection… A deeply felt collection of candid verse."

KIRKUS

AVAILABLE IN PAPERBACK, EBOOK, AND AUDIOBOOK FORMAT.

BUY ONLINE AT AMAZON, B&N, AND WATERSTONES.
ALSO AVAILABLE IN SELECT BOOKSTORES.

hawkshawpress.com